The first battle to regain Earth took less than a minute

A sharp *whump-crack* tossed one of the aliens into the dry mountain air. The blue-crested *kepwoi* seemed to float into the doorway, its long tubular weapon at throat level in the double-bend of an inhuman forearm.

Two more blasts, and a beam of red light ignited the stand of young maples to Erlanger's left. He kept pulling the trigger. The aircar began to quiver, to yaw. The Ceejay in the cabin door fell, the beam weapon still firing, now cutting a smoking trench in the packed ground before the cabin.

The aircar wobbled, now two feet up, now four. Obviously stricken, it slewed sideways into the cabin wall, rebounded, wobbled. A massive blast of heat seared Erlanger's face as he jerked back to the cover of rock, only to look up again to see a spinning, tumbling ball of fire—a stick-figure of flame—fall back into the clearing . . .

MICHAEL BANKS AND DEAN R. LAMBE

THE ODYSSEUS SOLUTION

BAEN
SCIENCE FICTION
BOOKS

THE ODYSSEUS SOLUTION

This is a work of fiction. All the characters and events portrayed in this book are fictional, and any resemblance to real people or incidents is purely coincidental.

A Baen Books Original

Baen Publishing Enterprises
260 Fifth Avenue
New York, N.Y. 10001

First printing, February 1986

ISBN: 0-671-65553-1

Cover art by Stephen Hickman

Printed in the United States of America

Distributed by
SIMON & SCHUSTER
Trade Publishing Group
1230 Avenue of the Americas
New York, N.Y. 10020

DEDICATION

*For Rosa and Julie . . . true Patrons of the Arts.
For Midwestcon . . . where the egg was hatched
and nurtured.*

Acknowledgments

The authors wish to thank their editor and publisher, Jim Baen, for his invaluable aid and encouragement. Aspects of alien astrophysics and xenobiology in this novel were developed through use of the WORLD BUILDER© computer program, which was originally written by Stephen D. Kimmel, a true friend and colleague. Helpful comments about communications satellites were provided by Dr. Charles Sheffield of the Earth Satellite Corporation. Finally, we wish to thank Patricia Greeson of the News Office, Tennessee Technical University, for allowing us to use her beautiful campus.

Prologue

At the fringes of the stellar system, the Cweom-jik vessel *Nest Maker* reentered normal space and decelerated, the velocity of the massive, egg-shaped craft an ever-decreasing fraction of lightspeed. Deep within the yoke an organic computer gathered and correlated data. Part of the near-sentient shipbrain confirmed earlier data regarding the new star system. The initial data suggested planets II, III, and IV as possibilities, but by the time the ship had reached the orbit of the innermost gas giant, shipbrain had rejected the second and fourth. The third, however, looked interesting indeed.

Another part of shipbrain scanned the electromagnetic, gravetic, and null-space multidimensional spectrums. As expected, gravetic and null space were blank, but—surprise!—modulated activity was high in the electromagnetic bands, and large amounts of information were channeled to linguistic and cross-cultural subroutines. Hundreds of years before, a robot probe's report had triggered *Nest Maker's* one-way mission. The Cweom-jik had expected easier prey.

The great ship, its external dimensions rivaling those of the smaller moon of the fourth planet, came to relative rest within what should have been the orbit of the system's fifth planet—although no planetary body existed there. Shipbrain analyzed, considered, extrapolated. Within its master programming, values were assigned to the complex factors that represented the intelligent lifeforms on planet III. Shipbrain knew that the status relationships, the very lives, of the 1500 *kepwoi* and their 2500 *een* mates aboard *Nest Maker* were dependent on the suddenly less-certain success of this mission of conquest and colonization. For their part, as the preliminary analyses became available, not a few feathers ruffled over aspects of the data. Subdominant *cweomki* squawked at subordinates as the bizarre characteristics and the inharmonious culture of the target lifeform became apparent. All *cweomki* were restless, eager to establish new roost-homes, new *zomua* for the Flock. The greater danger did not quell their lust.

Soon enough, in less than two rotations of homeworld Piveea, shipbrain completed the analysis, and made recommendations. Yes, the third planet, although a bit cooler than Piveea, could sustain *cweomki*. Yes, the aggressive, bipedal lifeform that controlled the planet did resemble an ancestral predator, the hated *zlekk*, but that was mere coincidence. And, yes, the plan for *Cweom-jik* conquest did include considerable risk, for the *zlekk*-like beings—the "humans" —measured three fours socially and two fours technologically. Among humans, groups within groups within groups existed in illogical bonded chains, but a united opposition would certainly develop in response to invasion by a superior species. That threat was acute; the entire *Cweom-jik* mission could be destroyed, for these eggless creatures used the First Four Forces. Humans possessed crude star-yoke weapons, those messy, inelegant bombs that for a time had hampered *cweomki* unity so long ago.

Therefore, shipbrain recommended a subtle cultural attack: The human civilization, though advanced in some ways, was quite fragile in its system of economic interdependence and cooperation. The doubling device could be translated into human technology, and introduced secretly. It was a simple thing, requiring only equal amounts of the constituent elements of the thing being duplicated. Use of the duplication device would spread rapidly, and the economic framework of the target civilization would disintegrate. True, some few might recognize the danger, but what could they do?

Then the *Cweom-jik* could arrive openly, with impunity. The fleet of planet landers would leave their roosts within the shell of *Nest Maker* and appear dramatically in the skies of planet III. Any resistance would be disorganized, discountenanced by the majority of natives, and easily excised. The *Cweom-jik* would appear as friends ready to help rebuild the shattered human socioeconomic system.

As with the matter duplicator, the foolish featherless bipeds would recognize their folly too late. Another world would join the Flock.

Chapter

ONE

As he rolled onto his back and cupped his head in his hands, Erlanger grinned at recollection of his grandfather's tales of the Old Times. According to one story, he was now supposed to smoke a cigarette. Of course, Grandfather Owens had been a boy before the Collapse and the arrival of the aliens, a time when cigarettes and cigars were made in "factories." What few machine-made tobacco products still survived in duplicated form were reserved for the top dogs, those who answered directly to the *Cweom-jik*. Men like Erlanger had to be content with rough local tobacco or maryjane and a corn-cob pipe.

Erlanger did not feel like smoking anyway. His gaze fell on Marla's smooth thigh, as moonlight filtered through branches dappled the young woman's skin with a changing pattern of white and shadow. Aware of his attention, Marla smiled dreamily and covered his view with her long denim skirt—more coquettishness than modesty, for modesty had been a stranger to that grass-covered river bank the past half-hour. She twined a finger in the light brown locks over his left ear, and giggled softly: "I swear, Brent Erlanger, I thought you'd never noticed me, but uh'umm, when you do take to a woman, you do right proud."

Erlanger wasn't listening. Above the rustle of the breeze in the oaks behind them, and the distant sounds of festival gaiety from the town common, he thought he had just heard the sharp snap of a twig. When Marla tugged on his hair, he turned and kissed her nose. "I noticed you, Marla, have to be blind not to, but you're special in more ways than one, and . . ."

"Marla Barlow, have you no shame! Rutting there on the ground like some animal . . ."

Erlanger twisted his neck quickly and painfully. Above them stood Heather Barlow, the Mayor's spinster sister. He struggled into his pants, and felt quickly through the grass for his shirt and socks. As he grabbed his boots and belt, he was still one sock short, but that was only a tiny part of the price he would now have to pay for Marla's charms.

Sticks and small pebbles bit into his bare feet as he scrambled into the trees. Behind him, he heard a slap and Marla's sobbing cries. The rough bark of a massive red oak scratched his still uncovered back as he tried to don his boots. He hadn't run far enough to fail to hear the next shout, however—"And don't think I didn't see your face, Brent Erlanger, you disgusting tomcat. My brother will see to you."

"Ah shit," he muttered as he brushed musty leaves from his heel and fumbled with stiff leather laces, "fat's in the fire now."

The next morning Erlanger awakened with a groan. He rubbed his stubbled chin and decided that shaving was not at the top of his list this morning. Once again he had let lust overpower common sense; his failure to avoid discovery almost guaranteed that he wouldn't have to worry about shaving for much longer. And Marla? He felt responsible for what was going to happen—or had already happened—to her. A scolding at the least, maybe a whipping.

He sighed in resignation. He shouldn't have been fooling around with her, but ... He grinned and shook his head at recollection of her supple body against his. Oh, well, there was no use worrying over how he had gotten into the mess. The problem now was to figure a way out of it.

It was funny, though, how he'd allowed her to pull him down so close to the festival—almost as if both of them didn't give a damn, though the stakes were high enough, especially for him.

The festival made it easy, of course. A group of Ceejays had flown in for one of their random inspections, and the Mayor had declared a three-day holiday in their honor. Along with everybody else in town, Erlanger endured the opening ceremonies, and watched the Mayor present the aliens with a token bag of seeds and nuts. The *Cweom-jik*, in turn, gave the Mayor some gadget for the duplicator. Then most of the town headed for the beer booth, while the Mayor and his cronies conferred privately with the tall, feathered rulers of Earth. Over his first mug, Erlanger had wondered whether the aliens actually ate that ceremonial birdseed, or simply tossed it aside as they did so much that was human. But he kept such thoughts to himself, as any sensible person would around Ceejays or their human vassals.

He had spent the first few hours among the blackjack, big wheel, and other gaming tables, and racked up a hefty sum in winnings. The thin, metallic tokens, made of some alloy that duplicators invariably rejected, made a dull weight in his pants, and he had done his best to relieve his pockets of the burden. Food and drink were plentiful, as were other games, and he happily indulged in whatever came his way—including Marla, the Mayor's daughter.

A healthy 18-year-old, Marla was kindly disposed that evening toward older men who shared her taste for beer. The Mayor, of course, did not approve of young women who indulged in alcohol or older men, so her activities were quite covert. But she had seemed to single out Brent early on, and after their third shared mug behind the hoop-toss tent, they arranged to rendezvous later on the river bank well back of the fairgrounds. It would be dark there, out of the blazing lights of the hovering Ceejay aircar, which illuminated half the town and provided a rare excuse for people to enjoy themselves well after sundown.

All had been fine, more than fine, until that bitch, Heather Barlow, had tracked the illicit lovers to their grassy bower. Fortunately, Erlanger knew, the Mayor was closeted with the aliens for the evening, and Marla's aunt could not pass on her glad tidings immediately, although she had probably tried. He had stumbled back to the festival for more beer to calm his roiling emotions, and eventually made it to his bed at some unremembered hour. Now, in the grim light of an overcast sky, the morning half gone, he ruefully considered his options. There were only two—he could leave town or he could stay and be hung.

He shrugged his wide shoulders and stared out his apartment window. Two stories below, Main Street was starting to pick up traffic as people, horses and wagons, and the occasional methanol-burning public vehicle crowded into town on festival-related business. The grey clouds promised rain, and there was a chill in the air that crept through the thin glass in front of him. He turned away from the window and surveyed his possessions.

In the center of his one-room apartment, the over-stuffed mattress was piled high with things he considered of value—a motley collection of hoardings that marked his thirty-year existence. As soon as he had rolled out of bed, and the night's events had come reasonably clear in his pounding head, he began to sort and pile.

As his hands roved through cupboard and closet, he gave little thought to the limited choice between leaving his birthplace and doing a short jig on a high platform. He could stay and die, or leave and *maybe* die. Given the choice, "maybe" had a better ring to it.

He sighed and tried to ignore his grumbling stomach as appealing odors from somebody's late breakfast wafted through the old building. The sorting process began to take on more purpose. The clothes, fair weather and foul, he stuffed into a sheet that would have to serve as a carrying bundle. After the first culling, he went through the too-bulky pile again, and threw out almost half of what he had packed— including a rare, unduplicated dress shirt, handmade by some forgotten temporary mate. He was left with his most serviceable coveralls, shirts, and boots; no need for niceties where he was going.

His stash of money he left on top of his battered dresser, where old Dennison, the building manager, would find it. The coins and bills were strictly local, stamped with a large "MIL" on their faces that indicated they could be used only in the Milford area. That restriction was an edict of the *Cweom-jik*, a rule that helped them maintain a tight grip on commerce, in the same manner that they controlled every other aspect of human behavior.

Brent frowned as bitter thoughts of the Ceejays and their rules drifted through his mind. Most people seemed to accept the order of things, but the presence of the aliens was something that had always bothered him. As a child, he spent many hours with his Grandfather Owens, a man who had been alive before the Collapse, the greed-driven fall of human civilization that the aliens, ostensibly, were here to reverse. The popular myth, taught to children and reinforced among adults, was that the Ceejays had happened upon Earth shortly after the duplicators had ruined the world's economy, and had offered to work with mankind, in their generous wisdom, to return humanity to the pre-Collapse state through proper management of the double-edged cornucopia that matter duplication represented.

Certainly, those strange birdlike aliens had helped initially; they provided technological devices for duplication, as well as badly needed raw materials and component charts for the duplication process. But they kept their secrets, knowledge that humans lacked about the molecular structure of items to be duplicated. And over the years of occupation, the *Cweomjik* gained more control, as illiteracy flourished, and unauthorized human use of duplicators diminished.

Some items couldn't be duplicated at all, or so the aliens claimed—the energy sources and weapons that they used, for example. And the Ceejays always seemed to demand more for their aid—more labor, more artifacts, more respect.

Erlanger shook his head, as he noticed that his fist had clenched the now-discarded dress shirt into a ball. Those stories told by his grandfather of the Old Times when men made what they needed, either individually or in "factories," seemed fresh in his mind. When people had more freedom . . . when local officials did not decide life or death at whim . . . when a man could travel whenever and wherever he wanted . . . when there was something called "democracy."

Somehow, the aliens did not seem to be helping humanity all that much. The only real technology beyond what his grandfather had called 19th Century—powered vehicles, weapons, communications devices, and the like—was in the four-fingered claws of the Ceejays and their designated leaders, the governors and the mayors.

"Yeah. Technology," Erlanger muttered, as his fingers brushed the smooth suppleness of his small toolkit, the symbol of his vocation as artificer. The pouch that contained those tools was a pre-Collapse, unduplicated item made from the skin of cattle through a now-forgotten tanning process. Sturdy yet lightweight, it closed up like a saddle bag, and easily could be carried over one shoulder. This he placed on the hardwood floor, next to his bundle of clothing.

There was little else. He rarely kept food in the room, for it spoiled too quickly or attracted bugs. And if he excluded his set of carving knives, he had no weapons. Clothes and his toolkit, not much for a man's life. And he only hoped that he would need the latter, since he doubted very much that he would be manufacturing any more of the various decorative gizmos that the aliens prized so highly. With luck, however, he might find some small town, far away, that was in need of an artificer or mechanic, where they would not ask too many questions about his background. He was good at his trade—repairing kitchen things, pumps, wagons, and the occasional bicycle. Better still was his skill at making the unique creations that the Ceejays considered "art," with which they decorated their aircars, their roost homes, and apparently exported to their other planets—wherever those distant worlds might be. Human artifacts were prized by the aliens, as much as human labor was required by them.

So, that's it, he thought, conscious of his increasing hunger. He would have to leave the bulk of his equipment—the saws, the hammers, the foot-pedal lathe, and all the rest—at his workshop on Maple Street. As late as it was, he did not want to be poking around town any longer, and it would look odd to be carrying those larger tools. With a sigh and a last look around his rummaged apartment, he grabbed up the sheet full of clothing and slung the toolkit over his left shoulder.

He listened for a movement on the stairs, then took the rear exit from the building, which gave way to an alley where there was little chance of being seen. The bundle made an awkward balance to the toolkit, and he shifted his grip as he stood beside the remains of an old powered vehicle. A "pick-up," his grandfather had called it, though not much identifiable was left after decades of salvage for duplication. He noted the high-pitched voices of a group of children who played near the alley's mouth, but the area was otherwise empty. A half block west, then he turned north on Mill Street and headed for the Littlemee River.

The bridge would have to be avoided, for by now the Constable—perhaps the Mayor himself—might be looking for him. Or maybe not, since no one had come pounding on his door. The Mayor had most likely had a late, busy night too, although Erlanger was sure that it was not as much fun as he and the Mayor's daughter had found.

In any event, he was certain that the Mayor's sister would be carrying tales as soon as she could. Heather Barlow had a couple of years on Erlanger, and thanks to her pinched face and sharp tongue, he was not the only unattached male to have rejected her advances. Now that rejection would be repaid with interest. The last man who had been caught in a similar compromising position with the lovely Marla *had* been hanged. True, that man had been a relative stranger from Perintown with no special skills, but Erlanger was not about to test his neighbor's good will. All Milford knew that the Mayor had big plans for Marla— public scandal would be squelched in a most direct fashion. Thus he was hardly being overcautious in disappearing, and it would be even better if no one saw him leave.

With a casual, inconspicuous stride, he reached the river bank without incident. Fortunately, the preceding summer and early autumn had been quite dry, and the river was low enough to cross at this point, if one did not mind wet feet. Just as his right boot entered the muddy water, he heard a shout. He turned slowly and his empty stomach clenched.

"You, Erlanger!" It was George Welch, the town Constable. There was no mistaking the man's silhouette, though Erlanger had barely made out the voice.

"Hold up there," Welch added. The Constable was maybe 30 feet away, and Erlanger tensed for running flight. Then he saw the pistol, a slug-thrower, one bit of Old Time technology that the Ceejays allowed their trustees to have. Erlanger had seen the thing in use, and knew how large a hole it could make in a deer—or a man. He forgot about running and slowly removed his foot from the water.

Welch caught up with him, breathing hard from the efforts of moving his 250 pounds of flab at an unaccustomed pace. Despite his predicament, Erlanger could not help a sly smile—every constable or sheriff he had ever seen was out of shape. Had they not had guns, there would be no law, no order.

"Morning, Constable," Erlanger said, carefully.

"Where the hell you think you're going, Brent? The Mayor wants to see you—*now!*"

Erlanger stepped back from the barrel of the pistol, which Welch had thrust so carelessly at his face.

"Just going fishing." He straightened up and tried to look self-righteous. "Besides, what's his nibs want with me? This is my day off, and he can call Jenkins if he needs something fixed. Or if the Ceejays want to buy any of my wares, tell him they're all on display at Sally's booth."

Welch smiled, not quite leering, and stuck his free thumb in the black plastic gun belt that strained around his waist. "Oh now, you *know* damn good and well what he wants. Half the town saw Heather Barlow dragging Marla up from the river bank last night . . . and you coming in from the woods, all hot and lathered. He knows you were knocking off a piece down here, and he don't like it one damn bit!"

The accused swallowed, but the dry lump stayed in his throat. "Well, what of it?" he finally managed. "She's old enough, and I'd hardly be the first. The Mayor shouldn't get his feathers ruffled over people having fun when he calls a festival."

The pistol poked the thinner man in the chest for emphasis. "Barlow can do any damn thing he pleases, boy, and right now he pleases to talk to you. I imagine they'll set up the trial right quick," Welch added with a smirk. "Should add a bit of spice to the festival."

Erlanger thought furiously. If he could get this fat slob to drop his guard a little, maybe divert his attention, he might be able to get the jump on him. He glanced around covertly. No one was in sight, and nothing suggested itself, except—"You know," he said, as he stepped to one side of the Constable, "right here's where I had her."

Welch looked down, then licked his lips. "Right here, on those rocks? She's soft, but she ain't that soft!" He sniggered.

"No, of course not. We were right up there, under the trees." Erlanger pointed back toward town, to a small grove of oak and locust on the hillside.

The big man turned his head to look at the supposed spot of lust, and Erlanger was on him. He swung his toolkit and connected with the side of the Constable's head, while his right—now free of the bundle—grabbed for the wrist of Welch's gun hand. The pistol fired, but the bullet whined harmlessly off the rocks to their left, and Welch went down as Erlanger hooked a foot behind his fat ankle. Bent over, Erlanger wrenched the gun from the stunned man's grasp, then punched him in the face, twice.

Welch lay still. Erlanger picked up the gun and his own things, checked the Constable's belt, and relieved him of a sheath knife as well. Without looking back, he stepped into water that soon flowed over the tops of his boots, and hurried across the river.

On the opposite side, he plunged into dense brush, ignoring scratches to his face and hands as he pushed aside blackberry and other creepers, and pulled himself up the steep bank. Finally, shielded by a large tree stump, he paused to catch his wind and look back.

Welch was stirring, so at least he had not added murder to his outlaw book. He continued up the hill until he found the old road, then headed west at a full run. Several hundred yards later he left the road, which had turned slightly south, and took a path that was, according to his grandfather, once a track for "railroads"—massive passenger- and freight-carrying vehicles. The steel tracks were long gone to the duplicators, and the going on the smooth roadbed would be easier than on the westbound road below. That old pavement, when it was not cracked and jumbled, was hard on the feet.

For the first time that day, Brent Erlanger allowed

his hunched shoulders to relax. Uncertain as he was about where he was going, what he might do, he felt good, even relieved. He had not realized until now just how deadly boring his life had become. He chuckled at the thought—deadly it might be now, but not boring.

Chapter

TWO

Two hours later, after alternately running and walking, Erlanger allowed himself rest. He was completely beyond familiar territory now. A while back, he had skirted the next village, Fairfax, and that detour had taken him south to another river bank. This river was a good half-mile wide, and could only be the Hiyo.

Judging from the position of the sun, the great river headed west, the way he had decided to go. Grandfather Owens had told him many times about the ruins of the mighty city that lay to the west, perhaps a day's travel away. But human deputies patrolled the districts between towns, and killed anyone who could offer no passport—an effective deterrent to wanderlust for most people.

The Governor's deputies, even the odd Ceejay overflight, gave Erlanger little concern. Rumor had it that the deputies kept mainly to the old roads, because bands of outlaws lived between the towns and in the wild country where roads were few. Such bands—if they existed—could be a real problem.

What worried him more than outlaws at the moment was the gnawing in his stomach. Water was easy enough to find, but he had left town in a bit of a hurry, without a thing to eat. It was still early enough in the season that he might find some apple trees bearing; maybe pears—grapes, too, might have been planted in these parts. Or perhaps he could bring down a squirrel or a rabbit. Hell, he thought, why think small? He patted the heavy revolver in his belt—this baby could put a deer in the pot. Saliva moistened his dry mouth at the prospect of fresh meat.

An instant later the gun was in his hand, and he was fading quickly into a dense thicket above the high water mark. All thoughts of dinner vanished, and a cold lump returned to his throat. Upriver, barely a hundred feet away, a group of six men walked out onto the smooth gravel of the river's edge. They were talking quietly and pointing in his direction. At first, he was sure that he had been spotted, but looking downriver, he saw the object of their attention. A body had washed up on shore.

The six, dressed in rough stained clothing that his nose could have tracked in the dark, carried an assortment of weapons. The largest two had long knives through their belts, while the others had staffs or spears of some kind. As they moved toward him, he became painfully aware of just how thin his cover was. Only chance had prevented him from being spotted thus far, and they were sure to see or hear him as they drew near.

By their ragged dress and arms, he had to assume they were outlaws—and not friendly. Erlanger knew that their superior numbers would overwhelm him easily, even if he used the gun. Sure, he had some knowledge of how to use the pistol—you pointed it and pulled the trigger—but he didn't have hands-on experience, and Welch had given him more practice with the other end than he cared to have again. But it was his only hope if things went as sour as they looked to become. It might be possible to befriend this bunch, fall in with them, but he would not take long odds on that.

Still, they were almost upon him and it was worth a try. He stepped out into full view as they came abreast of his hiding place. They stopped and swore— barely 15 feet from him—and one, a burly old guy with a bushy beard, moved toward him with hand on knife hilt.

"Who the hell are you, sneaking up like that?" Hairy Chin demanded, waving a metal staff menacingly with his free hand.

"Ah . . . be easy, friends. I'm Brent Erlanger. Used to live in Milford, back to the east, artificer by trade. But . . . I had to leave a bit sudden."

"So?" Hairy Chin must have made some sign, for the whole group moved several steps closer, and the two at the flanks shifted out of his direct line of sight.

None had yet noticed the gun, for Erlanger had concealed it under the leather tool pouch that was draped over his right arm. Now he brought the weapon into clear view. "Don't come any closer, any of you. No need to get riled, I'm on the outside of the towns, same as you."

"Now ain't that something?" the old grey-beard said, his eyes narrowed. "Do you have six shots in that collector's item, boy, or you just bullshitting us?" Hairy Chin reached for his knife, as did two others. Torn Shirt, on the far left, made a noise like a mare in season, and stuttered, "Let me have 'em, Pop. This townie's jus' bullshittin'."

Erlanger squeezed the stiff trigger. There was a roar, and his arm was pushed up and away. He gripped the pistol desperately, as Hairy Chin flew backwards with crimson blood gushing from his destroyed face. The rest of the band scattered like chickens before a cat—heading upriver, a couple in the river even. Erlanger, still gripping the gun in both hands, ran downstream, then ducked into brambles and willows along the hillside. Echoes from the shot reverberated from the rocky cliffs on the distant shore, and now two corpses graced this side of the Hiyo.

Slowly and carefully, as silent as a town man could be in the woods, Erlanger made his way up the steep river bank to an overgrown road at the crest. Suddenly conscious of his relative exposure, he stepped back into the bushes and checked both directions. Nothing. Even the background sounds of birds and insects, chirps and clicks that he noticed only in their absence, had vanished with the abrupt gunshot. In the distance, at the west end of the road, he could see a large number of buildings, two and three stories tall. In the late afternoon sun that was just breaking through thinning clouds, heat waves shimmered and danced on old concrete pavement, and he had to squint to be sure that no shapes moved among the decayed structures.

Satisfied that there was no obvious danger, he stepped back to the road, then thought better of walking down the middle, opting instead for the narrow pathway that paralleled it—a sidewalk, apparently, just like those few short sections that survived in Milford.

As he neared the first buildings, he noted that they resembled the older ones in his home town as well—quite similar to his former apartment, in fact. But no people were here, no signs of recent habitation. Dark windows gaped at him, empty holes with occasional intact glass panes that broke the gloom with their reflections. Tiny sounds returned, but these were the voice of abandonment—the scurry of paws, the buzz and flutter of wings.

Could this be the fabled city, at least the beginning of it? he wondered. Not that he had expected to find civilization, or even anyone living in the city. After the Collapse, cities had become hellholes of death and destruction; rapidly bereft of food and water, cities fell first to brutes, then bacteria. Many of his grandfather's tales had been about the post-Collapse years in Sincee. Erlanger dimly remembered his mother, who had died when he was seven or eight, and the way she would try to hush Grandfather when he told him those horror tales of weapons and human prey, of filth and plague. Now, in the empty suburbs, a bit of that boy returned, and he felt the small hairs rise on the back of his neck as a shiver ran through him.

He shook his head and moved on—aware that an edict of the *Cweom-jik* had cleared all cities years ago.

He had moved some distance from the river, generally north and west, he thought, although the sun was getting low and it was difficult to be sure.

At one point he walked up on a concrete bridge, which crossed, not water, but other roads, and the added elevation gave him a view of greater congestion further west, but he was not really sure what he was seeing. One end of the concrete bridge was broken and blackened, and while there were remnants of ancient powered vehicles aplenty, he could not imagine what had taken such a massive bite from the sturdy bridge. Many of the old cars and trucks had been stripped—no doubt to supply raw materials for duplication at some time, but others were intact and a few even contained human skeletons. Mindful of what his grandfather had said about city diseases, he gave those shocking, grey remains a wide berth, but not so wide as to fail to notice that some of the piles of tattered cloth and bones had once been children.

Though most were badly weathered and illegible, he spotted many signs bearing what he assumed were names. Most meant nothing to him, but he tried to puzzle out some of them; he felt he owed his grandfather that much. Chester Owens had been insistent that his grandson learn to read and write, and while well aware of the risks, he and two other Old Timers had conducted secret classes for over two years. He had been proud of young Brent, the best student in the class, he claimed, but Erlanger never got a chance to graduate.

As he moved slowly through debris-littered streets, Erlanger's reverie was abruptly shattered. Now well past suppertime, not to mention dinner and breakfast, he sniffed a familiar tangy odor drifting in on the light breeze from the river. He followed his nose and among large houses with faded, once-white columns and rusty iron fencing, he spied fruit trees. Rotten, bird-pecked apples dotted the base of several gnarled old trees.

He began plucking all the yellowish-red fruit within reach. He soon began to drop more of his treasure than he gained as hunger overcame common sense. Finally he put his hoard down in the tall grass next to the stand of trees, and retrieved one of his shirts from the clothing bundle.

Quick half-knots in the sleeves and collar turned the buttoned shirt into a makeshift fruit basket, and the hungry farmer returned to his harvest. The apples were small and a little bitter—no doubt the trees had not been pruned or maintained in several generations—but he did not mind. He spotted a tangle of blackberries and picked some of them too. Soon his hands were scratched and purple-stained, and he stretched out in the thick grass to enjoy a few more apples.

Not too far off he could see a faded blue sign.

"B-U-S—S-T-O-P," he read aloud, his lips twisting around the letter sounds. "Bus" he was not sure about, but "stop" he had learned very early in the game, when his grandfather and his old friends had to caution the children against speaking too loudly, or ever mentioning the reading lessons outside of family. Erlanger sighed and tried to clean his hands. So many secrets, so long ago. He let his thoughts drift back.

Grandfather had sent him on some errand, he could not remember what. He ran as fast as his short legs could go, but the Carltons' dog had just had puppies, and they were out in the yard, next to his house. A boy simply had to stop and play with them.

He felt the shadow before he saw the Ceejay aircar pass overhead, and grinned as it seemed to stop right over Grandfather's house. His young freckled face changed to a frown, however, as he recalled the basic teachings: Grandfather did not like Ceejays, but no one should ever say so. The frolicking pups were forgotten as the boy recalled his errand, and started for his own house. At his back, the sky blossomed like the setting sun, and the startled lad turned just in time to feel the heat of that soundless flash that took Charlie and Alice and Miss Tucker ... and Grandfather.

His father warned him that he must never, never mention that he had been to the illegal school. He felt a little guilty, and withdrew within himself. He was sure that he had failed, that he could have warned Grandfather. But his father convinced him that the Ceejays had ways of finding things out; that nothing he could have done would have helped. And then, two years later, his father failed to return from the official trading visit to Perintown, and he was completely alone. Oh, the Stantons had been kind when they took him in, old Buster Stanton made him an apprentice in his artificer shop. But as he entered his teens, he began to overhear the rumors about his family, about his grandfather, and he made few friends.

A large black deerfly buzzed his ear, and Erlanger blinked. He had almost nodded off in the waning afternoon warmth, his stomach now satisfied.

He stood up and stretched, and checked all directions for dangers that his inattention might have missed. Apples and berries are fine, but scarcely an adequate diet, he thought, and he began to consider fish. He had some hooks in his toolkit, but all his line was at his workshop. A pole was no problem, any handy willow would do, but proper line was needed. He could unravel threads from the bedsheet, but that would take hours to braid a reliable length. Certainly, there would be fish in the big river, and one of the signs he had passed earlier had pointed to the north for something called "Eden Park."

He spotted an area of small shops. As he drew closer, one broken window displayed a familiar word. "FISHING LIC" read the grey, metal-looking letters. The "Lic" part was a mystery, but fishing was just what he had in mind.

The sun was almost down, and the interior of the shop was very dim. What he could see, however, was not encouraging. Someone—many someones—had torn the place apart. He stepped gingerly through the shattered metal door frame, and began to explore.

He pushed aside an overturned counter, and felt glass crunch beneath his boots. Dust wrinkled his nose as he suppressed a sneeze, and tried to see into the back of the ruined shop. He tripped over something, and as he looked down, he could not believe his luck. A fishing pole, or at least most of one. The light, springy pole—apparently one of the artificial substances, a plastic of some kind—was missing its top section, but the handle actually included a metal reel. The reel was corroded and useless, of course, but he recognized nylon line when he saw it—after all, he had paid dearly enough for such fishing line when it came his turn at the Milford duplicator.

As he gathered up the valuable line, he noted the dim outline of a back door. Through the cracked door panel, he could see another room, and an open rear exit. He was just about to clear aside the rubble that blocked his way when he froze. Voices! Human voices.

Only weeds and brambles were visible from his vantage point, but the voices seemed to be moving away to the northwest. More outlaws, he thought, or perhaps the men from the river bank.

Erlanger decided that a short retracing of steps would be in order. At least, if he headed back east, he would be in an area he had already covered. With full night almost upon him, he would need the relative safety of familiar surroundings.

Carefully, he crept toward the front of the shop. Once he winced as something long and brittle made a sharp snap-crackle, but he paused for some minutes and heard no outcry.

Once outside, he remained close to the buildings, and regained the road without incident.

Chapter

THREE

The night was uneventful, but hardly pleasant.
About a mile from the place where he had found the
fishing rod—and heard voices—he discovered a three-
story brick building with a metal stairway on the
outside.

The steps up the wall, more like a ladder really,
were a surprise. Not only did they provide easy access to the flat roof, but the bottom section could be
pulled up, and the whole thing was still quite safe
and sturdy. Once on the empty roof, with the stairs
raised, he had little fear of being surprised while he
slept; but that bottom section, although unusually
light in weight, did make a terrible squeal of protest
when pulled up.

The early autumn chill was a challenge to the extra clothes in his bundle, and twice he awakened to
distant cries, animal cries or howls to be sure, but
troubling nonetheless. Thus, his sleep was far from
comfortable, and Erlanger had risen with unaccustomed stiffness in every joint.

In the morning light he could see the wide river

below, and green fields of what he assumed to be the
park in the opposite direction. Closer to hand, on the
roof itself, he noticed a large bulge. Although it was
stained with bird lime and grime, it was semi-
transparent. As he brushed dust from this plastic
dome, and leaned against it for a closer look, a section shattered and fell through to the room below.
Inside, it looked like an ordinary apartment—dusty,
true, and with some furnishings he did not recognize,
but apparently otherwise undisturbed.

He sat back from the edge of the intriguing hole
and rubbed the stubble on his chin. He ought to be
thinking about food, but he still had plenty of apples,
and the strange sights had piqued his curiosity. He
gathered his things and considered the easiest way
into the intriguing room, into what was obviously a
private dwelling over a shop of some sort. As he
headed toward the outside steps, he noticed a lower,
square bulge in the roof that had the look of a trap
door. He knelt down and pulled, and much of the
wooden frame came away. A few more jerks, and he
was looking into another large hole—this one with a
wooden ladder to one side.

Now mindful of dangers from decayed wood and
metal, he placed first one foot, then the other on the
ladder. There were little creaks of protest, but the
wood held. He tossed his possessions to the bottom
and descended quickly.

He was at first disappointed by the four rooms he
found. The air held dust, musty odors, and a lingering hint of rot—the latter from a large, yellow metal
box in the kitchen area, but there were few surprises.
Several devices, 'lectric or 'lectronic he supposed,
had no obvious function that he could identify, but
most of the furnishings appeared little different from
those he had seen in Milford houses. Oh, he was
pleased to find knives and other useful eating and

cooking utensils in kitchen drawers and cupboards, but as he stashed these items in his increasingly awkward bundle, he pondered the lack of uniqueness in the Old Times objects.

He was turning to leave the rooms when his foot caught on the red, patterned rug. Like all the floor coverings in the apartment, this one was laid out wall to wall, and was of no familiar fabric or weave. Near the bed, however, the edges of a cut rectangle were clearly visible. Must have got wet and curled up, he decided, although a quick glance revealed no obvious ceiling leaks. He kneeled and pulled up the rectangle.

"Aha! Another trap door." Erlanger fumbled with the recessed metal catch, and opened the hidden panel. Plastic. The rare, black material covered packages, and he slowly pulled the heavy objects to floor level. The small, wrapped package on top contained a pistol and ammunition, but he scowled in frustration when it became obvious that dripping water had rusted the weapon to useless scrap. And even to his untrained eye, the cartridges were too small for the gun in his belt.

A yet smaller packet held coins, gold coins! He whistled as he counted his find. Gold could be duplicated only from high-grade ore, or large amounts of old jewelry, and was greatly prized. Suddenly he was a rich man—at least a rich outcast. The larger, heavier bundles were even more astonishing. Books! Lots of books. Why, his grandfather had dared to keep only one, and it had been destroyed with its owner, so many years before.

Many of these books were water-stained, their pages gummed together, but some were in good condition. As he carefully opened one of the latter, a whistle escaped his lips again. The book was heavily-illustrated with drawings of machines. Clockwork and pistons he recognized readily, but many other pictures were a complete mystery. And the other intact books were even more strange, with unfamiliar titles, long, puzzling words, and truly odd symbols next to numbers and letters.

He returned to the main room, his new treasures in hand, the gold in his pockets. He could hardly carry all the books, but two were added to his clothes bundle for leisurely study. The remainder he rewrapped and returned to the hiding place. He doubted that anyone else would happen along, but maybe the water that had destroyed books and gun would now be kept out.

His stomach growled, a reminder that even rich men with books have to eat. He considered the door that led out of the main room, but a sharp kick at the painted metal pained all the way up his spine. A glance at the unfamiliar locks convinced him that he would have to retrace his steps up, then back down to the street.

From his vantage point on the roof, he could see no easy way down to the river, so he opted for a probable fishing spot in the park.

It was not the best looking fishing hole he had ever seen, but it had fish. The grasshoppers he caught in the tall grass proved appealing and the carp that rose to the bait were indeed appetizing.

As he finished his third fish, Erlanger considered whether to try for more in the pond, and smoke them for later over the fire he had built. No, that would take too much time, he decided, and fresh ones seemed easy to catch.

Casually, he pulled another apple from his pocket, and then felt nature call. To his left he spied a small building near the trees. When he got closer, he chuckled aloud. "Men" and "women" he read, chiseled into the concrete privy—just what he needed. Habit took him toward the "Men" side, but a rank odor changed his mind, and he headed for the other side. He doubted that any of the opposite sex were around to object.

Inside, the porcelain fixtures were dirty, and empty of water, of course, but still served their intended function. Wonder of wonders, there were even rolls of most-appreciated paper, although the outer layers crumbled into grey snow at his touch.

Now feeling much better about his world, Erlanger paused in the doorway. The strange odor had penetrated to the women's side as well, and he wondered what had died—fairly recently—in the other room. Made bold by his success in apartment exploration, he stepped through the mystery door. It took several seconds for his eyes to adjust, as the men's room lacked the hole in the roof that had illuminated the other side. But the carrion smell was almost overpowering, along with another, somehow-familiar stench. "Smells like cat shi—"

He did not complete the thought; did not have to. A loud roar drew him erect. His heart began to race, and he turned his head slowly. Outlined in the doorway was a cat, larger than he had ever seen or imagined. And a noise behind him proved that the deeper recesses of the room held another. Very slowly, he inched away until the small of his back pressed up against a hard sink. He felt numb, without thought, without plan. The two monsters, probably a mated pair, looked large enough to bring down a bull. They had to weigh over 500 pounds, and even if they did look well fed, no animal likes uninvited visitors in its lair.

He could barely make out the one farther inside, though its yellow-green eyes glinted in the weak light. The other had not moved from the doorway, although its tail, hooked at the end, swayed back and forth in

an almost hypnotic rhythm. The skin was pulled back
from the jaw in a frightening grin, the teeth thus
exposed . . . teeth that could snap a thigh bone like a
twig. Erlanger felt his legs grow weak at the thought
of those long, brown teeth in his flesh. Neither cat
moved. Gradually, the paralysis of thought lifted,
and the cornered man remembered his weapons. The
gun and knife were both at his belt. Maybe I won't
need them, he thought feebly, as he ran his tongue
over dry lips. Maybe they're just as terrified of me as
I am of them. But what the hell are they?

Stories had come down for generations about dangerous wild animals, but Grandfather Owens had
scoffed at many of those tales, and suggested that
such yarns were merely another way of keeping town
folk under control. But the old man had agreed that
there were once places called "zoos," animal places
that might have been emptied when things fell apart
during the Collapse.

No tale, no story to keep young children from wandering into the woods, had prepared Erlanger for
what he now faced, however. While he could not be
sure about the other one, far back in the gloom of
metal stalls, the cat that blocked his escape was
white. Not straw-colored like lions were supposed to
be, not striped like tigers, not black like leopards.
Erlanger shuddered slightly as he restrained a full
shrug, his hand sliding slowly to the pistol.

Just as his shaking fingers curled around the grip
of his most powerful weapon, the cat in the doorway
snarled and hunched its shoulders. The noise was
incredible within the small room, and the snarl was
answered with a matching howl from the other cat.
Erlanger fumbled with the gun. Some part of it caught
in his belt. The damn beast was about to spring, its
rear legs bunched!

The pistol came free, and the floor saved him. While

covered with years of wind-blown grime, the surface was still smooth glazed tile underneath, and the big cat was unable to gain firm purchase. It scrabbled for sure footing, found none, but leaped anyway. As it flew toward his right shoulder, Erlanger fired. The cat's body crashed into the wall two sinks away from his rigid stand.

His dazed eyes lingered on the dead attacker too long. With a soft pad of feet, the other cat was on him. Reflexively, he threw up his arm, and felt the pistol connect solidly within the gaping mouth. His grip on the weapon slackened, as the cat bit down and twisted, and nerveless fingers released the gun when claws raked his ribs. He kicked out desperately, and the big cat gave ground just long enough for his left hand to snatch out the sheath knife. He slashed inexpertly across one foreleg, and pressed his slight advantage to slash lower, across the ribs. The cat's teeth found his shoulder, and both went down to the floor. Erlanger stabbed and slashed blindly, while his weakened right hand tried to choke and push the massive head away.

Then it was over. He lay gasping, his heart pounding in his ears, while blood both feline and human cooled on his ripped clothing. As he tried to push himself up, he winced at the pain in the torn muscles in his right shoulder. It was all he could do to keep from screaming. Shock had set in, and he shook his head to try to clear his vision.

He was never sure how he made it back to the pond, to his meager possessions. He woke in pain, with chills, beside the dying fire where he had cooked fish no telling how long before. After he had crawled to the pond's edge, and drank cooling water, some rationality returned. He inspected the injuries, sure that he was dying, and was pleasantly surprised to find that only his shoulder was seriously wounded.

Thankful that he had found the metal pots earlier, he stoked up the fire and boiled water to clean up as best he could, left-handed. Somehow, he still had the killing knife, but the gun was missing. No matter; the need for safe shelter outweighed any possible attraction that a return to the cats' den might hold.

Having cleaned and covered his wounds as best he could, Erlanger walked slowly away from the ponds, looking for a safe spot. He spotted what appeared to be a tower through the trees, and he made for it, pausing frequently to catch his breath.

When he reached the tower base he found a flaking steel door, barely held in place by rusting hinges. After several minutes of concentrated, exhausting effort, he was able to force the door from its frame and pull himself up winding stairs. At the top of the first flight, he fell into a rounded room where large, corroded pipes offered shelter from the rain that was beginning to blow through the broken windows. He had just enough strength to set his cooking pots beneath dripping rain water before he passed out on top of the lumpy bag of clothing.

Chapter

FOUR

The days following were a chaotic blur for Erlanger. Somehow, despite loss of blood and a raging fever, he survived. The old stone tower proved to be a serviceable shelter through his recovery period, and before a week had passed he was making short forays to scavenge what food he could find. There were, oddly enough, plenty of berry bushes and fruit trees in the vicinity. In lucid moments, the injured man had wondered whether the area had once been a farm. Odd that it should be so close to the city, though.

He was soon strong enough to make his way down to the shallow ponds for a catch of fat carp. After several trips, his confidence returned—he'd seen no additional cats, and it seemed likely that the pair he had killed were the only ones around. Occasionally, as he passed the weather-worn restrooms, he could smell the cats' rotting carcasses, but he had no desire to make a closer inspection.

A more thorough search of the ruined city held little appeal, either. He had no reason to assume that his treasure-finding luck would hold, and he now had every reason to fear dark buildings. The items from the "Fishing Lic" store had been ample, and as for the room with the mysterious books ... well, he could return there, should he ever feel the need.

Erlanger was not quite sure how many days had passed, but as the sunny afternoon warmed his healing flesh, he felt the time had come to move on.

He pushed slowly up from the dusty floor, winced slightly at what the movement did to his right side, and started to collect his possessions. "Got to find some friendly people."

Early the next morning, his familiar bundle and toolkit over his shoulder, he found himself treading towards the mighty river. He hoped to find a bridge to carry him across. Safety, he was sure, lay on the opposite side. He was even willing to swim if he had to, to gain the southern side. No telling how long he would be living in the open, and further south was certainly the appropriate direction, considering the winter weather in these parts.

An hour's trek up and down the riverfront proved disheartening. A stiff breeze from the muddy water brought constant grit to his eyes, along with a general odor of rot. He found evidence that at least five bridges had crossed the Hiyo at one time or another, carrying vehicle traffic over vast roadways. Now there were none.

Or at least, next to none. The Ceejays, who had leveled all cities, had not done a complete job on one bridge. A pair of enormous arches stretched above him, as he stood on cracked concrete at the base. Rusted steel beams, dotted here and there with clinging flakes of yellow paint, supported fragments of roadway that extended over open water about a third of the way across the river. Rubble—stone and more

twisted beams, rose from the water to meet the shortened span.

Worth a try, Erlanger thought, as he gazed at more
steel than he had ever seen in one place before. Even
if he had to swim the rest of the way, the head start
from this end of the broken bridge would justify the
effort required to climb to the level of that shattered
road. He kicked aside a thin metal sign to gain a
better view of the challenge, and as the sign turned
over, he had a minor revelation. That long word had
been seen frequently, but never made sense. Suddenly he realized that his grandfather had shortened
the name of this place for some reason. Cincinnati,
not Sincee. He shrugged and kicked the sign again.
What difference did it make? Invocation of the true
name would not restore the bridge.

And the bridge was going to require more than a
little effort, he saw now. He would have to climb at
least 80 feet, although the broken concrete and twisted
metal appeared to have adequate hand and foot holds.

He swung his two loads so that they would balance
reasonably well as they hung over his back, and approached the base of the ramp. A chill traveled down
his spine.

Glad that none of his few friends were here to see
the case of shakes that his task brought on, he wiped
damp palms against his soiled pants, and carefully
mapped his route up the face of the steep wall.

Forty minutes of effort brought him over the edge
of rugged, grey pavement, where he stretched out to
calm his labored breathing and rub circulation back
into cramped fingers. The climb had not been that
bad—just slow going, hard work, and no little pain.
But he hadn't looked down, even once. He'd made it.

Once he felt sufficiently rested, Erlanger began his
journey to the foreshortened end of the bridge. After
a brief walk, perhaps 300 feet, he stood looking down

at the roiling water. While the wind was much stronger at this point, there were adequate beams and cables to ease his descent, and he began without hesitation.

Fortunately, while the rubble began as a few projecting beams at the top, it widened quickly into a gradual slope of tortured metal and collapsed stone. Once at the bottom, his scuffed boots stood only three feet from the rushing water. Large blocks of concrete, green with river slime, led into the water.

Erlanger sat on a convenient upthrust block, and pondered the remainder of his crossing. That chill returned to the back of his neck as he considered the struggle through uncertain currents laden with toolkit and clothing bundle. From here, the river looked a lot wider than it had from the shore. He wasn't about to simply jump in and start stroking. No way to tell what might hinder or even snare him; further out, he could see ripples of white water that surely marked underwater hazards.

He looked about carefully, in hopes that something would suggest itself, and sure enough he spotted a log in a collection of debris caught by chunks of the bridge.

With a cautious eye toward his footing, he moved onto the pile of flotsam. Foul odors caused him to draw back momentarily, and he wrinkled his nose at the smell of something long dead. No doubt it had drowned and been river-tossed among the debris.

The mass was unsteady as he stepped on a solid-looking pile of brush and let it shift with his weight and stop moving before he leaned fully in that direction. Six similar steps, and he was within reach of his chosen log, his river boat. As he leaned out to snag the log, the debris beneath him separated, and he found himself in the water.

It was cold, but not intolerably so, and he quickly caught hold of the log he was after.

He clung to the log for a timeless interval, while cold air and water spray rasped in his throat. It was all he could do to keep his head up, his chin on the rough wood, and both arms draped over the side. By the time he found the strength to climb astride the log and lift his soaked load from his back, the current had carried him over a half-mile west, downriver. And that current was growing stronger.

Erlanger finally achieved an unsteady balance, with clothes and toolkit steadied by both hands on the log as he leaned forward. He began kicking to break out of the current, and finally succeeded in heading the log toward the southern shore.

Eventually, he felt something reasonably solid beneath his tired legs—the muddy bed of the river rising to meet the shore. Fighting the pull of the water and the muck that sucked at his boots, he guided the log and its precious cargo to the river's edge. He sank to the sandy bank, where he wearily pulled his two bundles to dry ground.

He lay on his back for a long time, unnaturally hot and exhausted. Then he moved to inspect his possessions. Surprisingly, his books were not very wet. The larger of the two volumes, the one with the title *How Things Work*, had a new water stain on its cover, but was otherwise dry. The other one, *Inorganic Chemistry*, had some wet pages, but they could be dried without damage. His clothing bundle must have absorbed most of the water that had penetrated the sack, thereby protecting the books. The small cloth bag containing the coins was soaked, but a little water wouldn't hurt gold. His tools, on the other hand, would have to be dried before they rusted.

The sun was high, just past noon he figured, as he opened the books to help them dry, then sat back to let the warmth work on him, too. Strange, how very tired . . . not much of a climb, really, and not that long a swim either . . . almost as if I'm still sick . . .

Grandfather stood above him and glared at him, his face stern. "Look what you've done, boy! Screwed around that dead city too long, and now you're in trouble. Sure, you got some good finds, but I told you never to explore alone!"

"But, I had to . . ." Erlanger began, strangely small before the older man.

"You got to get the hell out of that blasted place and find some real people, people with your kind of spunk and ability. To hell with exploring now; the name of this game is survival. Find the right folks to join up with, and then plan, then explore. Those damned *Cweom-jik* got to be pushed off this planet, and there must be people somewhere working at doing just that. You need to be with them, not traipsing around hill and dale, taking what scraps of my world you can find."

Marla strolled up beside Grandfather. "Leave him alone, old man. Leave him to me." She smiled sweetly at Erlanger. "We have better things to do, don't we, Brent?"

Grandfather turned, in an odd slow motion, to face the young woman, who for some reason was nude, except for a garland of flowers in her hair. As the old man turned, he slowed even more. Marla turned her head, and she, too, slowed. Then both froze. A shadow crept over the two, and it was suddenly very cold. Erlanger looked up to see the sun blotted out by the bulk of an enormous *Cweom-jik* aircar. Then, a flash, thousands of times brighter than the sun. Grandfather was gone . . . Marla was gone . . .

Chapter

FIVE

Erlanger sat up on the cold, muddy beach. Through a tangle of tree roots and other river bank trash, he looked at the ruined city. His head ached, and he shook it to clear the hallucination from his brain. Grandfather was certainly long dead, and Marla was but a remembrance of his equally-dead past. But they seemed so real.

He chuckled over Grandfather Owens' words, almost hysterical, as he wondered how his unconscious had fed him the dream, had tried to tell him something. Well, maybe that was the way to go. Hook up with rebels—if there truly were any—and fight those damned birds. Nothing of his old life was left to him now. He could do whatever he wished, almost like the people during the Old Times. He was free.

What was it that Grandfather had said once about freedom? "There will always be free men, and you won't find them bowing down—not to other men, and not to aliens!"

A chill wracked his body, and it was difficult to think clearly. Grandfather had not been talking about outlaw bands, he was sure of that. From the one bunch he'd seen, there was little freedom there. Sneaking around, hiding out—that was no way to live. But if there were rebels, a really constructive organization, he was more than willing to join. If they would have him. Any village he might happen upon, on the other hand, was sure to have leaders who would be suspicious of strangers.

His face felt hot, yet his legs and feet were cold. Something caught his wandering attention on the opposite shore. He squinted, and his vision cleared. There, over the city's northern edge, a large blur about a mile from the river bank . . . a Ceejay aircar!

Suddenly, a bolt of light erupted from the underside of the flying machine. Smoke and debris rose from the point where the flash struck the ground. The damn Ceejays were bombing some target over there. Erlanger scrambled to gather his possessions, and ran up the hill from the river's edge. His legs felt rubbery, and air burned in his lungs as he gulped short breaths. He looked back from the relative safety of a grove of small trees with yellowing leaves. From this higher position, he spotted other moving shapes downriver from the aircar. Six figures were dashing about, throwing things into what looked like a small boat.

Who were they? The ones that he'd heard days ago while crouched in the back of the "Fishing Lic" store? He strained to make out what they were doing, and began to voice his thoughts aloud. "Not another outlaw band?" No, those types shunned the city, or so he had heard. Outlaws favored areas near the remaining population centers, the towns, where they could prey on decent folks. The group over there, at least from what he could see at this distance, looked to be wearing the same type of clothing—uniforms

perhaps, the colors of which were obviously camouflage.

Faint sounds drifted through the air. The Ceejay
aircar was blasting again, although it was difficult
for Erlanger to hear above the slap and gurgle of the
great river. The people across the water must have
had the same problem, for only now did they turn
and point in the direction of the alien activity. The
small party immediately dropped their burdens, and
began running back into the ruins. "Makes sense,"
Erlanger muttered, "they wouldn't want to be caught
in that boat, or on the open riverfront." Almost like
watching those "movies" Grandfather used to talk
about, he mused. "You still there, Grandfather? No,
hell with you, old man, send Marla back . . ."

The Ceejays were making random progress toward
the river. Now and then the aircar would stop and
another building would suffer further ruin. As the
aircar drew closer, more details of the oblate sphere
were apparent, and Erlanger's attention focused again.
He could see strange shapes cut into the aircar's hull,
and there were projections, ominous spikes that had
to be weapons.

The humans had disappeared, and Erlanger wished
the unknown group well, outlaws or no. A childhood
legacy from his Grandfather, just now claimed, led
him to cheer silently for the people with the boat. He
rubbed his eyes and watched the alien vessel float
toward the riverfront, toward the now-abandoned
boat. His mouth gaped in surprise when a hatch
opened on the lower side of the aircar and the boat
and all it contained rose quietly into the Ceejay machine. Never before had Erlanger seen such Ceejay
power, such frightening technology. Perhaps there
was much more that he didn't know.

The mysterious hatch closed, and the aircar flew
slowly toward a derelict structure along the road

that paralleled the river. Erlanger was forced to turn away when further blasts began, so bright were the actinic flashes. A low rumble reached his side of the Hiyo, and the ground vibrated beneath his boots.

After several minutes the dazzling shots ceased. All the riverfront buildings, everything that had stood along that section of the concrete bank, was simply gone. In their steed, a softly glowing mound of molten metal, broken here and there by stone and smoke, snaked toward the water.

His feverish chills now replaced with shudders of raw fear, Erlanger contemplated the devastation caused by one *Cweom-jik* aircraft. Those six people, outlaws, fugitives, explorers—it no longer mattered—must have been hiding in the center of that long, hot mound. "Poor bastards didn't have a chance, not a snowflake's chance in hell," he cried quietly, as his right fist clenched around his toolkit. He brushed at wet eyes with a dirty knuckle, and watched the deadly grey aircar hover above the river for several dozen heartbeats. Finally, the Ceejays drifted silently off to the west and disappeared into low clouds.

Erlanger rose unsteadily. He had none of the faiths of the Old Timers. Most of those religious beliefs had died with the Collapse, but he felt like thanking some higher power for his good fortune, for getting him across that river before the Ceejays arrived. Too bad about the six with the boat, but he had escaped. If that aircar had appeared while he was on the bridge, or in the water, he might be just another small patch of black ashes in an unlamented drift downstream. Apparently those rumors were true; Ceejay overflights did hunt down renegade humans, and they were quite effective in the disposal of same.

As he stared towards the clouds that had swallowed the aircar, a wave of dizziness turned his legs to jelly, and he fell to hands and knees. He shook his head sharply and the moment of nausea passed. As he regained his feet, however, his pulse raced, and he still felt hot and weak. "Must be nerves from seeing that attack," he said to himself, and headed up the hillside to the high plain above the river.

By the following evening, Erlanger knew that he was going to die. Fever and terrible weakness were constant, and he had several more hallucinations as he plodded along. His shoulder wounds, which had seemed to be healing, were open. Now an angry red, and with a vile odor, the torn flesh added a stabbing torment to his every movement. He rested beneath a portion of a broken overpass, once a part of the wide roadway labeled "I-75." He had chosen this road because it seemed to bear due south, and the route had been easy. Too, there was a possibility that he might find people along this roadway. He no longer cared how friendly those folks might be, so long as there was a chance that he could get treatment for his injuries. But any chance seemed dim indeed, as the fading sun cast long shadows across the cracked concrete before him.

In lucid moments that grew more and more infrequent throughout that day, Erlanger had realized that his wounds were badly infected, that the fever, weakness, and hallucinations were terminal signs. Only a matter of time, he thought, before the bugs in my blood get me. Either that, or I do something stupid like walking off a cliff while talking to Grandfather. For most of the day, he had simply forced one foot in front of the other. A couple of times, he remembered to forage for food, but there was little to be found.

Now, as he sat beneath the concrete overhang, he knew that he couldn't continue any further. Sure, a town might be just over the next hill. People there might be willing to provide medical attention to a total stranger. His infection might not be too far advanced for treatment. A lot of maybes, too many ifs. He almost didn't care. Tears of pain had replaced grim frustration long ago. It was coming on dark, and he could feel a storm in the air. So nice to sit here, so nice to sleep . . .

His head jerked up, and he grimaced at a new stab of pain. No! He couldn't just give up, couldn't die here against a nameless wall of concrete, not after all he'd done. That would be admitting defeat to the idiots who ran Milford, to the Ceejays . . . to Grandfather. He thought he heard the old man chiding him again, and cocked his head to one side. No, just last year's leaves whispering to him on the evening breeze.

Onto feet, must get up. He leaned into the rough concrete at his back, and with heels and his one good arm, he pushed himself upright. He almost fell as he struggled with his two bundles, but when settled on his back, they seemed to help him balance. He faced the wind, which increased as clouds now completely obscured the setting sun. Again he willed left boot, right boot. Dizziness returned, but his feet kept moving south. Occasionally he stumbled as frost-heaved tarmac tried to trip him, or young trees reached from the road's edge to slap his legs.

Once begun it was easier somehow to keep walking. The cool wind felt good on his forehead. Voices waxed and waned behind him, but he ignored them; he had to keep walking. The sounds moved closer and took shape beside him. Erlanger continued his slow pace southward. The voices became sharper, more insistent, and he wondered, in a detached way, why he didn't recognize these new ghosts. Now a hallucination was standing in front of him. His feet were forced to stop, and he wavered before the blurry apparition. It . . . she started to speak, and her arms waved wildly.

Marla! Marla again, but not lovely in flower-bedecked nudity this time, Marla dressed in strange clothing. Erlanger smiled, his lips formed a familiar greeting, and he opened his arms to embrace her. Sharp stones at knee and palm were the last things he hugged.

A hazy form, a dream, was bending over him. Was someone talking to him? Random sounds, vague snatches of conversation drifted in and out.

"Looks bad, but you know we can't . . ."

"The way station is only . . ."

"Damnit, no! We have to . . ."

Hands, firm hands were on his tired body, were lifting him to float as a ghost, with the ghosts. It felt so good to drift, to give up all responsibilities. Erlanger smiled into unconsciousness.

Again, that vague human shape hovered over him, but he perceived many changes. The cool wind was missing, the sharp gravel no longer stabbed his skin. He lay on some soft surface. A fire burned nearby; he could smell the tang of wood smoke, and feel the radiant warmth. His eyes opened slowly. Marla was there. He felt a sharp prick on his arm, like an injection, and Marla was holding a syringe. Why had Marla cut her long hair—hair now much darker in color? She had aged too, and . . .

It wasn't Marla.

Erlanger tried to sit up, and something pulled painfully at his ribs. He looked down to see large bandages there. More bandages covered his upper arm and shoulder. He was otherwise naked, although a thin blanket covered him from the waist down. Probably just as well, he thought, in the company of strange women. He stared at her, and she met his gaze squarely; her green eyes and mature face revealed nothing. Soft eyes set in a round face. Nose narrow. Lips full. Not unlike Marla's face, yet here a woman, not the ripe, late adolescence of the Mayor's daughter. He closed his eyes and fell back.

"Feeling better?"

"Better than what? My side hurts like hell, and so does my head. But I'm obviously alive, so I guess that's more than I had any right to expect." He tried to sit up again, and succeeded. "What town is this?"

She hesitated. "Not a town, it's a way station."

"On the way to what?"

"Just an underground room, what you see around you. We're about halfway between Cincinnati and Lexington, but well off the highway."

Cincinnati he knew, had escaped from. Lexington was a strange word. He decided not to reveal his ignorance. "So, what do you do here besides rescue strays?"

She smiled, a small, fleeting expression that seemed to brighten the room. "Let's just say we're here to help you heal. We found you on this highway, and we're more than a little curious about you and your tools."

His toolkit! What had they done with it? And his other treasures? He made another silent resolution to reveal as little as possible. "So? What's so curious about me, just a guy with a bad case of cat scratch?"

That smile again. "Ah, so that's what got you. Very nasty. But you're a fellow human, on the lam, and carrying interesting things."

He tried to smile in return, but discovered deep scratches in his face that he didn't remember acquiring, and gave up the effort. "Nasty doesn't come close. Huge, pure white cats ... but I still don't understand what's so interesting about me—"

She had turned her back to adjust the fire in some kind of enclosed woodstove, but she jerked around, her eyes wide. "Birdshit! The Cincinnati white tigers!

We've heard of them, but never saw them. They once made that zoo famous—you're damn lucky to be alive."

He tried to make a casual gesture, as if he routinely slayed dragons before breakfast, but his wince of pain spoiled it. "What about my tools?"

She stared at him thoughtfully. "Let me put it this way—if you know how to use that toolkit, we may have some use for you. And, since you're obviously on the run, maybe you have some information we can use as well."

"Who's this 'we'?"

"That will have to wait for now." From the stove, she produced a small pot of rich-smelling, warm broth. "Try to drink this."

Erlanger stifled the next question, and complied. He found himself suddenly very sleepy, and with the pleasant taste of chicken broth still on his lips, he fell asleep.

The next time he awoke, he heard raised voices—a male and a female voice. As he cautiously opened his eyes and struggled to sit up, the voices stopped. He was chilled suddenly, and pulled the blanket around his shoulders. The stove was out. He looked around, seeing the way station for the first time. He was lying on a wooden bunk that was built into one wall. The floor and walls were of stone.

His nurse and a strange man sat at a small table—staring at him.

"Hello." It seemed appropriate, so he said it.

"Good afternoon," the woman responded. The man nodded, expressionless, and stood. He was taller than Erlanger, maybe six feet four, and solidly built. His dark hair was close-cropped, and a weathered face showed through a thick black beard. He stepped over to Erlanger and stuck out his hand. "I'm Alan Wysocki."

Erlanger returned the man's grip, although his present condition didn't permit a match for Wysocki's obvious strength. "Brent Erlanger, late of Milford, artificer by trade. Thanks for taking me in." His gaze shifted to the woman to include her with his gratitude. She smiled again, longer this time.

Wysocki released his hand, and pulled a chair nearer to his bunk. As he sat down, Erlanger noted that Wysocki was wearing the same type of clothing as the woman—close-fitting, but lose pants and jacket, made of a lightweight, sturdy material. Beneath the jackets were light-colored pullover shirts. Both pants and jacket were in green and tan camouflage patterns . . . the group on the river bank!

He frowned, not sure that he could trust his memories. "Were you on the river bank, loading a boat, a couple of days back?"

"Three days ago, yes," Wysocki replied. "How do you know?"

"I was watching from the south shore. I saw them, the Ceejays, take your boat like they were sucking up a feather. Then they blasted the waterfront. Thought sure everybody over there was dead."

Wysocki looked at the woman, then removed his own jacket and rolled up one sleeve. His arm was red and swathed in bandages. "Other one's just as cooked," he said, as he rolled down the sleeve, his teeth clenched. "I was lucky, at that, just brushed by molten steel. Two of us were killed."

"I thought I counted six," Erlanger said.

"Right. Lori and me, the others have already returned to Base." He picked up the camouflage jacket, searched the pockets, and came up with a battered briar pipe, tobacco, and a crude flint-spark lighter. As he talked, his fingers packed and ignited the pipe with practiced motions, his black eyes remained locked on Erlanger. "We were exploring, looking for useful items, when the damn Beaks showed up and started blasting. Never seen the like; don't think anybody has for years." Wysocki's face took on a grim cast, and Erlanger could see the fire of hate in his eyes.

Although he was far from trusting his wits yet at a gambling table, Erlanger was beginning to understand his benefactors. They had to be rebels. Luck was with him still. He hadn't found them; they had saved him, and he had already been accepted into the group. Or had he?

He had missed Wysocki's last words, as insight dawned. ". . . we're interested in what you were doing on the highway. And now you tell us you were in Cincinnati when those egg-sucking Beaks nailed us." The taller man leaned forward, and stabbed the air with the stem of his pipe. "Just what were you doing there? You were in the city, right?"

Erlanger tried to get comfortable on the narrow bunk, and met the challenging gaze. Had they searched his clothing bundle? Clearly, they'd looked through his toolkit. They probably already had his gold and books, and only needed him for what information they could squeeze from a sick man. He tried to sit up a little straighter. "Where," he asked, as he slid his feet to the floor with care, "is my toolkit and clothing bundle?"

"Take it easy . . . Brent, isn't it? You'd best lie back, you're still in no shape to argue. Your stuff's all there, in the corner." The dark-haired woman, Lori, gestured to her right as she moved closer to the bristling men. By craning his neck, Erlanger could see that his tools and clothing bundle appeared intact, and were where she indicated, among the stacked boxes.

"Yeah, well, bring me my clothes, will you? I suppose my pants are shot, but I got another pair in that bundle . . . as you probably know by now."

Deftly, she moved to his side, and felt his forehead with the back of her left hand as her right held his wrist in a peculiar fashion. She seemed lost in thought for about a minute, then nodded and smiled. "OK, tough guy, your fever is down; I guess you're entitled to get dressed."

Wysocki pointed sharply with his pipe again. "But just the clothes, Erlanger. Leave your tools be. They're fine right where they are for the time being." The woman looked at her companion sharply, but said nothing as she carried the soiled bundle of clothing to his side.

"Damn lucky we found you when we did," Wysocki continued gruffly. "But we still want some answers. Who and what are you, and where'd you get those books?"

Erlanger paused in mid-zipper. His denim coveralls were a bit whiff from their trip through the river water, but he had no others. Slowly, his fingers finished closing the pants, while he marshalled his thoughts. "So, you did go through my things," he finally said to the man seated before him.

"Damn straight. Outlaws might be carrying all manner of weapons, if that's all you are ..." Wysocki rose, and knocked his pipe against the side of the woodstove. He kept Erlanger in view the whole time.

"Oh, Alan, let him be. He's no outlaw—we both heard enough from his delirium to know that!"

As he fumbled with a shirt from the bundle, Erlanger looked back and forth from woman to man. At least he appeared to have one ally. "Hey, what gives with you two? I'm just what I said. The tools are mine, been mine for years. Artificer, remember? As for those books, since you've obviously been looking for that kind of thing yourselves, I found them in an apartment on the edge of the city."

Both were staring at him intently now. Wysocki

scowled, and snapped, "And I suppose you know how to read 'em too?"

"Some, yes. My grandfather taught me to read, or at least he tried to, before the Ceejays got him. That was years ago, of course."

"Who?" The taller man moved closer, his fists clenched.

Erlanger was forced to sit back on the bunk, and his own temper was beginning to flare. He didn't enjoy the cross-examination. "My grandfather, Chester Owens was his name, if that's any of your damn business . . ."

Lori moved up to take Wysocki's arm, to pull him back. "See, I told you, Alan, he's all right."

"Shut up, Lori. Let me handle this. Wouldn't put it past the Ceejays and their toadies to plant someone like this, to try to . . ."

She jerked harder on his arm, and literally pushed him back into the wooden chair. "Alan, your pigheadedness is just too much! Those wounds weren't faked. Brent damn near died. Besides, he wasn't even looking for us, we just happened to be . . ." She paused to catch her breath, and Erlanger admired her spunk.

"Actually," the injured man said, in what he hoped was the proper tone, "I was sort of looking for you, for rebels like you."

"What!" Wysocki half-rose, and Lori dropped her restraining hand.

"Well," Erlanger continued, "what other choice did I have? Milford was past history for me, and no other town was likely to welcome me with open arms. Damn sure I didn't want the outlaw life, even if I could've survived initiation. So I was looking for a rebel group, was hoping that something like your bunch existed."

"And just what makes you think we're part of some

underground?" There was ice in Lori's voice, and Erlanger was no longer sure that he had any friends in that cold stone room.

He held his palms open and tried to grin. "It's obvious, now that I'm thinking straight. And you've as much as admitted it . . . how you search the cities for useful Old Times stuff, how you recognize the value of books. So count me in. Where do I sign up?"

The woman's expression softened, and she nodded. Wysocki's face did not relax, however, when he said, "Ain't that easy, my friend. We need to know a hell of a lot more about you, about why you left your cozy nest."

Lori moved angrily away from the bearded man, and kicked at a canvas backpack on the floor. "Just what I've been telling you, Alan. He's got skills, and he's got the right motivation. Back off and use your head. We've got plenty of time to hear his whole story on the way to Base. Besides, we can call our people in Milford for a complete check-out on that end."

Wysocki glared at the woman, and almost shouted. "Nice work, Lori. Just blow everything into his big farm-boy ears. Could be a spy, and you know it."

"If he's a spy, I'm a vestal virgin! Stop being so damn paranoid, and go hunt us up some fresh meat. Erlanger's going to need more protein if we're going to start making tracks to Base in a couple of days."

Still scowling, Wysocki picked up a small crossbow—of a design that Erlanger had never seen before, and slammed out the door. "I won't be far off, Erlanger; you just remember that," they both heard through the vibrating wood.

"Don't worry, Brent. Alan will come around as soon as you go through debriefing at Base. We do have to be careful, of course, but . . ."

Erlanger leaned on his good arm, and searched the

room for his boots. As he spotted them drying behind the stove, he said, "Sorry to cause trouble. And thanks for the support. I do want to join up." A bit of dizziness met his first few steps toward his boots, and she offered more than verbal support, but he waved her off. "No, I'll make it; I need the exercise." He swayed for a moment more, then got his balance. "By the way, what did you mean about 'calling' Milford? Like some kind of telephone?"

She smiled that pixie look again. "Don't try too much all at once. Just get your boots, and plant your butt again. But in answer to your question, sure. Landlines and packed microwave links tie us to all our people in or near the towns."

His boots were dry and stiff. They would need a thorough oil treatment before he did any more serious walking. He wondered whether they had appropriate oil or grease among the many apparent supplies in the way station, and then his left boot clunked to the floor as he realized the implications of what she had just told him.

"Holy Old Time Religion! In all the towns? I had no idea you were that organized. Must be pretty secretive bunch, come to that. But what's a 'packed microwave'?"

She frowned and started to busy herself at the stove, laying a fire. "That's something else that will have to wait. And please don't mention any of this to Alan. He'd get really pissed, and he's suspicious enough as it is, what with two *Cweom-jik* aircars in this area in less than three weeks."

"Sure, Lori, I guess I can't blame him too much." He scanned the small room for something that looked like boot grease. "But can you at least tell me how far we're going? Where is this 'Base'?"

"It's a fair trek yet," she replied, as she struck a match to kindling. "I doubt if you've ever heard the name. Before the Collapse, it was quite a place . . . called Oak Ridge."

Chapter

SIX

They were on the road again for almost three days before Erlanger learned much more about their mysterious Base. The trip south had begun slowly, for Erlanger was still weak, despite the rich venison steaks that Wysocki provided. During the week they spent at the way station before Lori pronounced him fit enough to march again, little of consequence was revealed by either rebel. Not until the first day of the trek, in fact, did Erlanger learn the woman's full name, Lorilei, although both she and Wysocki had continued to question him closely, to ask about his life in Milford and his skills.

"Be dark soon, best start thinking about shelter," Wysocki said softly.

They had topped a small rise in the rolling hills through which they had traveled for the past two days, and Erlanger turned back to stare at the tall man. Wysocki gestured with his crossbow, a weapon that he used quite efficiently, and which Erlanger had felt quite often at his back. Clearly, he was still on probation, still under guard, for he was allowed no weapons and had been told to walk in the middle. As he paused to catch his breath, not yet in peak condition, the man from Milford spotted movement in a distant field. "Horses," he finally guessed aloud.

Wysocki merely grunted, but Lori moved down from her position at the lead to follow his pointing finger. "Yep," she said, "this area is lousy with horses. I'm surprised we haven't seen more herds. Of course, we've stuck to the old Interstate so far, and I guess there weren't many farms close by here before the Collapse. But this was certainly horse country ... still is, for what that's worth."

Erlanger grimaced, and hopped on one foot while he pried a small stone from the tread of his left boot. "Sure would be a hell of a lot easier than walking. Why don't you fence in a bunch and tame 'em? Farmers around Milford have plenty of horses, and the Governor's men ride patrols, so why are we wearing out shoe leather?"

Lori shook her head. "It's been tried, but it just calls too much attention to our people. Oh, we've got horses at Base, right enough, but when we're out on missions, it's too dangerous. We think the damn Beaks have some kind of sensor that detects body heat, probably an infra-red thing, and riding horses a couple of miles is just like waving a red flag if an aircar's anywhere around. We've seen them blast wild herds, too, so that's probably why there aren't many near the roads." She sighed, and smiled sourly. "Don't think I wouldn't rather be in a saddle, though, Brent. We're not stupid, just hard-won cautious."

As he rubbed his three-day beard, Erlanger enjoyed the way her lithe form moved when she made dramatic gestures. For all her obvious no-nonsense rigor, her voice was very pleasant, and he had come to enjoy listening to her thoughts.

Wysocki broke his reverie with another grunt and a none-too-gentle shove on his shoulder. " 'Nuff gawking, let's move. I think there's a building 'bout two miles ahead, off the road a piece, that'll serve for the night."

Erlanger shook the hand off his shoulder with barely repressed anger, and moved to walk beside the woman, who seemed in an informative mood once again. They continued in silence for a time—keeping to the tree line at the edge of the highway, as they had from the beginning. Feeling a need to at least put himself on a more familiar level with the man, Erlanger broke the silence with, "What the hell's the rush, Wysocki? Got a hot date at your Base?"

Lori turned sharply, opened her mouth to comment, then seemed to change her mind. Finally she said, "There's something funny about these Ceejay fly-overs, as you should well know, and there's no sense being exposed longer than need be. Besides, we can't count on the weather this time of year. We've got rain gear, but nobody likes slogging along in the wet."

"No argument there. Guess we have been lucky with the weather, at that. How much farther have we got to go, anyway? You're damn closed-mouth about this Oak Ridge place."

The woman looked back, and was satisfied that the other rebel couldn't overhear their quiet conversation. Wysocki was scanning the large valley they were entering. "I'm almost sorry I mentioned Oak Ridge, even though I'm pretty sure you're trustworthy. Alan doesn't . . . well, no matter." She smiled over her shoulder, and kicked—almost playfully—at a small pile of yellow and russet oak leaves. "Let's see, we ought to be about 30 miles south of Lexington, not far from what's left of Berea College, so another seven,

eight days hike should do it ... if your poor shoe
leather holds out, that is."

"Yeah, thought so," Wysocki said as he caught up
with the other two. "We're just north of the old Mt.
Vernon exit, and there's what's left of a maintenance
station ahead to the east. Was still a solid roof on the
place last time we were through."

As Erlanger turned in the direction Wysocki indicated, he noticed movement out of the corner of his
eye. "Hey, that's a—"

Wysocki pushed Erlanger to the left. "Into the
woods, but slow. Quick movements are sure to nail
us." Wysocki cursed softly as he directed the party
through the dense brush at roadside. "Another damned
aircar ... maybe the same one that dried us in Cincinnati. Hell of a lot of activity for Beaks, 'specially
this time of year. Something damn-all funny going
on, ever since you showed up, Erlanger."

"Alan, there's no cause to jump on him. We knew
there was unusual Ceejay surveillance, even before
we found Brent."

"Yeah, yeah, Lori." Wysocki swore again as a thin
tree branch slapped his face. "So it's just a coincidence. Spread out a bit. If them birds are scanning
the area, maybe they'll take us for deer, horses, some
animals. Drop to your hands and knees and hold
still."

All three played possum for the better part of an
hour. Erlanger felt rather silly, but he had to assume
that the rebels knew what they were doing, that such
a ruse had worked in the past. Finally, Wysocki moved
toward the open, gesturing for them to stay put.

Lori moved up close beside Erlanger's doubled-
over position, her hands and knees mud-stained from
the inelegant crawl. "Those Beaks are probably long
gone. We rarely have trouble avoiding them, away
from the cities like this." She brushed a twig from

her tangled hair, and muddied her forehead in the process. Erlanger grinned at her ineffective efforts to clean her hands. "Birdshit! What I wouldn't give for a hot shower." She grinned in return. "Long walk yet for hot taps. Don't pay any mind to Alan's paranoia, by the way."

His fears that a searing bolt of flame would strike through the overhanging branches at any moment had gradually diminished, and Erlanger eased himself to an upright posture. "Para- what?"

"Sorry. Medical term. Paranoia used to mean irrational fear, but these days, it's a fairly healthy state. What I mean is, Alan's just as puzzled as I am about all this Ceejay activity. And that blasting in Cincinnati . . . well, maybe the Beaks knew that some pockets of Old Times technology, some libraries maybe, had been missed, but there must be more to it."

As he sat next to her on a dry pile of leaves in the lee of a large elm, Erlanger brushed his own dirty palms against his travel-soiled overalls. "But that's no reason to think I had anything to do with the *Cweom-jik.*"

"One, maybe two aircars going over every couple of months, that's normal. You know the Ceejays leave most things to their human toadies, the day-to-day administration, the grain harvests. Fast as those aircars are, it's a long way from their permanent settlements in the tropics, and they tend to stay there once the weather turns cool here. No, there's got to be some special reason, and damnit, we ought to know what it is."

A long-legged spider crossed the toe of his boot and Erlanger decided to let it live, as he tried to think of a useful contribution to solving the mystery. "Never knew they stuck to warm places," he finally said.

Her deep-set, green eyes regarded him evenly, as if in confirmation that her trust was justified. "The

Underground has a pretty good picture of their habits. They had to come from a warmer planet, and one with lesser gravity, too, from the care they take in walking on Earth. Like our birds, their bones must be hollow; those big scaled feet don't take to cold ground either. Ceejay evolutionary history must have been based on some flightless ancestor, something like our dodo or moa, if you've ever heard of those."

Although very interested, he was only half listening. Some slight change in the forest sounds, perhaps a drop in the buzz and twitter in the surrounding branches, had brought his head up, his ears attentive. He hushed her with a finger to his lips, his ears straining to catch the sound that had drawn his attention.

"You two having a cozy chat?"

Erlanger might have screamed, but his throat constricted so rapidly that it came out as a muted cough. His heart pounded and his hands shook as he stood and faced Wysocki. "You son of a bitch! What's the game, see if you can make the new guy crap his pants? You had no call to sneak up like that." He looked at the woman for support, and it was apparent that Lori had been startled, too.

"That was childish, Alan," she finally said, as she bent to pick up her pack. "I assume that the sky's all clear?"

"Yeah, sure. No sign of the aircar. But there'll be no fire tonight, not with Beaks anywhere in the area."

"I thought Ceejays didn't fly at night, that they roosted or something like that," Erlanger said, as he tried to control his temper.

Wysocki's eyes narrowed, and he cupped his thick beard with his left hand. In his right, the cocked crossbow rose to target Erlanger's chest. "And who told you that, farm boy? You got friends in high places?"

The woman angrily brushed the crossbow aside as she stepped between the two men. "Knock it off, Alan. You've had your fun, playing woods spook. Brent's not stupid. Most anybody in the towns could figure out that the Ceejays avoid the dark. The way they light up an area when they land at night, it's obvious that they haven't any more night vision than a chicken. And he's not carrying a transponder; you can take my word on that."

"Not outside, anyways. Could be something new, implanted. Something even you missed." Wysocki continued to scowl, but he did release the tension on the bowstring.

"What the hell are you talking about? Transponder?" Erlanger looked from one to the other in confusion. He grabbed his clothes bundle so tightly that his knuckles were white.

Lori started to speak, but her companion gripped her chin. She shook off the rough calloused fingers and turned back to answer. "The Beaks give their trustees a little radio transponder, a gizmo that lets them track and locate their pets from a distance. That's how the Governor's patrols can travel on horseback and we can't. Unfortunately, they've gimmicked the nasty little things to self-destruct if tampered with or if put into a duplicator, or we'd have had copies of them—or at least been able to neutralize them—long ago. Now, this big dummy here thinks they've got a new version, a transponder that's implanted inside your body. But I'm satisfied that you're not equipped with anything your mother didn't start you with, so . . ."

"That's quite enough, Lori. More than he needs to know." The tall, bearded rebel headed off toward the old highway, his back tense and straight.

"Alan, you really do . . . oh, the hell with it. C'mon, Brent, it's getting damn dark, and if we're not to have a fire tonight, I at least want a place out of the wind and damp."

"Me too, Lori." As he followed the two rebels, Erlanger's thoughts were in turmoil. He almost tripped as his boot caught on an exposed root. His cheeks slowly grew warm, and the tips of his ears turned red as it suddenly occurred to him *how* Lori had been satisfied that he carried nothing unusual under his skin.

Although adequate for bodily needs, venison jerky and dried fruit did not make a very satisfactory meal. And the evening was growing chill, despite the blanket that Erlanger had been given as they left the way station. He still thought a fire, even a small, smokeless blaze, would have been safe—especially inside this huge, barn-like building. Wysocki had vetoed any fire, however. The rebel leader had argued that there might well be human patrols in conjunction with the increased *Cweom-jik* activity in the air. Whether the Beaks could smell smoke at any distance was an open question (though Lori was sure they could not). If the Governor's patrols were in the area, however, any fire was a bad idea.

Erlanger muttered to himself and tried to find a more comfortable position on the hard concrete floor. Some kind of storage barn for road maintenance equipment in the Old Times was how the rebels had explained it. The building was far enough from the highway for reasonable security—or at least so the man from Milford thought. Wysocki had felt otherwise, and he and Lori had gone to scout around after they had eaten their cold dinner.

Erlanger got up and walked outside the main door. Long shadows and dim forms, tree trunks and bushes, were all he could make out. No movement. He was beginning to worry.

After a slow and cautious walk of about 100 yards, the darkness lessened. To the right, against a wall of trees, some great machine stood. Erlanger heard small sounds. Mice, maybe bats? He drew closer and tried to picture the scene in daylight. He rested his hand on what appeared to be the rear of the machine. Rust and perhaps yellow, yes yellow, paint came off on his fingers.

The sounds were louder. He felt around the machine. There were four wheels with flattened, rotted rubber tires still almost chest high, and then a curved blade like some monstrous drawknife. A wheelhouse sat on top, toward the rear. Unsure, not a little afraid, but intrigued by the rhythmic sounds that he couldn't quite identify, he pulled himself on top of the great blade for a look into the mysterious cabin. His mouth dropped open in shock, and "humph" escaped his open throat. His grip slipped from dew-slick metal, and he landed solidly on his butt, far more embarrassed than injured.

"Now who's a sneaky bastard, Erlanger?" Wysocki growled. Once again, the wicked point of the crossbow bolt was sighted on Erlanger's chest. Behind the mostly naked, thoroughly angry man, Lori clutched her shirt to her full breasts.

"Sorry, I . . . I was worried about . . . sorry." Erlanger scooted backward on hands and buttocks, gained his feet awkwardly, and stumbled away from the lovers.

When the pair returned to the building some time later, Erlanger feigned sleep. But he was to sleep little that night.

"Could I see that?"

Wysocki scowled as he took the strange, palm-sized device from his eye, and started to return the plastic object to the button-down side pocket of his camouflage jacket. Lori held out her hand and shook her head sharply. "Christsake, Alan, let him look at the map. What's the harm in that, at this point?"

She took the flat plastic microfiche reader from the bearded man's hand, and passed it to Erlanger—a peace offering of sorts to end the strained relationship of two against one that had prevailed for the last two days. She showed the artificer how to focus the eyepiece and move the tiny rectangle of film, as he held the device up to the clear sky. Erlanger whistled, amazed at the clarity and detail.

"The curved lines represent topographic levels," Lori explained. "Now you can see the ridges we've been climbing, the beginning of the Cumberlands."

Erlanger nodded, not sure what all her words meant, but intrigued by the skills of the Old Timers. This "map-fiche," as they called it, had obviously been made from aerial surveys. He located the precise cut through the rolling hills that represented the Interstate they had been following, and was able to match a couple of distant rocky peaks to the southeast with the numbered images on the film. He would have stared much longer had the woman not gently tapped his elbow.

"Thanks, Lori. That thing's incredible. Once we get to your Base, I hope to . . ." Erlanger looked down at her feet, unable to meet the green eyes next to him. "Lori, Alan, I'm . . . well, the other night . . ."

Dimples formed in her cheeks as her mouth turned up in a brief smile. "Forget it, Brent." She tossed the map reader to Wysocki, and hooked her thumbs in her packstraps. "C'mon, daylight's burning up, and I'm looking forward to the comforts of a way station tonight."

As Erlanger turned to follow her shapely posterior, he chided himself for the direction of his gaze. Lori wasn't available, not that way. He hoped the sharing of the map marked a thaw in the chill that had existed from the morning after his discovery that he was odd man out. Most of the previous day he had simply plodded along in silence—always conscious of Wysocki's eyes at his back. He had silently cursed his embarrassment, had rehearsed a dozen ways of making amends. He should have known better, should have realized that Lori and Wysocki had more in common than membership in the Underground. Thinking back, there had been plenty of clues—glimpses of gesture and regard between the two. Gotta stop thinking with my balls, he said to himself, these people are offering me my only chance. Can't mess up now.

Fresh meat, a hot meal, even hot water for a rough bath, such was the luxury of an Underground way station. As Erlanger warmed his feet at the woodstove, he wondered aloud about the smoke from this welcome fire. Granted, they had seen no further evidence of Ceejays, or of anybody, for that matter. He wondered about that too.

"Not to worry," Lori answered, as she sopped gravy with the last piece of corn bread, and brushed yellow crumbs from her lips. "These way stations were well designed. Smoke filters, heat traps. The original Base personnel were one sharp bunch, believe me." She paused, and looked down at her empty aluminum plate. "And we're getting that sharpness back."

Wysocki turned his head and fixed his distrustful look on the Milford runaway. He touched the woman's hand, a gesture that Erlanger now saw as the affection it was, and said quietly, "That can wait until he's checked out, Lorilei."

She nodded and sighed, as she leaned back against his shoulder. She closed her eyes, and changed the subject in response to Erlanger's second question.

"As for why we haven't seen any people, well, this region never was all that highly populated. There were a few towns here and there, and the hill people have always been pretty closed off, from what we can tell from the pre-Collapse records."

She rose to put more water on to boil for clean-up chores, then continued. "Besides, as we understand it, these Interstate highways were designed to bypass population centers, so even if the riots, famines, plagues, and goddamned alien attacks hadn't killed off better than 70 percent of the human race, there still wouldn't be many people around here. Not too far off, though, there's a settlement called Bailey's Switch, whatever the hell that means, but we haven't any reliable contacts there, so . . ."

Erlanger jumped up and began to pace the limited clear space between stockpiles of supplies. "Horseshit!" he shouted, startling the relaxed couple. "You can't mean that! 70 percent . . . I had no idea that it was anything like that."

"Probably much higher in many places. Records ain't that good, but it's a reasonable guess." Wysocki continued in a voice more gentle than Erlanger had ever heard from that burly chest. "Sit down, Brent. None 'a your stomping around's going to mean diddly-squat to the dead. Save your energy for tomorrow.

"Our world was just too tightly balanced on a thin edge. Didn't take much to push us over. The cities were too dependent on long lines of transportation, of communication, of energy. The duplicators just tore our guts out. Molecular duplication was pie in the sky, instant Lotus Land. Nobody wanted to work; nobody gave a shit. Hungry? Just stuff a duplicator's intake chute. New shirt? Just throw in some old clothes, twiddle the dials."

Erlanger had calmed somewhat; his long fingers

rested on his denim-clad knees. He listened intently to the longest speech he had ever heard from Wysocki.

The iron door clanked shut as the man tossed a couple of split oak branches into the fire. "We were just too fuckin' high on a pyramid of ignorance," he added as he returned to Lori's side. "Literacy had been falling for generations, and damn few understood how anything worked, how things were made—least of all the molecular composition of things. So, once the obvious sources of raw materials for duplication were gone, and that was green-apple-quick in the cities, the Four Horsemen rode right in."

"Four Horsemen?" Erlanger raised an eyebrow as he fumbled to pour another cup of nettle and bark tea. "That's another name for the Ceejays?"

"Not quite. Much older, strictly human invention. Keep forgetting you ain't read much yet. Beaks just came in to mop up the pieces, to collect the spoils of what we'd let fall." Wysocki's dark eyes almost closed, as if in pain. He spat angrily at the hot stove, then gestured with his empty cup for a refill of the bitter brew.

Erlanger filled the other man's cup, then sat on one of the bunks that folded down from the wall. He fingered the broad leather straps that held the narrow bed. Finally he looked up from his tea. "All those years, *working* for them, making things for them, helping bring in the harvest to feed them."

"You just did what you had to do," Lori broke in softly. "What choice did you really have?"

"And now, if you pass muster at Base, you do have a choice," Wysocki added, softening a little in the face of Erlanger's troubled sincerity. "You've got some basic skills, and a mind that can be trained. At least Lori thinks so, and I suppose I have to go with her judgment." He said this last with a wry grin and sideways glance at the lovely woman by his side.

Erlanger put the cup to his lips, winced, sipped anyway. The tea was hot, but it was good. He swallowed and sighed. After a moment he spoke again. "If only we hadn't invented the duplicator, or had somehow been able to keep it from wrecking the economy ..."

Lori looked questioningly at Wysocki, received a negative headshake in reply, but went ahead anyway. Apparently she thought her partner's mania for security a bit overdone.

"Brent, are you aware that within the space of a few months at least eight people—that's how many we have record of—claimed to have invented the duplicator?"

Brent didn't say anything, but his eyes began to widen.

"How likely is it for that to have really happened?" Lori continued. "Eight different people in widely separated locations simultaneously invent something that makes mincemeat out of physical law as then understood. They had to have been dupes, or brainwashed plants, or maybe just greedy traitors. We don't know the details, and they don't matter. We do know that no human being could have created from the ground up the alien technology implicit in those devices."

Lori paused to brush a strand of hair from her eyes. "No, Brent, the duplicators were a gift to humanity from the *Cweom-jik*, the opening salvo in their invasion of Earth."

For a moment, Erlanger didn't even feel the scalding liquid that slopped from his cup onto his thighs.

Chapter

SEVEN

The three hikers were well into the mountains now. Green rolling hills and grassy river bottoms had given way to distant rocky spires and rough cuts of naked stone on the edges of the Interstate. Twice the previous day they had to pick their way through rockfalls that all but blocked the old highway. The broadleaf forests had thinned, and scraggly pines dotted the steep hillsides. More in the open, with less immediate cover, Wysocki prodded them to watch the sky, and to avoid making a standing silhouette at ridgetop. Their pace had slowed, and Erlanger was grateful for the poncho that the last way station had provided for the driving, sometimes rain-soaked winds of the narrow passes.

As they caught their breath in the lee of a massive granite boulder, Wysocki clapped him on his still-tender shoulder. Erlanger grinned, and welcomed the comradely gesture. The night before, as they roasted rabbits in the crumbled stone fireplace of a camp ground, Wysocki had returned the Constable's knife to Erlanger. He was off probation, at least as far as these two rebels were concerned, although Wysocki explained that he would still have to go through some unspecified screening at Base.

By late afternoon, still in full light, they reached a side road to what Lori called a Forest Service cabin. Though hardly in perfect condition, the wood and stone building had survived the many winter snows reasonably well. After evicting a pair of outraged chipmonks, Erlanger started a fire—easily smokeless with a ready supply of dry deadfalls. The flat, open area in front of the cabin had seen little regrowth over the years, and the whole rocky area seemed devoid of life.

They had eaten the last of their fresh food the night before, and now Wysocki called for a hunt while there was still daylight. His plan called for Lori and Erlanger to act as beaters, coming in from the west, while he curved around the other way with his crossbow. Along the way, they could pick any greens or ground nuts that might add to the stew. In less than an hour, Wysocki had pinned a young doe neatly through the neck. He and Erlanger each carried a hind quarter, while Lori brought up the rear—her pack stuffed with greens, along with the liver and the heart. They were a merry, bloody band as they headed for the stream that Wysocki assumed to be behind the weathered cabin.

As they topped the last rise, Wysocki dropped in his tracks. Erlanger, a little behind him, crouched down and peeked over the rise in the direction Wysocki was staring. Lori crawled up beside the two men.

A mere 50 feet in front of them, where the clearing before the cabin was at its widest, a Ceejay aircar rested. Two of the aliens, apparent weapons in their four-fingered claws, waddled in their awkward strut in the space between their vehicle and the cabin.

"What did you leave inside?" Wysocki hissed in Erlanger's ear.

"My clothes bundle . . . and the poncho." The younger man found his voice despite the fear that squeezed his throat. "I brought my toolkit for butchering." At that thought, his adrenalin-primed nostrils twitched at the blood-warm meat that lay beside him. He almost vomited.

"Good. Lori?"

"Just the poncho and blankets," she whispered.

"Yeah, same here," Wysocki replied. "We may be able to get away; we left no obvious technology; just average outlaws. Maybe they won't make much of a search."

Erlanger paled as he recalled what he carried with his clothes. "The books! The books are in that bundle."

"Ah, shit. That tears it."

Erlanger began an incoherent apology.

"Quiet, let me think." Wysocki squirmed back from the ridge, and began to paw through his backpack.

His chin buried in gritty, brown moss, Erlanger continued to watch the Ceejays. He had seen aircars at close range before, in official visits to Milford, but now he tried to really take in details. The craft was a flattened ovoid on its side, while the open hatchway toward the front end was more of a vertical pear-shape. That figures, he thought, as he tried to ignore a cloud of gnats that danced inches from his eyes. One of the aliens, a *kepwoi* or male by its shorter stature and brilliant bands of blue feathers, entered the cabin. Erlanger tensed, ready to flee. A third alien, a dusty brown female, emerged from the hatchway and twisted her long thin neck to adjust some instrument on the grey straps that crossed her downy breast, then waddled to speak with the other eight-foot female who leaned against the front of the aircar.

Stretch a turkey and top it with a duck, he could

almost hear his grandfather say, as he strained to control his breathing. Something about their behavior, their movements? He clenched his teeth as he felt a tug on his leg, and slid down the pebbled slope to join the other two.

"What's happening?" Wysocki whispered.

"Two *een* outside now; the male went into the cabin. Something's odd about the way they're walking."

"Yeah, well you'd walk funny too if you had to balance on two clawed toes forward and two back." Wysocki began to stuff his shirt with several round, metallic things about the size of apples. He shoved a heavy blue pistol in front of Erlanger's startled eyes. "Think you can use one of these? No need for silent weapons now; it's all or nothing time. You claimed to have shot men and tigers."

Erlanger nodded dumbly. His gaze flickered rapidly from Wysocki to Lori. She nodded grimly in return. White teeth showed as she bit her lower lip, and a thin line of sweat banded her forehead. "Ah, that's not the same kind of pistol. How does this work?" He was almost in shock, his face pale, his fingers numb. These crazy people were actually planning to attack, to kill Ceejays.

The bearded rebel twisted his lip in disgust, and placed the younger man's shaking hand around the pistol. "Easy. See—.45 caliber automatic. Safety here. On, off. It's off now, so keep your finger outside the guard. Pull back slide to cock. Now cocked. Hold with both hands, so. Nine rounds in clip. No sense giving you a spare clip, we'll be lucky if you get off that one."

His tongue seemed to lock in his throat, and his teeth tasted bitter, as Erlanger grasped the cool metal. "But we've got to get away. We can't . . ."

The woman moved closer and brushed aside a short

lock of hair that was plastered over her left eye. "Sorry, Brent. No choice. Those are the rules. No time for initiation, I'm afraid. You get the 30-day course in 90 seconds. We're amazed that we haven't been spotted so far. Must be a lot of magnetic ore in these rocks or something. Just goddamned lucky that they're not watching their heat sensors, or radar, or whatever. We can't just crawl off now. We'd be nailed inside ten minutes, once that aircar's up again. Besides, we can't risk being followed back to Base. That's rule one."

She paused for breath, and stuck three of the round things on her belt. They had small clips for that purpose. Then she slipped a large white capsule into her palm, and stared at Wysocki sadly.

"But nobody ... I mean, I thought Ceejays had some kind of defensive screen?"

"Yeah, electro-weak force bubble around their aircars, around them," Wysocki said, with venom in his hoarse whisper. "But it slows them down—conservation of momentum, something like that—and there seems to be a rapid heat build-up inside the force bubble while it's turned on. Besides, they've gotten cocky over the years, what with the mayors and the governors kissing their tails. I didn't see any of the red bellypacks on any of 'em outside. We may just have a shot. Only game in town anyways. Lori, how many grenades you got?"

His stomach heaved again. "You've done this before ... the Underground, I mean. Attacked aircars?"

Lori held up four fingers and Wysocki nodded. She knuckled sweat from her eyes and explained. "None have made it back with a report, but we think so. These grenades are new, though. They put out an electro-magnetic pulse as well as the blast. We hope they kill the instruments, the controls. Time for a field test." Her last comment came out as a nervous giggle.

"Understand this good, Erlanger." Wysocki held up his own white capsule. "We can't be taken prisoner. We've got pills, but even if we had one for you, I couldn't trust you to take it. Things go sour, and as long as I've got breath, I take you out. Sorry, but that's the only way. Be a blessing compared to what the Beaks would do to you."

"We who are about to die, and all that nonsense," Wysocki muttered as he slipped into his packstraps. Lori did the same, and Erlanger slung his toolkit over his shoulder with little conscious thought to how little help a screwdriver would be. "Right," Wysocki continued softly, as if he were planning a summer picnic, "we'll spread out, creep around this ridge. Brent, you rest that piece solid, and aim for the male you saw. If he's still in the cabin, he'll be out damn quick. The go signal will be my first grenade. Got that? No firing until I lob the first grenade at the females. Lori, you toss for the open hatch. We can't be sure how many might be left inside. Now, let's make like snakes. You off to the left, Lori." He punctuated his last commands with a quick kiss on Lori's pale lips, and a squeeze of Erlanger's upper arm.

As Erlanger peeked through the tangled vines of yellowed mountain laurel, and tried to point his pistol steadily at the cabin door, a sharp *whump-crack* tossed one of the aliens into the dry mountain air. The blue-crested *kepwoi* seemed to float into the doorway—with his long tubular weapon at throat level in the double-bend of an inhuman forearm.

Two more blasts, and a beam of red light ignited the stand of young maples to Erlanger's left. He squeezed his own trigger reflexively. Blue smoke drifted through his field of view, and he kept pulling the trigger. He saw a crouched figure, running. The aircar began to quiver, to yaw. The Ceejay in the cabin doorway fell, the beam weapon still firing, now cutting a smoking trench in the packed ground before the cabin. The aircar wobbled, now two feet up, now four. He looked for another target, unaware that his finger spasmed to produce empty clicks.

As if from a great distance, he heard Lori scream: "Alan, no!" Wysocki was running toward the still-open hatch of the aircar; his arm came up in an overhand toss, and he spun off toward the treeline as orange light flashed from the alien vehicle.

Wysocki was almost to the top of the ridge. The aircar, obviously stricken, slewed sideways into the cabin wall. The grey shape rebounded, wobbled, seemed to straighten. Late afternoon sun glinted from its viewport as the unsteady craft swung around. A blast of massive heat seared Erlanger's face and he jerked back to the cover of rock, only to look up again, to see a spinning, tumbling ball of fire—a stick-figure of flame—fall back into the clearing.

Lori ran into view. She neared the blackened hatchway, now almost eye-level, and lobbed another grenade. Erlanger was on his feet and running, too. She'd be killed, fried like a bug in a skillet.

Before he could reach her, and before she could reach the still-burning remains of the man she loved, the aircar crashed into the cabin again. A great wind stole his feet; he slid forward on his chest. Splinters of cabin logs rained on his back. He twisted his neck and saw the aircar, nose down. Saw the cabin, the nearby trees, on fire. Lori was kneeling, was screaming, next to him. He found his feet, painfully, and reached for her.

"Lori!" he shouted. "Lori, we've got to move quick. These woods are tinder, the whole mountain's going up in a few minutes."

The woman didn't move, didn't hear. She stared at the disgusting cooked flesh that had been Wysocki, stared as if the rest of the world had stopped.

He jerked her to her feet. She might have been a life-sized rag doll, for all her animation. Her pupils were fully dilated; her mouth hung slack. Increasing heat warmed his back, and he tugged the unresisting woman down the dirt road, jogging south toward the highway. Branches cracked sharply, popped and hissed, as more trees caught the spreading flames. Fortunately the stiff evening breeze was from the south, but Erlanger was only dimly aware that the way he was heading, into the wind, was the proper escape path from a forest fire.

The cool air was a stabbing pain within his chest, and his right hand ached from gripping Lori's wrist. He paused to look at her, the dull red glow that erased the spreading dusk on the ridge behind them highlighting her. She still clutched a pistol in her right hand; Erlanger had dropped his at some point. Her fingers were like ice, steel hard, but he pried the weapon loose as gently as possible and stuck it in the thigh pocket of his overalls.

"Lori. Damnit, Lori, talk to me. We've got to run." He shook her shoulders, finally gritted his teeth and slapped her cheeks. She screamed and began to claw at his face. It took all his strength to restrain her, but at last he had her attention. She began to babble, to sob quietly, as he pulled her along. Gradually her color returned, then her reason.

"Get off this open road, jerk! We stand out like a pregnant sow." She yanked her wrist free of his sweaty grip and took the lead.

Erlanger grinned, a twisted rictus of strain, and followed her onto the rocky roadside trail. He wanted to hug her.

*　　*　　*

They kept moving for hours. The full moon helped, but not much. Loose rock, roots, deadfalls, and low branches were constant obstacles. There were only a few high clouds; the stars were clear to the south and the west and they were able to maintain their orientation easily. At their backs, smoke darkened the sky, smoke occasionally colored pink by the fire's glow as they gained a mountain crest. The fire did not appear to be spreading as rapidly as Erlanger had feared.

Her story began in fragments; pieces of her life emerged between labored breaths, as if her load lightened with each revelation. They stumbled into a chill mountain stream, the water to boot-top before they noticed the cold and the wet. Lori filled the canteen on her packstrap as she continued to spill her thoughts.

"He was a chemist. Did I tell you that? Yes, Donald, my husband Donald, was a damn fine chemist." He watched her face; she appeared to be dreaming aloud. Her hair was black in the shadow of a heavy pine bough. She didn't notice when he took the full canteen and hooked it to a belt loop at his hip. She didn't notice when he took her cool hand and urged her up the vine-covered bank.

"We were scouting the Asheville area for laboratory equipment." She jerked and seemed almost to awaken to reality as a twig snapped beneath her foot. "Do you know Asheville? North Carolina, it used to be. Mostly blasted ruins now, just like everything else. Found good stuff too; some kind of small research place, well out of the destroyed area. Donald and the others were really excited to find those spectrometer parts, the textbooks. Very successful expedition. Then, two days into the hike back to Base, the Beaks spotted us. 'Scatter,' Donald said. So we spread out. But they got us all. All except one. 'I alone am escaped to tell thee.'" Her voice had fallen to a whisper. Swatches of moonlight outlined the tears that streaked through the grime on her cheeks.

She stood silently against the rock of the cliff face, while Erlanger dragged more leaves and branches into the partial shelter of overhanging sandstone. His legs and feet were leaden, a massive ache. But he managed to seat her as comfortably as possible. She began to speak again as he removed her pack, and searched it for something of warmth. The greens, the deer heart and liver were almost nauseating now, and useless without a fire.

"I never thought I'd feel that way again. A piece of me died with Donald, don't you see. But after a few missions with Alan Wysocki, friends started to notice, started to tease me. Some said he wasn't my type, of course. That he was too old ... kind of funny, really, how it just happened, just snuck up on both of us. We just sort of melted together ... camped outside of Chattanooga, we were. That was over two years ago ... Alan understood that I wouldn't take another name, that I'd just be Lorilei ... first my father, then Donald ... and I couldn't risk ... just Lori."

She sighed and continued to mumble for a few minutes, as Erlanger wrapped his arms around her trembling shoulders.

Exhausted mentally and physically, the pair slept well past daybreak. His back and knees were stiff, his limbs cramped, and he stood like a man at the end of his days. Lori stared up at him. Life had returned to her green eyes, life and the pain of memory.

"Water!" she said, with a thick tongue. He passed her the canteen, and she gulped noisily. He offered his hand, but she ignored it as she rose on weak legs and reached for her pack.

She studied their surroundings and the position of the sun, and pointed to her left. She clutched his arm in a painful grip, then swore and picked up her pack. They walked silently the rest of that day.

Another night in the open, in each other's arms, passed without incident. Lori accepted his body warmth without comment, for a fire was too risky, but she was as mute as the mossy tree stump they sheltered against. The next morning she was more communicative, if only to point out edible plants to supplement what little dried food remained in her pack. Erlanger offered to set snares for small game, to search for a fishing hole in one of the streams they crossed, but his growling stomach was always over-ruled. Clearly, she had but one goal, to get back to Base.

Well past noon, the sun's warmth gentle on their faces, their general downward path brought them into a deep ravine. The upper edges of the narrow cut were naked rock, while the floor and lower reaches were covered with dense brambles and twisted vines. Whatever river had rushed through here and created this divide was long gone. Erlanger suggested an easier route, a return to the highway, but Lori insisted that the shadowed groove in the mountain side would be safer. Earlier, she had thought she'd seen a Ceejay aircar, though he had been sure it was just a hawk in a high search for dinner.

The spring floods had cleared a reasonable path, and they made good time—despite the irritation of deerflies and gnats that thrived in the moist bushes.

Lori, who had continued in the lead, suddenly gave a choked cry and fell prone. He rushed to her side, and scanned the ground for the snake he feared had struck. He knew little of snakes, but thought both copperheads and timber rattlers were possible in these hills. She jerked on his leg, and pulled him down beside her. Snakebite was not the reason she swore between clenched teeth. Tears welled again from the dark circles of fatigue below her squinted eyes.

"Not again. No more," she muttered over and over, while her hands clenched the remaining grenade at her belt.

Erlanger was not sure what he was seeing; he inched forward on his belly. Lori moaned something and tried to restrain him. Something not green, not brown. Dull grey, curved, artificial. Yes, Lori's worst fears were correct. A Ceejay aircar.

But what was it doing in this cramped ravine? Odd as those damned Beaks were, even a nonhuman pilot wouldn't jam a craft into this small area! His brow wrinkled. Over the damp smell of humus, the slightly acid odors of leaf-mold, his nose caught the clear sickly sweetness of rot, of carrion long dead. He crawled farther; parted the ferns and seedlings that obscured his line of sight.

He twisted his neck and tried to signal Lori. The aircar rested at an angle; snapped and crushed trees surrounded the nose of the craft where it had cut a long furrow in the rocky earth. He saw no signs of life, alien or terrestrial. Beside the open darkness of the pear-shaped hatch, two dung-colored mounds lay in a bed of flattened brown vegetation.

The woman crept to his side, the metallic grenade clenched in her fist, and stared past his shoulder. "I think it's derelict, a wreck," he said softly. "Looks like two dead *Cweom-jik* near the hatch." They peered at the silent alien machine for many hundreds of heartbeats, while only the buzz and chirp of familiar forest life greeted their straining ears. Finally he stirred, rose to his knees. "This thing got any shots left?" He gestured with Lori's automatic. She nodded with what he hoped was understanding, and he eased closer to the aircar.

Their patient caution, their fears, had been wasted.

The Ceejays had obviously been dead for some time, and the interior of the aircar—once he nerved himself for a quick peek—was a blackened shell.

For the first time in days, the woman's authority returned. She was all business, her back straight, her eyes glittering as she probed and examined. She gave very close attention to the alien corpses, in spite of the rank smells. The bodies were intact, although bloated and soft. No Earthly scavenger had touched them, apparently. Erlanger tried to inspect the aircar, but found little but soot and melted metal.

"Gotta be it," she muttered, as she removed a case of shiny instruments from her pack and began to slice the alien bodies. From time to time she dropped pieces of rotten flesh into tiny clear cups and jars—plastic containers that he had not known the pack contained.

Almost sickened by her activity, he looked away. "Lori, what the hell are you doing?"

"Don't you see? This explains everything. The increased overflights, the attacks. The Beaks have been searching for this aircar, this crew. My God, this is a great opportunity. Tissue samples!"

She grimaced as internal organs spilled from the belly of the female Ceejay. Odors even more vile filled the air, but her enthusiasm didn't diminish.

"Searching? But if this thing blew up, how did those two even make it outside in one piece?"

A grating noise answered him as she took a short, shiny saw to the thin bones of the alien skull. "No, no, Brent. They had to have landed first, then triggered the self-destruct. We know they did that in the early days of the invasion, when tactical nuclear weapons were still available on our side. They've never allowed an intact aircar, or any of their energy weapons to be captured. Something else brought these damned birds down, though, and I'm hoping by all the sainted heroes of Earth that it was a disease."

He pinched his nose and moved upwind. "Disease? You mean they were too sick to stay in the air, to make it back to their roost-homes in the tropics?" He slapped his forehead. "Hey, maybe that's what I noticed about the way they walked, the ones that we nailed back at the cabin. Maybe they were sick too."

Lori paused, and looked at him. An expression of pain, of bitter recall, washed over her haggard face, then she returned to her task. "They were slower on the trigger than they should have been." She almost spit out the words. "If only they'd been just a hair slower yet." Her thin shoulders shrugged, but her hands continued to cut and dig. "The tide might be starting to turn. If only these tissue samples aren't too far gone to tell us what we need to know."

By the time they found the kidney-shaped pond above a beaver dam, it was almost dark. He would have opted for a full bath, but had to settle for a rough wash-up, since Lori was more concerned than ever about a betraying fire. The cave they found in the hillside above the pond was quite cozy. Fortunately, it was too early for a bear to have claimed it for the winter. Something smaller—perhaps fox, perhaps coyote—had denned in the cave recently, as indicated by cracked, gnawed bones and smelly bits of fur, but there were no disputes for this night's shelter.

The still pond provided three fat trout. Sliced thin, raw, and cold was not Erlanger's first choice, but he managed to choke down the slimy meal. Protein was protein, Lori had argued with a shrug. Her clean face almost glowed. Her excitement was contagious and he found himself matching her question for question, as she talked more about the Underground and her life as a member. He tried to avoid painful areas, but at times she would fall silent as some question about the research or organization of the rebels reminded her of a lost love.

"No, that's all right, Brent. I've got to face it. Alan Wysocki was one hell of an electronics engineer. You wouldn't know it to look at him, to hear his woodsy talk sometimes. His team thought they were close to the basic principles of duplication. As soon as we got those electron microscope components back from Cincinnati, Alan was—ah damn, there I go again. Can't afford to lose much more salt water. Come sit over here, would you?"

He looped his long arm around her waist—for warmth, he told himself. As she smiled at him, only her eyes and teeth visible in the shallow cave, he tried not to think about how long it had been since his shirt had seen soap. She was far from festival costume herself, yet she smelled pleasantly female. He pushed his thoughts in a more appropriate direction.

"How can you tell if the Ceejays had a fatal disease? And mucking around with those bodies today, wouldn't we catch it?" He tensed at the last disturbing idea. She reached over and squeezed his hand.

"No fear there. Alien is alien, macro- or microscopic." At his puzzled frown, she continued: "Cross-infection, inter-species contagion just isn't in the cards, Brent. That's why those bodies were still in fairly good condition, even after several weeks. Only internal *cweomki* bugs had worked on them. Our terrestrial bacteria wouldn't have much effect until decay was far advanced to basic compounds. Not that we didn't try, of course. Biological warfare attacks, strains of Newcastle Disease, poultry, 'flu, psittacosis, you name it and some country secretly tried it, back there toward the end of the Collapse. Even while the right hand of what remained of human government was welcoming the so-called aid of the Ceejays, the left hand smelled a rat and prepared to fight."

She snuggled into the crook of his arm, and her voice became sharper. "But nothing worked, not even enough to provoke a response."

She was silent for several full minutes, and he thought the strain of the day's activities, the forced march of the last three days, had finally claimed her. She wasn't asleep, however. She squeezed his hand again and turned toward him, her lips only inches from his. "That's why these tissue samples are so vital, why we've got to get them to the labs at Base as soon as possible. This may be our first break in over 80 years. Either a natural Beak virus has mutated into a virulent form, or one of our attempts could have mutated, one of those twisty bits of DNA could have recombined in just the right way. It's a feeble hope, I know, but hope of finding the least chink in their fortress has kept us searching all these years."

She drew his head close, her hands gentle on his neck. "You've got to promise me, Brent. If something should happen to me, you'll get my pack to the labs. The Base really is underground, you see. Oh, there are plenty of historical reasons why we call the organization Underground too, but Oak Ridge is only a convenient shorthand. That city, that old research complex, was blasted just like every other high-tech area. Base is close by, under about 100 meters of limestone. I'll give you the trail signs, the passwords."

He quieted her fears as best he could, and assured her that the two of them would finish the journey, that there was no need for such morbid thoughts. She became more animated, more adamant about the importance of their new mission. He changed the subject in what seemed the most natural way.

Afterwards, as he sat in the lip of the cave, he wasn't sure how he felt—the future held sweet promise, and puzzlement. Kissing her had seemed the most logical thing to do, but logic had played little part. It hadn't been love, but it had been human passion, human communion in the face of those cold stars, and the slavery that at least one of those stars had brought to Earth. She had clawed his back, had bitten his lip, but he didn't mind. Once she called out, "Alan," but he was more flattered than jealous. He listened to the night sounds, the far-off groan of an owl, her close gentle snores. He stared at those so distant stars—not sure whether he had consoled a widow, or venerated a saint. He had not, he told himself, desecrated a shrine, though part of him wasn't sure.

Chapter

EIGHT

Cold, stiff, Brent Erlanger reawakened to anger. Slowly, he sat up on the narrow metal shelf that had served as his bed for the past three nights. As he bent to retrieve his only blanket from the damp concrete floor, where he found it every morning, his back muscles protested. Getting old? he wondered. More than likely, the enforced inactivity that came with being locked up in this little hole in the ground was responsible.

The door was locked by some mechanism that operated from the outside; Erlanger didn't even try to open it. Instead, he forced himself into the routine of calisthenics that he had begun the previous morning. He had no idea how much longer he would spend here, and he wasn't going to go soft, whatever the future held. As he exercised under the weak light from a wire-caged ceiling fixture, he let his thoughts roam back to another cave, one that had been made a lot more cozy by Lori's presence. The contrast between that natural cave and this small cell was sharper still, as he recalled the events that led to his imprisonment.

*   *   *

The morning after their intimacy in the cave had dawned gray, and Lori's mood seemed to match the overcast skies. She spoke little as she took the lead along the old highway. The squeak of packstraps and the rattle of loose gravel were Erlanger's only companions for most of that day. He had to strain to hear what few remarks she made, something about "Cumberland," as the cracked road began a steady upward slope. No warmth was added to their camp or meal that night, in the gloomy shelter of a half-destroyed overpass. She's mourning for Wysocki, he thought, as Lori made plain that body heat was all she meant to share against that cool concrete.

Two days, three. He tried to reason with her, to take time to hunt or fish, but she marched on, obsessed with a single goal. While she talked more—her conversation about the potential of the *Cweom-jik* tissue samples was almost lively at times—her eyes held a feverish glint. Another day, and the trek turned southwest. Beautiful scenery surrounded them, deep mountain vistas in the beginning of fall colors, but Erlanger could see little more than his tired feet.

"Norris," Lori said, as they crossed a dry valley, a former lake bed that narrowed into a bottleneck with remnants of massive concrete structures. "Used to be a hydro-electric generating station. The river shifted south when the upper dams were blasted."

Erlanger was awed. He had no idea what "TVA" meant, and she added little more. While the ruin was some ways off, his estimation of the size of the structure made all of Milford a pale comparison. Certainly as impressive, if not more so, than anything he had seen in Cincinnati. People had made that, had changed rivers to their will.

The next afternoon brought them to a small rise. Smashed ruins of a fair-sized city spread out in the

valley below. "Oak Ridge," Lori said, unnecessarily.
Erlanger grimaced. The destruction of human civilization before him was the worst he had yet seen.
Building foundations, steel girders, fire-blackened rubble, and blanched naked trees mixed with sickly overgrowth. The Beaks had given Oak Ridge special
attention.

Silently, soberly, Lori led him along an unmarked
path through the hills to the northeast of the destruction. She pushed aside brown vines, and they slipped
inside a low-ceilinged cave. Something a little odd
about that concealing vegetation, Erlanger thought,
but he didn't have time to study it, as he followed
her toward an apparent dead end of rough damp
stone.

In the gloom, Lori produced a miniature flashlight
from her breast pocket. The yellow circle of light
revealed a dark crack, and she squeezed around a
tight bend that would allow only one at a time to
pass. At her heels, Erlanger was astounded to find a
huge, open chamber before him. He paused, but heard
only her breathing and the distant echo of dripping
water.

At eye-level, against the near wall, Lori tapped out
a code signal. Within seconds, as if by magic, the
solid wall was split by a door. Bluish light spilled
into the chamber, along with three armed people
who quickly surrounded the two travelers. Erlanger
blinked rapidly. No question, all three weapons were
pointed at him.

He heard little and remembered less of the rapid
greetings and explanations among the four rebels. He
was rushed along an upward slope in a hallway cut
through rock. At some point in the maze of passages
and chambers, Lori and one of the rebels, a woman,
disappeared. The remaining "guards" urged him on.
While some stared, the people he passed usually ig-

nored him. Strange sights, odd odors greeted his puzzled senses.

Eventually, they had arrived at this cell. Then Erlanger was stripped, his clothing and toolkit confiscated. His questions, his protests, were not answered. He was given a thin jumpsuit and a scratchy blanket and the dull steel door clanged shut behind him. He saw people three times a day, but little conversation accompanied his meals or the exchange of the pot that served his sanitary needs.

Erlanger panted curses as he finished his exercise routine. His sweaty skin itched from many days without bathing. It should be time for Fred LaFayette, one of the original guards from the hidden entrance, to bring breakfast. His internal clock told him that LaFayette was overdue, and his stomach grumbled. He paced the cell a few times and tried calling through the small barred opening in the door. With ill grace, he sat on the noisy metal bunk. "If this is how Lori treats friends," he muttered, "who needs this outfit?" After what he estimated to be a good hour, LaFayette appeared. As usual, the hawk-nosed man was accompanied by another armed guard.

"Damn your eyes!" Erlanger swore, as he bounced up from the shelf. "You guys off on a three-day drunk? I'm starving in here . . . freezing my ass off. What's going on? Where's Lori?"

LaFayette smiled; the expression stretched his pinched face into a caricature of human kindness. "No lip, friend. Besides, you ain't allowed to eat this morning. You got an appointment with the doctor."

"What?" Erlanger frowned and scratched his matted hair. "What's with the examination? I'm healthy as a bull. A little soap and water's all I need."

"So you say. Lori's been through debriefing, and

convinced the powers that be to let you live, so now
you get to go through screening."

Erlanger started to make a speech about his ill
treatment, then thought better of it. Rights were relative. The old democracy his grandfather had told
him about guaranteed certain things to its citizens;
the *Cweom-jik* granted no rights—just some privi-
leges to a selected few. This rebel society would doubtless have its own concept of rights. While others held
the weapons and the keys, he was in no position to
make demands, at least until he knew what was his
to demand. His teeth clenched painfully; patient ac-
ceptance was still necessary.

"Let's get it over with. I've got nothing to hide."

The other guard stepped out of the cell and turned
right, while LaFayette held back to bring up the rear.
Erlanger followed the silent one; his bare feet slapped
the cool tile floor in unison with clicking boot heels.
Resistance was pointless, and Lori's last words to
him had made it plain that the Underground would
not welcome him with open arms at first. Apparently
their security had been threatened by Ceejay stoolies
more than once. Fortunately, the turncoats had been
discovered in time, and each had paid the usual trai-
tor's price.

He was escorted through a series of passages and
chambers not unlike the ones he had traveled through
on the way to the cell. Finished concrete predominated over natural stone now, and more people were
in the halls. Quite a variety of people. He stared at
several men and women whose skin color was the
stuff of legend in Milford.

This screening business bothered him. The notion
of a doctor puzzled him. Certainly, a doctor would
know quite a bit about torture, but ... What had
Lori said? Here he would be assumed "guilty until
proven innocent"? He tried to remember what he

medicine. Pain, he knew, could make people talk, but surely they wouldn't go that far?

He had visited what passed for doctors back in Milford. Once, he'd slipped with a wood chisel. Sometimes, when setting broken bones and such, doctors used drugs, duplicated drugs from Old Times that made people act silly, and yes, babble. Perhaps the rebels would load him up with drugs, and he would spill his guts. But damnit, he told Lori and Wysocki everything, certainly everything important.

As soon as the idea came to him, he found his face growing warm with embarrassment and anger. There were things, after all, that he would not want strangers, even friends, to know. Of course, the rebels wouldn't know the women involved; but that time he went to Perintown and . . .

He halted suddenly to avoid stepping on the heels of the guard in front. That man, whose name he had yet to hear, was tapping a series of numbered keys on the wall next to a blue door. The door opened, and the trio stepped into a long, white hallway. Erlanger felt a chill, and noted an odd, somehow familiar scent. The hall was lined with more doors. Damnit all, was the Underground nothing but mysterious doors?

He spotted an intersecting corridor about fifty yards away. Other than the doors and the intersection, and strange tubular light fixtures in the ceiling, little else was noteworthy. His guards led him past three doors and then entered a light green room. Journey's end—a hard bed, a lot of shiny instruments, and some electronic equipment, all new to him. The strange smell was even stronger here.

"Up on the bed, friend," LaFayette ordered. He winced at the constant repetition of the obviously insincere "friend," but sat on the bed without protest.

The second man left, and Erlanger spent a few

minutes studying the equipment spread around the room, some of it on small tables, some hanging in racks on the walls. A few things were obviously cutting tools, but he was careful not to stare too long, not with the grim-faced LaFayette hovering nearby, his right hand on his pistol holster. Some items he recognized. A "steth'cope" he remembered that thing was called. Cotton balls and some gauze bandages were also familiar. A big rectangular electric light hung above him, but it was turned off. Odd-shaped tubes and bottles bracketed the bed. The glassware did not inspire relaxation.

His survey was cut short by the arrival of a somewhat stocky but attractive woman with short, dark hair. She was dressed in white. Under other circumstances, Erlanger might have struck up a friendly conversation. Was she, perhaps, the doctor? His torturer? LaFayette seemed to stand straighter when she entered, and the guard's eyes were more on her than on him. But he still held a ready hand near his gun.

"H'lo, Lydia." LaFayette grinned. "This here is Mr. Brent Erlanger."

"Right," the brunette replied. "We're all set for him." She turned to face her victim. "You're the one who came back with Lori, so I've heard. I'm Lydia Rutledge, med tech."

Erlanger nodded, watchful. His neck felt stiff.

"Lori had a lot to say about you." Lydia smiled briefly, in a manner that suggested there was little more to be said about the perilous journey from Cincinnati. But Erlanger thought he detected a glint of unspoken interest, perhaps intrigue. He wondered whether he was correct. Grandfather had always told him that women were good at keeping secrets—except from one another.

"Shuck off the top of your jumpsuit, and give me your right arm," Lydia suddenly ordered.

Erlanger complied, as he watched LaFayette watch her. His own attention was quickly drawn to the med tech, to her ample cleavage specifically, as she leaned forward and pushed back his sleeve. She wrapped a short length of rubber tubing around his upper arm, tight enough to pinch the skin, and secured it with a half knot. This done, she began poking the muscle of his forearm.

"Good tone, but why is it that you hunks are so hard to bring up a vein?" she mumbled. "Make a fist." He followed instructions, fascinated. She kneaded his flesh for a few moments, said "Aha!" and turned to remove a needle-tipped syringe from a shiny tray. "This will hurt," she announced, and popped the needle through his skin. Erlanger felt a sharp bite, then a mild burning, as the amber substance in the syringe flowed into him.

He started to speak, found he couldn't think of what he wanted to say, and paused. He felt very relaxed, and imagined that he must look rather stupid, a big grin on his face. So calm, so soft . . .

The light, he hadn't noticed the light before. He blinked slowly. A gentle blue glow—or was it green? —less than a foot from his face. On, off, on, off. Not the big overhead light. Odd. On. Off.

"Take deep breaths," a new, male voice ordered. "Look at the light." The light continued to blink, now more slowly.

Suddenly, all the lights were on in the room. He tried to sit up, but his muscles wouldn't obey. He was pleasantly tired. He couldn't keep his eyes open. He practiced focusing them on Lydia Rutledge, who was sitting in a chair that wasn't there before. Come to that, he didn't see anything that had been there before. The walls were no longer the same, and someone had painted them yellow. The room even smelled more friendly. He stared at the short brunette. I'll bet, he thought, she has very nice thighs . . .

Lydia giggled. "Thanks."

Erlanger shook his head, and his vision blurred. Some of his drowsiness was wearing off. Had he said that aloud? He blushed. He realized finally that they had moved him. He had been unconscious, and he didn't have any idea of how much time had passed. "Is . . . where's the doctor?"

"That's all over, Brent." Lydia smiled warmly. "You've been through the wringer, and I'm happy to say that you passed." Her smile dimmed a little. "Of course, if you hadn't, you would never have awakened."

He felt relief wash through him. A dull hammer beat the back of his eyeballs, and his throat was dry. "What did I say? What did they ask?"

She shook her head. "You passed; let's just leave it at that."

He nodded. Maybe he didn't want to know.

Time crawled, then trotted. He fell asleep at least twice, and was awakened each time by Lydia, who alternately urged him to keep his eyes open and chattered loudly about nothing at all. Once, she gave him some sweet juice to drink through a bent glass tube. At last, the fog cleared, and he was able to sit up.

A familiar face, cleaner and more healthy than he'd last seen it, peeked in the door. Lori, his good "friend." The two women held a quick, whispered conference, then Lori moved to his side.

"I think it's time we have a cup of coffee, Brent. Feel up to walking?"

He wiggled his fingers and toes, then got shakily to his feet. Both women moved to catch him as he took a staggering step, but he waved them away. It was somehow very important that he stand alone. He still

wore the soiled jumpsuit, but someone had thoughtfully added doe-skin slippers to his feet.

"All right, then," Lori said, as the shorter woman
opened the door to let them pass. "This way, Brent."

Erlanger followed, still weak, but determined. Lori
turned right, took a few steps, then waited for him.
He trudged beside her and nonchalantly put an arm
around her shoulder. As they continued, he leaned on
her heavily, and she wrapped an arm around his
waist. He forgot the past three days, almost.

For several minutes, they passed many of what he
soon realized were corridor route numbers on the
walls. He felt almost normal when, after two more
turns and a short uphill climb, they came to a large,
cheerfully-painted area. The floor was carpeted, and
the room looked like a restaurant. Tables and chairs
were placed here and there. Lori led him to the near-
est empty table, sat him down, and went to get cups
from a steel counter at the back wall.

Erlanger looked around. Although the room could
have easily held sixty people, there were maybe ten
who were seated at various tables. Odd, he thought,
that there aren't many people around. Maybe it's the
middle of a work day? The soft buzz of conversation,
which had quieted with his arrival, resumed as Lori
returned with two steaming cups of black liquid. He
sipped the cup she offered, then made a face as the
bitter taste washed over his tongue.

"It's real duplicated coffee," Lori said in sympa-
thy. "I'm sure that was rare in Milford, but you'll get
used to it."

"Uh huh. I guess I'll be getting used to a lot of
things, now that I'm finally *in*."

Lori picked up her cup. "I knew that you would
pass. But Admin and Military couldn't go on my
word alone. We have rules about strays, whether

they're brought in, or wander too close on their own, and we can't be too careful."

"I guess I understand, but it's still a damn poor way to treat somebody who ... like I was being accused of something I didn't do. I was about to—"

"Hey, Doc!" A shout from the doorway interrupted Erlanger. He turned and saw a tall, heavy-set man with a red beard and, next to him, a lanky fellow with bristly hair and skin the color of the coffee in his cup. He tried not to stare as the two made their way to their table, but found that he was more than a little fascinated to see a human being who was so different from any he had seen before. He knew about blacks, to be sure, as well as orientals, and other racial types. According to his grandfather, however, the Milford area had never attracted a wide variety of people. Or at least, it hadn't during and after the Collapse. Grandfather Owens had been a little vague about why that was so.

Lori was on her feet instantly, and embraced both men. Erlanger felt a twinge of jealousy, but rose too.

"We heard you were back," the black man said, his smile wide. "LaFayette's mouth's been flapping for days, and we got most of the details about the mission. Sure too bad about—"

"We all knew the risks," Lori snapped. She sat down slowly, then managed a weak smile. "I ... I'm sorry, Cleve. I've talked so much about the whole mess that it's like a raw nerve."

The black man patted her shoulder. "Mind if we pull up a chair? We're not due back at the shop for another half hour."

Lori waved toward the empty area, and the two moved a table over, then went after their own coffee.

Once the newcomers were settled in, Lori made introductions. "Brent Erlanger, I'd like you to meet Cleveland Stearns and Phil Campbell."

Stearns nodded, and extended a hand. "Call me Cleve." His grip was surprisingly strong, and he chuckled. "Don't rub off none. We're all the same color to them damn Beaks!"

"I, uh, sure," Erlanger said. He shook hands with Campbell, who also seemed genuinely delighted to meet him.

"So," Cleve asked, "what do you think of our little town?"

"I haven't seen much of it, beyond lots of hallways, the clinic, and a nasty little stone cell. Just how 'little' is this place?"

"Never counted the square meters," Cleve replied with a slow wink, "but I think we have about a thousand people."

Lori nodded in agreement. "That's right, but Base can hold three times as many as it does now. There's a whole block of unoccupied housing on past G level, Cleve."

"Really?" The black man raised his thick eyebrows. "I've never been over there. Spend most of my inside time eating, sleeping, and working." He poked Campbell playfully. "Not like some I could name."

A grinning Campbell read the confusion on Erlanger's face. "Cleve's not a native like Lori and me," he explained. "We picked him up in cave entrance B-6 a couple of years back. And we were damn lucky he wandered in, too! He's probably one of the few people alive who knows anything about CMOS technology."

Cleve chuckled, as his long narrow fingers engulfed his plastic cup. "Yeah, I was all set to move into that cave. Thought I'd found me a home for life. Then these guys screwed it up by coming through the back wall. I don't know who was more surprised, me or them."

Erlanger felt himself warming toward the thin man;

at least he wasn't the only stray lamb. "What's 'sea-moss'?" he asked.

"Ho—you gotta ask about CMOS? I bet there's a whole bunch of other stuff you'll have to learn about before I can even begin to answer. Has to do with electronics—Old Time stuff, a generation removed from solid-state, which came after vacuum tubes. You savvy?"

The newest recruit shook his head. "Not really, although I have heard about electronics and computers. I've even worked a bit with 'phones, but that was simple enough: wires and switches, resistors, and suchlike. But there were some plastic boxes I never did understand; just wired them up like I was told."

"I know that feeling. How'd you come by that?" Cleve leaned forward, his elbows on his knees.

"I was an artificer, back in Milford. I sort of picked up what I needed to know along the way, with some help from old man Stanton before he died."

Campbell gulped coffee loudly. "Hey, that's great. We can use another hand. You'll learn quick enough."

"If Campbell could learn, anybody could," Cleve added. "I had to teach these children everything I knew before they could get most of their old micros back on line. Lucky for them I'd been around that stuff all my life. The basement of my folks' house was full of computer boards, radios, and all sorts of gadgets. My great-grandfather was what they called a hacker, and his interests—and his junk—stayed in the family, even after the Collapse. Of course, it had to be well-hidden when the Ceejays came."

As curious as he was to learn more about Cleve's history, Erlanger held back on the obvious questions. Something in the thin man's tone told him that it might be a touchy subject. Evidently, these rebels assumed that he was ready to jump in and go to work. If that was where he'd fit in best, then the electronics section would be what he'd join, but he didn't want to commit himself just yet. So much he didn't know . . .

"Sure is nice to feel welcome finally," he said. "I'm wondering about one thing, though. If this place was built to hold three thousand or more, how come there are so few now?"

The other two looked at Lori. She cleared her throat, and set down her cup. "Yes, well, that is something you'll be briefed on, our history. The Base was originally part of Oak Ridge complex, all that rubble you saw on the way. Oak Ridge was a research and development center for many years, operated by the old government of the United States. They studied nuclear and other forms of energy here—weapons too.

"Before the middle of the Twentieth Century, during a war as I understand it, but decades before the Collapse, Oak Ridge was established as a secret installation. After that war, a large amount of important defense research was conducted here, somewhat more openly. Then, this underground installation was built—again quite secretly. Apparently this complex was one of several in the country that was designed as a refuge against foreign invasion."

"Worked pretty well against the Beaks, too," Campbell said. "We're hoping that similar complexes still exist in other parts of the world, and that they are still staffed as this one is. We know of a few possibilities on this continent, and—"

Lori silenced him with a look, and Erlanger did not miss the significance. Even though he was cleared, thanks to the mysterious interrogation, he was not a full member, not yet. He hid his concern behind another attempt to train his taste buds with real coffee.

"Anyway," Lori continued, "more than two thousand people moved in here during and after the Collapse. I've always figured that they saw the breakdown associated with duplicators coming, and they planned to preserve civilization and current technology. Didn't quite work out that way, however. The hidden entrances can be defended by a relatively small number of people, and the founders did their best to keep the very existence of Base a secret, since the possibility of being overrun by outlaws was strong after the Collapse. We're pretty self-sufficient here, Brent. We manufacture a lot of what we need, and irreplaceable supplies are rationed—when they can't be duplicated or scavenged. I imagine it was the same way before the Ceejays attacked. We have large hydroponic farms on the lower levels, so the founders only had to sneak in fresh game occasionally."

Lori tilted her empty cup. Campbell got the message and went for more coffee, as her brief history continued. "The real problem was in maintaining technology. Vital parts failed, and there weren't any good spares left to duplicate. Duplicators failed too, and parts for them were practically nonexistent. Many tried to find the underlying principles of duplicators, but nobody succeeded. Of course, the companies that produced duplicators conveniently disappeared about the time the Collapse became obvious."

Erlanger raised an eyebrow. "All part of the *Cweomjik* master plan, as we now know. Before the Beaks appeared openly and the attacks on cities and high-tech centers started, we went underground in more ways than one. Some other research installations survived for a time, and maintained radio contact with Base. Then the Ceejays killed almost all communications."

"I don't ..." Erlanger stared into the dregs of his coffee, suddenly conscious of his need for a bath and fresh clothing.

"Those damned birds wanted complete control, even

as they offered to 'help' humanity out with its problems," Cleve said quietly. "You ought to—"

"No, no," Erlanger interrupted. "What I meant was, what happened to communications, before the Ceejays attacked openly?"

Cleve Stearns drew back from the table. "Hell, man, first thing they took out was the Clarke-orbit comsats." He caught that look from Lori again. "Ah, that's a whole 'nother story; it can wait 'til you're more in the picture."

Lori seemed about to take his hand, but pulled back. "Do you have any idea what it was like, Brent, right after the Collapse? The whole country, the whole world I guess, went outlaw! Everything went to hell."

Erlanger nodded. Grandfather Owens' stories were still vivid memories.

"About thirty years ago here," she went on, "replacement parts were critically low, and many of the original Base founders died. One faction wanted more direct action against the Ceejays, instead of the long-term research effort that was originally planned. Some were just fed up with hiding in a hole, and they argued that if the Beaks couldn't be pushed off Earth in their lifetime, it wasn't worth it. So they left—as many as half the population. Gradually, singly and in groups, the activists left to attack the *Cweom-jik*. And they never returned. Those who remained were dedicated to the long-range goals that we still uphold. We must find a way to turn Ceejay technology against them, or redevelop our own science until we have suitable weapons."

Silence followed Lori's final words. The unfamiliar coffee seemed to boil in Erlanger's stomach. Cleve broke the awkward moment with a broad stretch. "Time for us to hit it, Campbell. Let's leave Brent with the charming doctor. I'm sure Lori has a lot more to tell him. The rest of our crew will be back from lunch any time."

Campbell stood. "Come down to our shop soon, Brent. E-1103."

Erlanger smiled and waved them off, then turned to the woman who continued to puzzle him. "Speaking of lunch, or breakfast, for that matter . . ."

"Didn't you eat? Oh, yes, the pentothal. You would have made quite a mess if you'd eaten before your session." The light plastic chair rocked as she stood. "Poor boy, it's time you found the commissary. But I can't stay; I have a lot of lab work ahead of me this afternoon."

He would have liked to have known more about her work—she had never told him that she was a doctor—but she discouraged conversation as she led him farther into the maze. Some minutes later, they entered the pleasant dining room on C level. The lighting seemed to suggest a bright spring day. Food was set out in steam trays along a wall of windows, and he could see people at tables beyond the windows. When they're not trying for the old stone cell effect, he thought, this place sure doesn't feel like a cave.

"Heartburn City." Lori grinned. "No, it's really pretty good. Oh, and Admin arranged for quarters too. Before I forget here's something you'll need . . ." She handed him the slim folder that she had been carrying. "Here's a map of the complex. Your quarters are on this level. Block C, Room 88." She looked at a square, old-fashioned analog clock set into the wall. "Sorry, I really have to go now. There's a lot for me to catch up on." She made eye contact briefly, but just as he was about to speak, she shook her head—as if in answer to a question she didn't wish to hear. "I'll see you soon, Brent; probably late tomorrow, after you've talked to Administrator Boone, and with the job classification people. There should be a memo in your room about that. If you have any problems, just pick up a phone and punch 411; that's the Base information number."

She stared at him again for a long moment, then she was gone.

Erlanger rubbed at a bunched muscle in the back of his neck. Maybe it's still aftereffects of the interrogation drug, he thought. He frowned and headed for the serving trays.

Fresh fruits and vegetables, including a surprising number of tree-borne fruits, were offered. He wondered how they grew trees underground. His nose recognized beef, in a stew, as well as venison, rabbit, and chicken. His mouth began to water, and he postponed investigation of how the rebels handled food supply in favor of more immediate demand.

He filled a shallow bowl with the beef stew, and loaded a plate with most of the vegetables that he thought he could identify. At the end of the serving line, fresh bread beckoned, and he took almost half a loaf. Nobody seemed to be counting rations. He passed the shiny coffee urn and shook his head. Water would do.

Alone at his chosen table, for he certainly knew no one else in the room, he alternated grateful bites with attempts to read the map that Lori had left. He felt someone approach his back, and looked up to see LaFayette, his former jailer.

"Hiya, Fred," he mumbled around a carrot. "Heard I passed muster? No hard feelings; you were just doing your job, I suppose. Have a seat."

"Yeah, for a minute," LaFayette answered. His eyes were still prison-guard slits as he took the chair and leaned toward Erlanger. "Just curious about what you have in mind."

"In mind?"

"Yeah, with the Doc."

"You mean Lori?"

The big man scowled. "Don't play games! Hell yes, Lori. How many other doctors you know? I think you're taking advantage of her!"

"I don't know what you're talking about."

"Like hell you don't. With Wysocki gone—and there's been some talk about that—you seem in with her pretty solid."

Erlanger dropped his spoon in surprise. LaFayette's accusation was certainly contrary to the signals he'd received from Lori during the past hour. His face hardened. "I don't see it's any of your business, Fred, but I don't have anything 'in mind.' I'm just trying to fit in here. Guess I'll find out more about that tomorrow."

"Listen, friend, Wysocki was tops around this place, and only you and Lori know what happened. A lot of folks are taking his loss real hard. Just you remember that."

"You've heard the story straight. He died like a man." LaFayette's face pressed close, but Brent didn't flinch. He tried to change the subject. "Tell me something? Why is everyone calling Lori 'Doc?'"

LaFayette's harsh expression softened a bit. "Guess you can't be all that close to her, at that. She was one of the last to be trained by the original medical personnel, but she doesn't play sawbones that much, nowadays. Heads up research—she would rather go out with the search teams. Like the one you ran into. She always wants more bio-medical research equipment."

"You do medical research here, too?"

"Yeah, mainly has to do with Ceejays. That's one possible line of attack, so they say. But she can tell you about that, if she wants." He pushed back his chair. "Keep in mind what I said, you hear?"

"Sure," Erlanger said, as he watched LaFayette carry his puzzling emotions from the room.

He returned to his now-cold stew. As he ran a last piece of bread through the thick gravy in the bottom of the bowl, he studied the map again. The underground complex had, it appeared, twenty-four levels in three clusters, like truncated pyramids. Levels with odd numbers were on the right-hand, or north side of the complex, while even-numbered levels were opposite, in the south cluster. The floors of the levels varied by about ten feet, and the three clusters were arranged in a split-level configuration, like some of the Old Time single-family houses in Milford. The two main clusters did not interconnect directly, but shared common tunnels to a third installation to the east. That one carried no labels, and was apparently unused, for the most part. Little description accompanied the different areas of the map, so he was only guessing. He had to guess at a lot of the words too. Each of the three clusters had its own hidden tunnels to the outside, and he supposed that all of those were well guarded.

The floor plans of almost every level were similar. Six blocks were sectioned off by passageways, and the blocks were labeled A through F. Blocks contained rooms of differing sizes, and some blocks on the lower levels were huge, single rooms. Hydroponics—whatever that word meant—was an example.

With some concentration, he found his present location on the map, and traced a route to C-88. Although the wall clock announced midafternoon, Erlanger felt as if sundown were long past. He gathered the remains of his meal, took the bowl and silverware to the wall alcove where others had taken theirs, and headed in what he hoped was the right direction for his new home.

C-88 was unlocked; indeed, no external lock was on

the simple hinged door, just a knob. He entered, and was relieved to find the lights on. He was pleased, as well, to find a latch on the back of the door. He scanned the room quickly: a small bed, a couple of chairs, some cabinets and drawers set into one wall, and a shelf. An unfamiliar telephone hung next to the shelf. Directly across from the bed, a smaller room proved to be a private bath—a luxury he never had in Milford.

The little room's clean, cool porcelain was a welcome sight, and he used it with a gratified sigh. The day had been exhausting. He found the idea of a shower very tempting, and all the necessities—towels, soap, and back brush—were laid out on the vanity. He just didn't have the energy, and settled for a quick wash of face and hands, after sniffing suspiciously at the scented cake of soap.

Even the bed smelled pleasantly fresh. He shrugged, and thought how service improved once a visitor was given a shot of babble-juice. He slipped out of his jumpsuit, and turned down the covers. The sheets and blanket were a little better quality than he was used to. Years ago, he'd enjoyed truly fine bed linens at Wilma Shively's cathouse, but Wilma did have connections. Or, more than likely, she had enough on the bigwigs of Milford to get whatever she wanted. The ceiling lights were in his eyes, but a search for their controls was too much effort. He mused about his past for a time, but Milford seemed so far away, and he drifted off to sleep in the warm comfort of his new life.

Chapter

NINE

The lights were still on when he awoke. Erlanger scanned the unfamiliar furnishings, momentarily disoriented. His survey revealed a small digital clock that he hadn't noticed the previous day: 7:03 AM. Seems right, he thought. For the first time in many days, he felt quite rested. "But after more than twelve hours in the sack, who wouldn't," he muttered. He rolled to the edge of the bed and sat up. The effort revealed a few stiff muscles, and slight pulling of the pink scars on shoulder and chest. He stood and walked back and forth, stretching and bending. He felt fit, despite his recent ordeal.

He entered the bathroom. Too many days had passed since he had bathed thoroughly. The last time had been in a stream, no soap, while an armed woman stood guard. He slipped off his smelly jumpsuit and stepped into the shower stall.

Erlanger emerged from the bath clean and refreshed. He would certainly appreciate fresh clothing, and the closet and drawers had remained unexplored when he fell asleep. He opened the thin closet door slowly.

His own clothes—now clean and crisp—hung inside! He turned quickly to the drawers. Fresh underwear and socks filled the first one he opened. The next drawer down brought another surprise, his toolkit.

Still naked, he spread the leather kit out on his bed. All his familiar possessions, at least all that had survived the Ceejay attacks, were there. They looked to have been cleaned too. Even the gold coins remained. He shook his head in wonder at his new treatment by the Underground. Then, he enjoyed the simple pleasure of drawing fresh garments over clean skin.

"Now what?" he said aloud. Maybe he should try the telephone; try to ask someone where he should go. His stomach voted for the commissary again, but he knew he had appointments today. A yellow square of paper on the back of the door caught his attention. Had that been there before? Funny printing, the letters were made up of tiny black dots. There were several numbers, then his name, then the message:

"0900 HRS: BASE ADMIN/ADMIN-11/INTERVIEW 1340 HRS: EDUCATION & PERSONNEL/EH-14/IN-PROCESSING & TESTING

PLEASE REPORT PROMPTLY. CALL 411 FOR INFORMATION OR DIRECTIONS."

They don't make it easy for someone who doesn't read much, he thought. But if he understood the first line correctly, he had plenty of time for breakfast. His bedside clock now read 7:52.

A few false turns and careful use of the map returned him to the commissary. Two lines of people snaked out the door, from which wafted inviting aromas. Evidently, he had picked the most popular breakfast hour. He joined the end of one line. There were no familiar faces, but he didn't expect any. After all, how many would he recognize here? He smiled at a few who made eye contact, but he felt uncomfortable about opening a conversation. He noted several more racial types among the group—blacks, like Cleve Stearns, as well as short people with dark skin but thin, silky hair. Two of the latter, particularly striking women with deeply tanned faces, high cheekbones, oval-shaped eyes, were speaking to each other in front of him. Their voices carried an odd lilt, and they were speaking English only part of the time.

The line moved quickly enough. When Erlanger reached the serving area, he found a wealth of choices. He loaded a tray with orange-colored melon slices, something that looked like thin oatmeal, and scrambled eggs and bacon. The coffee smelled appealing this morning, and he decided to give it another try. He couldn't resist a couple of fresh rolls that were topped with a brown, sugary glaze.

Once again, he chose a small, unoccupied table in a far corner. As he ate, he glanced about. Nobody seemed to be watching him, and he silently kicked himself for the feeling that he was still under guard. He relaxed and began to enjoy his breakfast. He sipped his hot coffee, and realized that he had learned to like the unfamiliar taste.

"Mind if I join you?"

"Lori! Sure, have a seat."

As she set her tray on the table and slid into the chair, her leg brushed against his. He felt a familiar spark, but she moved quickly, and her face showed no change of expression. She ate her fruit, then paused as she buttered a sweet roll. "I see you found your room . . . and the shower." That fleeting smile appeared, a quick flash of dimple lines. "I trust you're feeling almost human again."

He toyed with his coffee cup, unsure. Lori was friendly, and yet not. "Had a nice shower. Nice laundry service, too. I didn't think I was ever going to see my own things again."

"Everything there, I trust?" She watched him, her face impassive.

Erlanger nodded. "Well," he finally said, "how are things in the medical department? I should have guessed that you were a doctor, from the way you treated me in that first way station and all."

"Bio-Med, we call it. I don't practice in the clinic though . . . but do take on the odd case." Those dimples blossomed again. "My field is research. I head up the group that is trying to understand *Cweom-jik* biology. Knowledge is power; or at least, we hope it will be, and that our research will lead to a practical weapon. Those tissue samples I brought back may be the break we need. They were the first ever."

Her face seemed to glow as she talked. Erlanger began to understand the importance she placed on her work. He felt a sudden pride in having been a part of the tissue sample discovery, despite his subsequent "initiation" by the Underground. "So, have you made any progress?"

Lori frowned and shook her head. "Not really. We're still doing a lot of time-consuming tests; we just don't have the necessary equipment." She sighed, and sipped her coffee. "That's always the way. The Base founders provided for the treatment of human injuries and illnesses, and even good veterinary facilities. But they couldn't have foreseen the Ceejays, the need for research into truly alien biochemistry and physiology . . . Even with duplicators, we're limited in—"

Erlanger's eyebrows rose. "You still have working duplicators?"

"Ah, yes. No harm in you knowing now, I guess. But as I was saying, we have all the necessary equipment for human medical emergencies." He had the feeling that she was deliberately avoiding something as she continued, "but only limited provision for original research. Oh, the Base clinic is good, and we have three operating theaters, as well as a hundred beds, between here and South Cluster."

"That's the side that's not in use?"

"For the most part." She frowned, then said, "we could activate South Cluster if we had to; power's no problem. Only the livestock area is operational there now. We raise as much of our food as possible, so as not to draw attention to the Base through hunting or trade."

He began to tidy up the dishes on his tray, unsure of what to do with his hands. The rebels were obviously well organized, and he was eager to contribute. "You know, whatever I can do to help you, I'll be . . ."

Lori smiled, then laughed, and for a moment she seemed to be the woman he thought he had come to know on the trail. "Not in my labs, I'm afraid, Brent. That would take years of specialized training. I studied under Dr. Ramundo for a long time—after basic math, biology, chemistry, history, and English." Her face grew more serious. "You'll find that we maintain a lot of traditions here, or at least we try. Anyway, your slot will be up to Connie Sue in Personnel. I understand that your testing is scheduled to begin today."

He fumbled with the button on his shirt pocket and pulled out the yellow sheet that he had found on his door. "I guess I understand this schedule."

"Good. What will happen is that you'll be interviewed about your background and experience, and then you'll be given aptitude and ability tests. Those tests will measure your skills and potential for training."

He nodded, and smoothed out the folded memo.

"That's sort of what I thought. But how do I get to these places? And what's 'Admin'?"

Lori took the yellow paper. "OK, E level is two down from here. You can find room 14 on the map I gave you. Administration offices are two levels up. Be easiest if you take Blue Elevator."

He had also spread the map out on the table. "Elevator?"

Surprise registered, then she realized his ignorance of many aspects that Base residents took for granted. "That's right, they would have walked you around, standard 'blind man's bluff' security treatment." She scooted her hand around on the map. Their fingers touched for a moment, but she gave no sign that it was more than accidental contact. "Here, see? Blue's at the end of this corridor. This place is a real labyrinth, but you'll get used to the conventions here in no time; won't need a ball of string or trail of bread crumbs." He looked up, puzzled at her unfamiliar references, but she continued to trace a finger on the map. "Elevators are simple. Up and down arrow buttons beside each door. Push one if a car's not there, and once the car arrives, push the panel button inside for the level you want."

As they leaned their heads together over the map, he became aware of her scent, something more than fresh-scrubbed woman, something that hinted of flowers and musk. Suddenly, she drew back, rose tinting her cheeks, but her voice remained level. "Any room or passageway that you're not supposed to enter will be locked," she said. "You'd need the proper access code to work the locks, anyway, so I suggest you try to pick a straight route to wherever you're going. The security patrols won't recognize you yet, and some of those people come on strong."

He had wondered about the many guards inside. "And what about this Admin?"

"That's a longer walk from Blue Elevator, I'm afraid, but maybe I can get you there. You'll probably be interviewed by the old man himself." She glanced at the wall clock. "Good, we've got a little time yet, and you should know about Milford."

He had started to return the map and yellow schedule to his pocket, and his hand paused. "Milford? My Milford?"

"Right? I was talking to one of my friends in Communications. We've had a report from the Milford Underground."

Erlanger's hand slowly dropped to the table. Rebels in Milford? Not so long ago, he would have sworn that everyone in his home town was either loyal, or so cowed by the Ceejays as to make no difference.

"Your story checked out, of course. That Heather Barlow had set you up for the gallows, just like you told us. I gather that wasn't the first time that dear, sweet Marla spread her legs and invited a man to wear a very tight necktie." She smiled as she said it, but he didn't miss her change in tone. Was she simply amused, sympathetic, or maybe jealous? He felt slow heat rise in his cheeks.

"But that's all in the past, you'll be happy to hear. There's been a general house-cleaning in Milford government. Mayor Barlow and his cronies didn't meet the Ceejay quotas—with a little help from our affiliates. That's part of our long-term plan and we've succeeded in a number of towns. Anyway, the Beaks killed your Mayor and his bunch of thugs, and our people are now secretly in charge."

He stared at her in amazement. The extent of the rebel organization far exceeded his initial assumptions. A number of new thoughts flashed through his mind. "Hey, that's terrific! I had no idea of—say, that means I could safely return."

Her green eyes met his in a level stare. "Perhaps.

Someday, if that's what you really wish. For the moment, however, I'm afraid you'd be a bit of a security risk."

Erlanger started to respond sharply to the implied distrust, then considered the Underground's point of view. He thought more about Milford, about what he'd left there. Marla, well, Marla had been a brief bit of sport in the grass. Even without the danger from her father, just how much did he care for that little sexpot? As for the rest of Milford, what few friends he'd had—more like drinking buddies, really—would not be greatly missed.

Lori rose and gathered up her tray. She recognized his need to think to himself a moment, but now she broke into his reverie. "It's 8:45, Brent. I've got to talk with Dr. Speigel some time this morning; he's in charge of the Bio-Medical Department, so I can escort you to Admin."

When they left the commissary, he almost put his arm around her waist, as he had days before, when the slope had been steep or the night wind chill. As appealing as the idea was, he chided himself for even thinking it. He suspected that such an action would be met with cool resistance, if not outright hostility. This was a different woman, a competent woman at ease in her environment. He wondered whether he would ever see that "old" Lori again, whether that person had ever been more than his own distorted projection. This Lori wore a shell with no sign of vulnerability, no weakness.

As they passed through the grey corridors, they chatted about inconsequential things. Lori seemed almost eager to discuss neutral topics, historical aspects of the Underground, and features of the Base. "We sometimes find useful items in the rubble outside," she said as they passed the open door of a storeroom. "Books, lab equipment, spare parts, and the like. But it's dangerous to scavenge so close, so we don't do it much, and only in short sorties. This far south, the Beak overflights are more frequent than they were where you grew up. There aren't any towns that close, but we still have to worry about stray hunting parties. Of course, the immediate area is also dangerous in places because it's so damned hot."

"What?"

"Radioactive. Oak Ridge still processed U-235 and plutonium when the Ceejays nailed the complex. Granted, with that high a background count, it makes it easier for us to ... well, never mind that. There's also an occasional problem with outlaw bands." She gestured for him to turn left, and Erlanger scowled. He wondered when people would finally finish sentences around him. Lori continued. "But stuff has been piling up for over 80 years, especially over in South Cluster. Somebody got the notion, and the time, to start cataloging it about a year ago."

She paused, and leaned her head into an open door. "Just thought I'd say hello to ... nope, not here." They moved on. "Quite an undertaking," she continued, "but a lot of good is coming from it. A whole library of medical books turned up a couple of months ago, and some of the electronic equipment has proven functional. We think that most of what we're finding was not part of the original Base stores. Things were obviously brought in over the years, as salvage after the Collapse. People just hauled it in and dumped it, and nobody bothered to keep an inventory, especially during the schism years when so many left or died."

A man and a woman, in what he had come to recognize as the uniform of the security guards, approached them as they reached a level part of the long corridor. The passageway angled off to the south, but Lori stopped beside large steel double doors. A wide stripe of blue paint crossed the middle of the doors.

"Hi, Doc," the chunky female guard said. "Is this the new recruit?"

"Yes, Bonnie. Meet Brent Erlanger."

Erlanger shook hands with the woman, who then introduced him to her partner, Vic. The two guards exchanged pleasantries with him for a minute, then continued on their rounds. Lori moved to the keypad next to the elevator doors, and punched in an access code, then the up arrow. Within seconds, the doors slid aside with a whooshing sound, and Erlanger stared into a small room with a floor that seemed to vibrate slightly.

"Hey," he said, as he followed his guide inside, "I thought you said I'd have no trouble with this thing. What was that you did on the numbered keys? And howcum there are so many guards running around inside? Don't you people trust each other?"

The doors shut and Erlanger felt his breakfast head for his knees. "I'm sorry, Brent; when you grow up with security, some things just come automatically, by reflex. You'd have looked pretty foolish there, without an escort, although Bonnie and Vic could have checked on your appointment and keyed the elevator for you. I'll make sure that you're issued your private codes for the open areas. As for the patrols, bear in mind that Base began as a very secret military operation, and that orientation produced lasting traditions. Then too, this is a hell of a big place, so . . ."

Before Lori could finish her explanation, the unsettling motion stopped and the doors opened to a short, cheerfully-painted hall. A few steps from the elevator a middle-aged man sat behind a metal desk. Lori smiled at the older man. "Hi, Doug. This is Brent Erlanger, for an appointment with the administrator."

He did something with his hand and the metal door across the hallway, which bore large white letters "OFFICE OF THE BASE ADMINISTRATOR," made a buzzing sound. Lori pulled the door open, and Erlanger followed her into a plushly carpeted hallway.

Lori mumbled greetings to the few people they passed, but her mind seemed on something far away. She led him past several offices, then to the end of a short corridor. There, she knocked on a heavy wooden door.

"Come in," a muffled voice replied from within.

At Lori's nod, he preceded her through the door. His first glance told him that the occupant of this room was someone special. The carpeting had a thick, clean blue pattern, and the walls seemed to be of polished oak. Hundreds of books lined shelves from floor to ceiling on two walls. There were pictures on the walls of spacecraft and of Earth and Moon taken from spacecraft. He took a hesitant step closer to the classic NASA "Earthrise" photograph. Man had been there, before the Collapse, before the *Cweom-jik* had smashed human greatness. Erlanger felt awed.

"Catches your throat, does it not, young man?"

The quiet remark, and the soft click of the closing door brought Erlanger's attention to the old bald man behind the massive oak desk. His sensitive face was etched with hundreds of wrinkles, but Brent felt that such a face—now emotionless—could easily burst into a brilliant smile. Although intimidated by a curious feeling of power that seemed to fill the large office, the younger man felt at ease.

"So good to see you, Lori." The old man spoke in a slightly high, yet firm voice, with none of the tremolo that Erlanger associated with the aged.

"Glad to be back, sir," Lori replied. "I had to stop by Admin, and I knew that Mr. Erlanger had an appointment with you." Erlanger glanced at her. Her voice, her posture, carried an unusual deference.

"Ah, Brent, this is Winthrop Boone, our Base Administrator."

"Have a seat, son," the old man said, as he reached across his desk to shake hands. Erlanger nodded as he exchanged a light yet firm grip, and settled into the leather chair in front of the desk.

"Thank you, Lori. If you would excuse us now."

"Yes, sir." She turned smartly and opened the door.

"Lori," Boone said softly to her retreating back, "we all share your loss." Her head bobbed, and she muttered something as the door closed with a quiet sound.

Erlanger stared at the man in charge, who returned the look with deep-set blue eyes that projected a sharp intelligence.

"Now then, young man," the administrator said, at last.

"Sir?" Is this some final test?

"I have been waiting to meet you. Lori's reports have been most positive." He paused, and opened a cream-colored folder. "And our other data . . . well, I am impressed. Not that I should have been surprised . . . genes will out, as they say."

The old man continued to turn pages and appeared to scan their contents. Erlanger expected Boone to don glasses, but the old blue eyes could still focus. What "other data"? Erlanger wondered, uncomfortable in the silence.

"Nothing here to be shy about," Boone continued, as if mind reading was one of his talents. "We all have our little peccadilloes, so to speak; things we would prefer that others not know." The old man smiled, but the added wrinkles did little to calm Erlanger's rising anxiety.

"Of course, this material is confidential, rest assured of that. Everyone here has undergone the interrogation you experienced yesterday. I am sure that you understand the necessity. People spend an inordinate amount of time worrying about sex and love, those secrets of the soul, and they always wonder what they may have revealed under the drugs. In those respects, you are not remarkable, if that is any comfort.

"But enough of your file. I want to formally welcome you to Oak Ridge Base, and to our common cause, the elimination of the *Cweom-jik* from our planet." This time, as a smile returned to the creased face, Erlanger began to relax.

"Thank you, sir. I'm honored to be accepted. It's as if I've been searching for your Base for—"

"Yes, I am not surprised." Boone occupied his hands with a dark briar pipe, tobacco jar, and silent lighter. The sweet smell of Kentucky burley filled the air. "My commendations for the way you handled yourself on the difficult retreat from Cincinnati. We are all saddened at the loss of most of that mission, of course, but your actions in the company of Alan Wysocki and Lori made the difference between success and total failure. We do need people like you, people who react intelligently in a tight spot."

The younger man squirmed in the comfortable chair. He felt blood rush to his cheeks. He certainly didn't think of himself as a hero, yet he wasn't about to contradict the administrator. He stared at his hands and mumbled "Thank you."

"No—indeed, we thank you." Boone patted the folder on his desk. "Most of what you might tell me about your life, your background, is in this folder. There is no need to question you much further on that score. Instead, I would prefer to tell you a few things about your own life that you may not know."

Erlanger looked up, and sat straighter in his chair. That was a remarkable statement from a man he had only just met.

Boone continued, as if he failed to find anything odd in his remark. "Your grandfather, Chester Owens, was a hard-headed, independent thinker, but you knew that, I am sure. He taught you to read, despite the danger, and no doubt he shaped many of your attitudes—especially as regards the *Cweom-jik*."

Grandfather Owens a part of the Underground? Suddenly he had so many questions. Administrator Boone held up his hand, as if to signal that such questions should wait.

"No, Owens was not one of us. Too independent. From what I understand, Owens simply was not group-oriented. He lacked our long-term commitment. Records indicate that he was considered as a local operative, but was never passed." Boone leaned forward and paused to relight his pipe. "Chester Owens was considered to be overzealous. There was no question about his dedication to the cause, but he was thought to be unreliable—a 'hot-dog', if you know what that means."

Boone puffed his pipe for a moment, regarding his visitor quietly. Erlanger began to feel uncomfortable again, as if he should somehow defend his grandfather's memory.

"Then, in your case, we simply could not be sure of your interest, your loyalty. You made trade items for the aliens, after all. You were never contacted. Of course, recent events have changed your status."

The new recruit nodded slowly, and began to reply.

"In the case of your father, on the other hand, the record is quite clear. You should be proud."

Boone sat back, aware that his last remark would

need time to be integrated. Erlanger was stunned. Why, his father had never, in Erlanger's admittedly dim recollection, so much as complained about the Ceejays. Helmut Erlanger had been a quiet man, one who ate what was set before him, as the old saying would have it.

"My father was . . . a rebel?"

The old man set down his pipe. He smiled sadly. "Yes, he was one of us. One of the best of us. Helmut Erlanger was killed during a spy mission to a *Cweomjik* supply dump east of Milford."

"Thank you for telling me. It's a good thing to know."

"Yes, I thought you would want to know. Now, there are one or two questions that I have for you, if you do not mind."

Erlanger was still lost in his childhood. "Sure."

"Those books that you discovered in Cincinnati, were there many?"

His accidental discovery of that dusty apartment seemed so long ago. Erlanger let his gaze wander around Administrator Boone's impressive bookcases. "Ah, well, I didn't count them, but there must have been a couple dozen more. Most of those had what I guess you'd call technical titles."

Boone nodded as he cleaned his pipe into a square metal ashtray. "Good, good. It is a shame that the two books you took did not survive, but I am pleased that there are more. Technical books are quite rare, you see, and not just because of the alien destruction of libraries. I believe that publication of technical materials slowed considerably before the Collapse— something to do with literacy and computers. Of course, we are always searching for computer media— disks, tapes, cartridges, and memory cubes—but those are even more rare, and seldom decipherable.

"In any event, I hope that you will consider joining

an expedition back to Cincinnati. We would like to retrieve those books and look for other materials. That search team you encountered was our first mission in that location, and you are, perhaps, more familiar with the area than anyone else in our organization."

Although his breakfast seemed to turn leaden in his stomach, Erlanger met the old man's challenge squarely. "I'd be glad to do that, sir."

"Please note that I am not asking that you return immediately. Furthermore, while I think such a mission would be a good idea you may well fit in better elsewhere. I do not give all the orders; we are essentially an oligarchy." Those many wrinkles bent into a smile again. "I advise, and I listen, but all department leaders vote on important matters. And a search mission, with its potential for exposure, is very important indeed."

Erlanger doubted that the administrator was telling the strict truth about his actual authority here, but he wasn't about to contradict the old man. Perhaps Boone had just tossed out that idea to test his reaction. His thoughts in turmoil, he suddenly remembered one of that morning's surprises: "Not to change the subject, sir, but why were those gold coins returned to me? Surely they're valuable anywhere. I'd be happy to donate . . ."

Boone leaned back and laughed, a dry, rasping sound. "Thank you, son, but we do not have much need for treasure; much of the reserve from Fort Knox was shipped here during the Collapse. Keep your coins, although here they will just be a lump in your pocket."

Erlanger asked if they might return to the subject of his father, and they talked for some time. Finally, the administrator looked at his watch, a personal article that was apparently quite common at the

Base, although Erlanger had seen very few in his home town. "Well, young man, I believe you are going to be a real asset. But it is past eleven, and you will be wanting lunch before your testing this afternoon. We had best say goodbye for now."

He was lost. The elevator had been no problem; E-level, with its preponderance of light green or cream-colored corridors, had been found with ease. Once out of the elevator, he had followed his map with care. Not enough care, apparently.

"Eh, hi there," he said to a young man with wiry, brown hair, who approached the intersection that he couldn't seem to find on his map. As the man, who wore some kind of tool belt, smiled quizzically, Erlanger continued: "I'm new here, and . . . could you tell me how to get to Room 14?"

The man stopped in front of him, and seemed to hesitate; his expression became suspicious. Have I violated some other security rule? Erlanger wondered. After a moment, the stranger's eyes lost their hooded look. "Better than that, I can take you there." He stuck out his hand. "I'm Tom Delano, by the way."

"Brent Erlanger. Thanks but no need to go to that trouble . . ."

"Thought so. I figured you were the one who brought the Doc back. Right proud to meet you, Brent."

"More the other way around. I mean, Lori brought me in. But I have an appointment at 1:40, 1340 I guess you'd say . . ."

"Naw, that's for computers." Delano checked his wristwatch. "No sweat, 1:25 it is now. I gotta check in with Personnel too. C'mon this way."

Delano took the lead through the maze of corridors, and lapsed into a rapid, relaxed conversation. He was, he explained, a communications tech, and Erlanger took him to mean that he worked with telephones, so he mentioned his own background in

Milford. Delano quickly launched into a discussion of "microwave bursts," "fiber optics," and several other technical terms that left Erlanger completely confused. He tried to remain attentive, but most of his concentration was occupied with the route they were taking. There were fewer doors here, and Erlanger supposed that the rooms behind these doors were larger than those on the other levels he had visited.

"Exactly 1:30," Delano announced, as they stood in front of the door labeled: "PERSONNEL PLACEMENT (Dept. of Education)." Delano hurried into the room and, with a mock salute, he greeted a woman behind a grey metal desk. He turned to shake hands again. "Gotta run on in, Brent. Great meeting you. I'm sure we'll see more of each other. Carolyn, here, will see that you're taken care of."

"Thanks, Tom." Somehow a first-name relationship came easily with the talkative young man. "I hope so too." He turned to the dowdy, fiftyish woman. "Carolyn" didn't seem appropriate with her, but he saw no nameplate. "Hello," he finally said, "I'm Brent Erlanger. I'm supposed to . . ."

"Yes, yes indeed, Mr. Erlanger." She hummed softly as she flipped through a pile of folders on her desk, then extracted one. "Here we are." She picked up a phone. The device must have had some type of sound-screening capability, for Erlanger was startled to see her lips move without being able to hear either side of the conversation. She hung up the phone, but her eyes remained fixed on his shirt buttons. "Dr. Nguyen will be with you shortly. Please have a seat." The local version of Heather Barlow? Erlanger wondered, as he settled into the middle of a row of brown plastic chairs.

He expected another prison-cell wait, and tried to make out the contents of a bulletin board to the right of cool Carolyn. A number of papers and charts were displayed, but he was too far away to make out the printing. He had no more than stretched out his legs, and received a silent frown from the grey lady, when a petite, black-haired woman stuck her head through the door behind Carolyn's fortress.

"Brent Erlanger?" she asked, with a toss of her long, straight hair. He nodded in reply and stood up.

"Come on in. I'm Connie Sue Nguyen." She took his hand as she ushered him through the door. The handshake was formal, but warmer than he would have expected. Her eyes looked into his, and he could not help but notice her good looks.

"Nice to know you, Doctor."

"Call me Connie Sue, Brent. We're going to be working together for a while, so we may as well be friends." She smiled broadly as she talked, a happy expression that added laugh lines to the intriguing folds in the corners of her dark eyes. She appeared to be somewhat older than he was, but to him her looks were so exotic that he was unable to estimate exactly.

She continued to walk backwards. He followed, as she explained: "I'm the Base Psychologist. Educational Director, too, if you want full name, rank, and serial number. I have to find out what you're made of." She actually winked. "Your aptitudes, achievement levels, propensities, personality profiles, Rorschach projections . . . all that."

"Sure, Doc—, Connie Sue. Where do we start?"

"Through here. My office first, for a few preliminary matters. Now this way."

She turned down a short hall and into a vast room that was sectioned off by eye-level partitions. Several people were in the cubicles they passed, but none looked up from the books or papers in front of them. Some of the quiet people appeared to be sitting before teevee screens, and they had funny plastic earmuffs on their heads. Erlanger had seen similar screens at least, for the Ceejay communications console in the Mayor's office was somewhat similar to the ones he saw here, but few of these teevees displayed pictures. Instead, most screens, which seemed to be connected to typewriter keys, were filled with printed amber words.

He would have liked to study the machines more closely, but she urged him past the cubicles with a gentle hand on his waist. "You'll have your turn in a bit, Brent." They climbed four stairs and entered a glass-walled office that overlooked the cubicles. The room was colorful and comfortable, with just a hint of her scent in the air to identify its regular occupant. Low bookshelves lined three walls; the desk was stacked with papers of various sizes; and green plants hung from the ceiling. Several unfamiliar electronic gadgets and switch panels surrounded, and were actually built into, the desk.

The psychologist swiveled around to face one of the strange teevees, and waved Erlanger into a soft armchair beside the desk. Her fingers moved rapidly over the typewriter part of the machine, but they didn't produce the clickity-click he expected. "Now, Brent, let's start getting you into the computer."

His mouth dropped open. The fabled computer! So that's what they were. He wanted to ask a hundred questions. She silenced him with a smile and a toss of her coal-black hair. Then she proceeded to ask an endless series of her own questions, while her fingers flew over the keys. Questions about his parents, his education, his artificer apprenticeship, questions about his thoughts on this and that, questions about things he had never thought about, questions about his dreams even. It continued until he began to wonder whether he understood anything at all. She paused from time to time, while the computer made soft noises, and he pondered whether some of her questions had a hidden intent. He suspected that many did.

At last, just when he felt that his throat would squeeze shut without a drink of water, she finished a battery of items that seemed to concern his relationships with other people, and leaned back. "That's super, Brent. I've got a good KMPI profile. Sorry to pound on your head like that, but the whole idea is not to give you time to think before you answer." She stood up and stretched. It made for an interesting distraction from his dry throat.

She came around beside his chair and pulled him to his feet with a surprisingly strong grip. Is she this friendly with everyone? he wondered, as he met her dark eyes again. "Think you can stand more?" He nodded and she continued to talk as she moved toward the exit from her office. "What I want to do now is begin your APT sequence, a series of tests of your potential abilities. Actually, the computer will give you the tests. Heck of a lot more convenient that way, and faster."

She led him back to the partitioned row of cubicles again, and had him sit before one of the computer screens. She moved his hands to the keyboard. "I know you've got questions of your own, but try to hold them for a while, OK? Now, have you ever worked with a microcomputer or terminal before?"

He shook his head, now a little frightened of his ignorance before this charming woman. "No. No, I've only heard snatches, old tales, really. I met a black guy yesterday who . . ."

She smiled, and his fears lessened. "I didn't think you had. Nothing to worry about, really, it's not going to eat you." The tip of her tongue touched her upper lip, and he missed her next words. ". . . typewriters?"

He guessed at her question. "I've poked at old

broken typewriters, but in Milford no one was allowed to read and write, so . . ."

"Well, you know the basic idea, and the same thing applies to a computer terminal." She leaned over his shoulder and he was very conscious of her breast pressing against his back, and the light brush of her long hair. He struggled to concentrate on the screen as her fingers tapped the computer into life. The machine beeped a few times, and words appeared on the screen:

—OPERATOR?

Connie Sue typed NGUYEN rapidly. Her hair smelled so fresh, with just a hint of perfume.

—PASSWORD?

She continued to tap the keys, and strange letter and number combinations appeared. "Don't worry about all this stuff, it's just to bring up the right file. Now, it's loaded. Since you can read, I've called up the testing series in English; if you couldn't read, we would run you through the same sort of thing in symbols and pictures." She paused and pushed another key. "Now, you'll be asked questions on the screen, or sometimes through the earphones . . . oops, better show you." She picked up the earmuff things, and placed them over his head. Her fingers seemed to caress his hair, or was that merely an overly stimulated imagination?

Her hands touched his lightly, as she guided his fingers. "You'll just touch the screen where it's lighted here for your answers. Either Y for 'yes' or N for 'no,' or the numbers one through five, if the question is multiple choice. Got that? Just those seven responses. It won't matter if you hit the keyboard by mistake, anyway, but be sure you touch the right number for the answer you want to give. As soon as you touch the choice on the screen, the program automatically displays the next question. OK?"

"I guess so." He frowned. There were now a lot of words on the screen and he struggled to read them, in between twists of his neck to look back at her. Why hadn't they built these cubicles so two people could sit side by side? Then again, the awkwardness did have its advantages. He smiled up at her.

She bit her lip, and leaned forward again. "Let's just try a practice series, shall we? Oh, don't hit these blue keys here: ESC, HOLD, BREAK, POWER." The words that he had yet to finish reading disappeared as she keyed quickly, and the screen filled with new material. This time, there were words and little pictures of folded boxes. "Now, would you read the instructions aloud, Brent, and then do what they say."

He stared at the amber letters. "The following series eval ... evaluates your visual pattern re ... reco ..." Too many difficult words. He stopped and felt his cheeks turn red.

Connie Sue patted his shoulder. "Afraid of that. Nothing to be ashamed of, Brent, nothing at all. Those damn Beaks do one hell of a fine job keeping the human race stone ignorant. The wonder is that you can read at all." Her hair brushed his cheek, as she changed the program with rapid keystrokes. "That should do it. Now, what does it say?"

"This is a test of how you see things and put them together in your mind. The folded box on the left side of the screen is a perfect match for one of the five unfolded boxes on the right side of the screen. Touch the number for the unfolded box that you think ..." He read, slowly but not without a little pride.

"Now you're cooking! The computer will give you that kind of instruction for each test. Remember that time is important, so work as fast as you can. Don't worry if you don't understand some parts—just guess, and move on to the next question. It's important not to spend too much time on any one question. Nobody gets all of them right, at least nobody I ever heard of." She smiled and patted his shoulder again. "OK, I'm keying the session to start now."

He hardly noticed her leave as the tests began. He was actually talking with a computer. Old stories, some from his grandfather, had claimed that such machines were much more intelligent than people, but he couldn't decide about this one. Sometimes, the machine was very intelligent, and at other times the questions were very dumb. The reading tests seemed difficult, and a lot of the number questions made no sense at all. He found the tests with little pictures to be most interesting, although often the multicolored pictures were very strange.

Erlanger lost all track of time, but he thought perhaps two hours had passed when the machine actually told him to relax. "REST BREAK," the screen said, "STAND UP AND WALK AROUND. TONE BEEPS WILL SIGNAL WHEN TESTING WILL BE-GIN AGAIN."

Each time a break occurred, Connie Sue somehow knew, for she was standing at his back, standing very close. During her second visit, she pressed the HOLD key, and motioned him out into the hallway, where they chatted for about 20 minutes. Her ancestors, she told him when he mentioned his surprise at the varied racial types at Base, were from someplace called Vietnam. Her grandparents had been scientists in Oak Ridge, and had helped establish the Base. He recalled the two women he had seen at breakfast.

"Probably cousins," she laughed. "Bet you couldn't understand a word they said."

"Yeah, I did wonder."

"One of Administrator Boone's long-standing rules,"

she explained. "Any language abilities present here when things fell apart outside, well, we've tried to preserve them. That's part of my job, actually. The world isn't just the old U.S. of A., after all, and we'll need those language skills someday. Fortunately, we have a lot of old tapes, so my Vietnamese and French are pretty good."

By the end of the day, Erlanger felt as if he had filled three barns of hay, and carried the horse, too. He certainly needed another shower. He groaned when Connie Sue told him that he'd have a lot more sessions, over the next few days. But her smile almost made him eager to return to that small screen and its demanding questions.

Chapter

TEN

"Yum, say, this catchy chicken is pretty good—think I'll go for some more." Erlanger pushed back his chair, and started to move toward the commissary serving line for a second helping, but hesitated as the grin on Delano's face turned to choked laughter.

"What the . . . ? You got something stuck, Tom?" Cleve Stearns also began laughing, and the new man realized that he had inadvertently entertained his lunch table companions again. "So what's so damn funny this time?" he said slowly.

Delano's Adam's apple moved convulsively as the wiry man tried to swallow and chuckle at the same time. His eyes watered, and he finally cleared his throat, just as Erlanger was about to leave the table again. "Kill me, you really do, Brent. Some of the things you come up with. Not to put you down, man, but 'catchy chicken' for Chicken Cacciatore, too much that is . . . especially for somebody with a name like Delano."

Embarrassed, Erlanger glanced quickly around the large room. Although he felt as if the entire Base was laughing at him, only the three who shared his table seemed to be in on the joke, whatever the joke might be. By the third of his testing sessions with Connie Sue's computer, Delano and Stearns had become his regular companions for lunch breaks, but now Erlanger was beginning to wonder whether or not they were becoming his friends. The third he had just met. He rubbed the back of his neck, where muscles had begun to tighten, and scowled around the table. "So I've never had chicken go swimming with tomatoes before, that doesn't mean I'm . . ."

Cleve Stearns laughed again, an incongruously deep rumble from one so thin. "No offense meant, Brent. You just tickled our craw some, that's all. We're a little spoiled here, compared to the plain folks, what with the meat 'n 'taters diet of most places outside. Sure do beat poke salad, hominy, and sow belly any day."

With Cleve's last comment, reminiscent of his stories about his days before he had joined the Underground and his later expeditions to all-black towns in the South, Delano burst into a fresh fit of chuckles. Erlanger shook his head, and eyed the two electronics technicians with suspicion, still unsure whether they were laughing with—or at—him.

"Oh, give it a rest, you two. Let the poor guy have more 'catchy chicken,' if that's what he wants. Man has a chance for good chow, he damn well ought to eat it. If Erlanger's going operational, he'll need all the muscle he can get, 'specially if I get him for basic training."

Gratefully, Erlanger stared at the third man at the table. Deep-set black eyes looked back. He had only met the stocky man minutes earlier, when Stearns and Delano had asked Billy Lee Pisgah to join their table. He knew little about his sudden ally, whom Stearns had called both Cherokee and Colonel in what little conversation had taken place while all were eating. He studied the new man more closely. Pisgah had a powerful build and a face that indicated far more exposure to weather than was typical of Base residents. His straight black hair was tied at the back of his neck with a leather thong, and the coppery tan skin around his eyes and mouth revealed little about his emotions. Not a man I'd want across a poker table, Erlanger thought, as the silence lengthened.

Delano wiped his eyes and nodded. "Sorry, Brent. Mean it, buddy. We're all a little starved for novelty and fresh bait is bound to feel a barb or two. Call it any damn thing you like, I believe I'll join you for more chicken. Just like *la mia nonna* used to make, it ain't, but if we didn't have to bitch about food, where'd we be?"

As they refilled their plates at the stainless steel counter, Erlanger took the opportunity to find out more about their table companion.

"Billy Lee? Seems kinda carved out of stone when you first meet him, I suppose, but he's a hell of a guy. Old Times, his ancestors were pushed to hell and gone, from east of here to way out west, and still kept their pride, so Billy Lee stands tall. Ranks number three or four in the Military Department, I guess, but makes no big deal about it. He either plans or leads most of the search missions outside, so he's seen it all and then some." Delano's belt of small tools clinked as he moved his tray over to the coffee urn. "He also likes to handle training for new recruits; you're going to be dragging your butt, but you'll wind up knowing how to keep it, too."

Puzzled, and not a little apprehensive about his forthcoming training, Erlanger returned to the table. He was no longer sure that he wanted any more of the spicy chicken, and pushed the tender meat around on his plate. He was pleased that Stearns and Pisgah were in the midst of a new discussion.

"Naw, Billy Lee, there's no point to another mission to the Research Triangle, as far as I can see." Cleve paused to take a long sip from the cola drink on his tray, a dark, sweet concoction that Erlanger doubted he'd ever learn to enjoy. "It's burned flat, with nothing higher than spring corn, you know that. And those poor dirt-grubbers in Carolina are almost as low. If we're gonna find any good stuff, north and west's the way we've gotta go."

"No argument, Cleve." Pisgah's lips remained thin, and he spoke softly. "If only Wysocki's team had had more time in Cincinnati . . ."

Erlanger looked up from the mess he was making of his plate. "But aren't we going back? I mean, Administrator Boone told me that another Sincee mission was planned."

"What you mean 'we,' white man?"

Erlanger dropped his fork, but noticed tiny wrinkles around Pisgah's eyes and was relieved when both Delano and Stearns broke into open laughter again. These fellows would take some getting used to.

The shared hilarity faded; Cleve emptied his glass with a loud slurp. Erlanger became aware that the murmur of background voices, the clink of cutlery, the shuffle of chairs had diminished. Most of the Base personnel on this shift had finished lunch and left. He felt the tightness of his cheeks, aware that his grin had been prolonged, and was relieved when Pisgah changed the subject abruptly.

"Think we eat pretty well, do you?"

As he used his napkin, and leaned back from his tray, Erlanger tried to figure out why a second Cincinnati mission might be a sensitive subject. "Ah, well, Colonel, your menu is certainly different. More variety, I guess, than I would expect, underground and all."

Pisgah frowned and glanced at Delano. "Billy Lee will do." He crossed muscular arms over his chest.

They were interrupted by a tall, fair-skinned woman who approached their table silently and passed a piece of yellow paper to Pisgah. The military man scanned the message quickly, and stood up. "Excuse me, gentlemen. There's a Beak aircar at Oliver Springs, and that's way outside the normal schedule."

As Pisgah walked rapidly away, Erlanger looked at the remaining two. "Trouble?"

"Hope not," Cleve said, "but Oliver Springs is about 12 klicks away, to the northwest. One of our towns, of course. One of our major grain suppliers, come to that, along with Solway to the east. Let's hope the Ceejays don't have any special reason for dropping in on them."

"Not a hell of a lot we could do, whatever the reason," Delano added through clenched teeth.

"Yeah," Cleve added. "What say we take Brent on a two-bit tour of our labs? Beats cussin' Ceejays."

"Well, here's my hidey-hole, Brent," said Cleve. "W.C. Fields there works around the corner. C'mon in an' see the bells and whistles."

"What? W.C.?"

"Cleve's little joke," said Tom Delano. "An Old Times movie actor who . . . hey, Cleve, Brent's never seen a movie. Gotta drag him to the theater, first chance we get."

They entered the long, brightly-lighted lab, and Delano fell silent as the two men looked up from a workbench covered with a crazy rat's nest of colored wires and strange equipment. Erlanger noticed a familiar burning smell, and finally spotted a soldering iron in the hand of Phil Campbell. At least he thought it was a soldering iron in the redhead's hand. The instrument was certainly smaller and had a more delicate point than anything he had used in Milford, but then this iron trailed an electricity cord.

The other man wasn't familiar. Cleve spoke as both Campbell and the stranger looked up.

"Oh, Dr. McKay, I wasn't expecting . . . was there something?"

The other man, shorter and older than anyone else in the room, smiled at Stearns' question. "Nothing pressing, Cleve. I just stopped by to see whether you could spare a couple of 40 nano-eff capacitors, and got to admiring Phil's work on this little color monitor."

"Yeah. Goes in that gas chromatograph in the corner that we're trying to rehab for Bio-med." Cleve pointed at a metal and plastic object that reminded Erlanger of a cross between a small writing desk and a kitchen counter—if either had been attacked by brightly colored beetles and spiders. "We got the CPU in shape, and can probably salvage the chart recorder from that Beckman EEG against the wall, but I just dunno about some of the other mechanical pieces."

Cleve scratched in his bushy hair, and surveyed his workplace, as if in search of inspiration from the electronic flotsam of humanity's better days. "Oh, excuse me, you ain't met Brent yet. Brent Erlanger, this is Dr. Peter McKay, Underground resident genius. He sneaks over from the Science Department to rob us blind every chance he gets."

McKay chuckled and extended his hand to the new man. Erlanger looked down into twinkling blue eyes in the face of a man who appeared to be in his midfifties. "Forget titles; call me Mac. Pleased to meet you, Brent."

"Dr. McKay is project liaison between Science and

Engineering Departments ... on Alien Technology. Well, you wouldn't know about that." Cleve frowned. "Half the time, though, I think he's just a frustrated tinkerer like the rest of us."

The older man smiled. "That I am, that I am. Now cut all this formality, Cleve. Damn nonsense anyway, even if we can trace a connection back to the University of Maryland Extension Service. Nothing against our databanks and facilities, mind you, but handing out home-grown degrees is a waste of time. We've got better things to do ... sometimes I think the department heads lose sight of the forest for the trees." He winked broadly at a puzzled Erlanger and patted Cleve on the back. "I'd love to stay. Thanks for the caps, Phil. And, nice meeting you, Brent, but I must get back to my children, really must."

"You have children?"

"What's that? Oh, I see. Well, yes I do, two boys and a girl, matter of fact. Have photos here some ... no, no time now. No, I meant I have to get back to my assistants; we have a prototype running in my shop and ... well, maybe later." The short man hurried out.

"Close your mouth before you draw flies, Brent. Mac's always like that, busy as a beaver running six things at once." Cleve gestured Erlanger onto a high stool before his workbench, and sat as well. "If anybody's goin' to nail down the goods on Ceejay science, though, my money's on Mac."

"Amen to that," Delano added as he, too, moved toward the door. "I've got a glitched IR scanner waiting; and you'd better hustle some, Brent. Near time for our Educational Director to play with your head again." He grinned and pointed the way to the Personnel offices as Brent followed him, with a backward wave to Cleve. "If that's all she wants to play with. And, hey man, you got any time after, stop back up and see my toys, right?"

*   *   *

Erlanger had expected to spend another busy afternoon at the computer, but Connie Sue had surprised him with the announcement that his testing was complete.

"Not that you're out of my clutches yet, not by a long shot," she had told him as they sat in her office above the rows of computer carrels. "But your profile is now complete, and has been passed up to Administrator Boone. He's taken an interest in you, Brent, and wants to see you in a bit."

He approached the blue elevator on B-level, after a crossover on C, and checked his pocket for the card of access codes that he had yet to memorize. He grinned as he recalled his pleasure in discovering that he would see more of Connie Sue. Her subtle perfume and feathery touch were still vividly familiar from the brief sketch she had just given him of his educational future.

"Your aptitude for math and electronics is excellent, Brent, so that's the main direction that your training will take. Of course, I've set you up for remedial reading, and general studies . . . history, specifically Base history, too."

"Good, I guess. I sure need to know more about this place," he answered.

"No great mystery, as you'll discover. It's all in the program." She leaned across her desk and placed a yellow piece of paper in his hand. "You'll have other training assignments, I know, as well as a work assignment, so you can come by here any time you're free, but make it a regular habit, h'mm? Here's your log-on code; just punch in this sequence on the keyboard of any computer in the first row. Any problems, you know where to find me."

She grinned and stood, and he found his feet as

well, although the obvious dismissal confused him. "You mean?"

"It'll all be clear in a bit." She squeezed his arm as she ushered him to the door. "Scoot on up to A-1. The Administrator is expecting you. You do know the way?"

With a start, he realized that he was standing in front of the Base Administrator's office, with little recall of the path his feet had taken in the past several minutes. Nothing had changed in this pleasantly-furnished area since he was last here with Lori. He suddenly recalled Lori with emotion for the first time in three days. He hadn't even seen her in that time. Was she avoiding him? Had Lori returned to her familiar surroundings, her own people and interests, and chosen to put their trying, brief encounter into some separate place in her past? Sure, he had been busy too. Perhaps, as Cleve had suggested at lunch yesterday, Lori might simply be working on a different shift. He couldn't really blame her, he thought, for an uneducated artificer from Milford was hardly in her class . . .

"Help you?"

"Wha—?" Erlanger jumped, and turned to stare at the elderly black man who stood beside him. "No, I mean, I'm supposed to see the Administrator . . ."

"Yes, I see. You must be Erlanger. Just knock, young man, just knock. Our Boone has some killed 'im a bear in some time." The old man shook his head slowly as he walked away.

What the hell does that mean? Erlanger wondered silently, as he rapped his knuckles gently against the wood.

"Come in, Brent."

He opened the door and stepped into the quiet office. "Hello again, sir. I was told that I should report . . ."

"Indeed. Do sit down, young man. Your test results have more than met my expectations, I am pleased to say, and I wished to discuss your future personally."

Erlanger slid into the cool leather chair facing the desk and tried to hide his surprise. Faint blue tendrils of Boone's pipe smoke hung in the air, a cloud that seemed to add to the aura of power around the ancient bald head. "Well, thanks, I guess, but I would have thought—"

Boone held up a deeply-wrinkled palm. Clearly he was not accustomed to interruption.

"We have several things in mind for you, Brent. First, and most obviously, there is your work here. Your test scores, and your past experience in Milford, strongly indicate electronics. Since you already know Thomas Delano, Kaz and I agree that he should be your proctor. You will begin working with Thomas on half-shifts immediately."

The Administrator paused to relight his pipe. "Secondly, there is the matter of your military training. Colonel Pisgah has put in a request to supervise that aspect of your entrance into our organization, and you may expect to begin that program within the next few days as well." This time, as Boone paused, Erlanger perceived that a response was appropriate.

"Thank you, sir. Yeah, Tom and I should get along great. But who's Kaz? And if I . . . well, with Colonel Pisgah and all, am I being singled out for some reason, sir?"

The added lines around the deep-set eyes, which might have been a hint of a smile, appeared in the aged face. "Yes and no, Brent. As for your first question, Kazuo Ohira is Department Head, Engineering. He is Delano's—and now your—immediate superior. I will not speak for Billy Lee Pisgah, as he is quite capable of indicating his own motivations to you, if he should so choose, but I suspect that he is impressed with your record since you fled Milford. Note, as well, that we select new recruits with great care here, and have only two or three in training at any given time. Thus, in that regard, yes, you are special. You are, of course, completely untutored, but I believe Dr. Nguyen has already laid out a course of study for you, which will supplement both your vocational and your military preparation."

The younger man smiled at the prospect of more sessions with Connie Sue, by official order. Then he rubbed his stubbled chin, as another question came to mind. "I'm confused now, Administrator Boone. You said Engineering, but I thought that Tom and Cleve Stearns worked with the science people?"

"Not directly, although the lines do blur on many projects." The old man leaned back and exhaled softly. "Our table of organization is rather atypical, I suppose, but it will make more sense as your education progresses. Aside from central Administration, we have eight departments: Agriculture, Bio-medical, Communications, Education, Engineering, Maintenance, Military, and Science. The Science personnel are generally involved in pure research—particularly with regard to the *Cweom-jik*—while engineers maintain human technology and implement that research. In so far as we have a government, the department heads are elected; they, in turn, choose the Head Administrator, and serve as a ruling council."

Erlanger nodded to indicate his general understanding, then began to ask about his specific duties.

Boone frowned and held up his hand again. "Those questions had best wait upon further training. There is, however, a choice that you will have to make in the near future."

"Choice? But I thought everything was . . . ?"

"Please let me finish, young man. You will recall that I mentioned the possibility of a second mission to the Cincinnati area? That plan has now been approved, for we have reason to believe such a mission would be quite profitable." Boone put down his pipe and seemed to adopt a more relaxed posture. "You must realize that there are many gaps in our records, in our knowledge of the pre-Collapse world. This Base has yet to recover from the major split in objectives that occurred almost 50 years ago, and we are only now beginning to make progress in our understanding of the alien technology. Those force grenades, with which Wysocki brought down the aircar, represent the first practical application of that understanding. Now, while I appreciate that you are unschooled in Old Times history and geography, bear in mind that Cincinnati remains in better condition than any of the centers of industry and technology on the three coasts of our formerly great country."

"But the Beaks were blasting the city again, when I—"

"Please. You are quite correct, although we have little information as yet about the extent of that new destruction. An assessment of that question remains but one justification for further missions in that area. We hope that fragmentary records support an even more vital reason. So. You have been there; you found hidden books there. We wish you to consider a return mission."

"Sure, sir. I've already said . . ."

"Not so fast, Brent. Your choice makes a difference in your training, in your whole life here. If you opt for external missions, the program you follow here will be quite different. Of course, we would be quite happy to have you settle in our little community, for I am sure you would become a valuable technician. On the other hand, I do not have to point out to you the life expectancy of a search team member. And then, there is the matter of hypno-conditioning. All search team members are conditioned by Bio-med specialists against the revelation of information about the Underground or the location of this Base. Or at least, we hope they are, if ever subjected to stress or duress by the *Cweom-jik* or the human scum who work for them."

He opened his mouth, realizing at last why Lori had called him a security risk, and why some conversations were still cut short in his presence. But he didn't have the chance to voice additional questions, for the Administrator stood suddenly, with surprising agility for his age. "I do not want your answer now, Brent. You will have several weeks to decide, during which you will follow the assignments as I have indicated, and as written here." He handed Erlanger a thin paper folder from his desk. "We want you to weigh this matter carefully."

"What the hell was the name of that thing again, Tom? That holo- what'sit with the wiggles of colored light dancing all around? Wow, that's really something."

Delano grinned at Erlanger over the top of his glass mug. "Told you once, dummy. If you're going to be *my* apprentice, you better get it right the first time. A Tektronix Model 2710 Triple-beam Holoscilloscope, that's what it is. Hell, it's the best 3-D laser holographic test instrument ever made 'fore we was squashed, that's what. Damn lucky to have it, we are." Delano winked at Stearns and downed half his drink.

Erlanger copied his newly-assigned teacher, and burped. His face reddened and he glanced around the crowded room of the Long Branch Saloon—still not quite believing his eyes. He had rushed back to E-level in the late afternoon, as soon as he could find his way there from Administrator Boone's office. When he finally found Delano at his workbench, the wiry fellow had immediately thumped him on the back, and welcomed him into service. It was close to quitting time, Delano said, but he ran quickly through a tour of the shelves and benches littered with equipment in various stages of repair. Erlanger worried that he'd never understand a fraction of the 'toys' that his new boss demonstrated. He was awed when told to stand in front of a small black tube while Delano laughed at his tiny full-color image, open mouth and all, on a nearby monitor. Still laughing together, Delano waved as his shift replacement took over, and the two of them headed around the corner to Cleve's lab. His new friends demanded a celebration, and Erlanger wasn't about to argue.

He rested his elbows firmly on the table and stared around again. The walls of the strange rooms seemed hazy, and he blinked rapidly. "Must be the smoke," he muttered aloud. He tried to focus on the long wooden bar that paralleled the back wall. A mismatched set of mirrors gave back seemingly random reflections of moving people, waving arms, and blinking lights from several faded and cracked signs. Authentic Old Times beer signs, Cleve had called them. One, with black and red lettering, championed something called Stroh's, while the flashing message "It's Miller time" was giving him a headache.

He turned away to watch a comely woman fill several glasses from the white plastic jugs that he'd recently discovered to be the source of a very fine 'white-lightning'—the pride of the Agriculture Department.

"What's that, Brent?" Delano asked as he signaled the "volunteer" barmaid for a refill. The agritechs brewed a mighty fine beer as well.

"Huh? When? Oh, did I shay—uh, say that? The smoke, sure's smokey in here, tobacco and maryjane."

Erlanger turned his head as the double doors clunked together again at the entrance. A familiar stocky figure stood just inside the swinging doors and stared around the boisterous room. Erlanger frowned as he tried to puzzle out the reason for the odd doors. "Only fill the middle half of the doorway; silly looking slats in 'em?"

"What? Shit, have another beer so's I can hear you, Brent. The swinging doors? Hell, man, wouldn't be the Long Branch Saloon without them doors. Oops, watch it!" Delano ducked back as a skinny young woman slopped beer on his shoulder and muttered an apology.

Cleve's chair squealed, as he jumped up and waved. "Billy Lee, hey, join us over here, Billy Lee; we got a free spot." The black man's voice boomed out, and Pisgah nodded and worked his way through the crowd toward them.

The background music changed to another tune that Erlanger had never heard before. He could almost feel the pounding bass through the seat of his rickety chair.

"Jesus, Mary, and Joseph, this place is hopping tonight," Pisgah said as he added his beer mug to their table.

"Hops . . . yeah, thass it, hops an' yeast; been wondering about that. We always had trouble getting 'nuf hops an' yeast in Milford. How the hell you guys do it?"

Cleve Stearns shook his head. "Don't mind Brent, Billy Lee. Getting one on. He's entitled, I guess, first time in the Long Branch an' all."

"How the hell we know from hops, Brent? We just drink it." Delano demonstrated, and emptied most of his fresh mug.

"Yeah, go along with you there. Time for 'nother

round; my treat. Say, how we paying for all this good stuff?"

Even Pisgah laughed loudly at his question. Delano took a final swallow and pounded his mug on the table, as he replied: "You'll find out, sucker; you're in the program now. You get to be 'volunteer' bartender or stock boy here 'bout once a month."

Erlanger blinked, his pupils large in the dim light. "No money? Whal thass all right then. Fill 'em up!"

Erlanger was feeling better than he had in many weeks. He looked up as two women walked past and sat at a table in the far corner. "Hey, thass Lori, my good frien' Lori. Think I'll ask Lori for a dance. Maybe back t' my room for couple drinks, huh?" He grinned at his drinking buddies, and slapped Stearns on the back.

"Brent, no. I don't think that's . . ." Stearns tried to hold him back, but he shook off the restraining hand.

His three companions watched sympathetically as he staggered over to the table where Lori was talking to a middle-aged blonde. He supported himself against the women's table as he leaned close to Lori. She said something, and shook her head. The blonde's eyes narrowed as she added to the conversation. Erlanger staggered back, and almost fell as he slid into his chair.

"Ho boy, Grandfather told me there'd be nights like this. Like t' freeze me out."

"Not Lori!" Delano asked.

"We tried to . . ." Cleve began.

"Nah, not Lori, I mean, she's kinda cool, yuh know, but okay. Said she'd talk t' me tomorrow. Just not tonight, you know. But that blonde bitch, who the hell's she?"

"Virginia Haywood," Pisgah answered. "Older sister of Lori's late husband, Donald."

"Virginia's our computer librarian and historian," Stearns continued, "and I suppose she passes for what little family Lori has left. Didn't like you much, huh?"

"Say that again. Hey, need 'nother beer."

"I don't think so," Pisgah said, with an edge to his voice. "I was planning to begin your basic tomorrow morning, but I believe we'd better make it the day after. I trust you two can pour him into bed?"

Chapter

ELEVEN

"Figured you'd show up here eventually." Delano looked up from his workbench, and shook his head at the slumped figure in the lab doorway. "How's the head?"

"Aah, don't ask," Erlanger replied softly, as he fumbled his way to a stool. By the time he had regained painful consciousness, stood through a long, cool shower, downed a half-dozen glasses of water, and grimaced past all but tomato juice in the commissary, it was well past ten by the commissary clock. Somehow he found his way to EK-0956, and Delano, where he thought he was supposed to be that morning.

"Here, bright-eyes, choke down a couple of these. You'll feel better in a jif." Delano tossed him a small white plastic bottle with large grey and black capsules inside, and pointed to the stainless steel sink against the back wall. "Actually, you know, you're not due here until after lunch. Your half-shifts with me are in the afternoons. Scheduled to begin training with Pisgah this morning ..."

He jerked around from the sink and moaned. "Oh no! I forgot to check that folder. Where do I . . .?"

"Relax, you idiot. You probably don't even remember that Billy Lee was with us last night, but like I told you, he's a straight guy. He put your start in the E-level gym off 'til tomorrow. Just don't screw it up then."

"No, I . . . thanks for . . . what should I do now?" Erlanger stared around the packed benches and shelves, and tried to focus on the high density circuit board that Delano was exploring gently with a fat logic probe.

"Send you back to bed, I should. Knew you wouldn't be worth shit today, but I've got just the job for scrambled brains. A four-year-old could do it. Been meaning to get that mess sorted for years." He grinned and drew the benumbed man around to the other side of the bench at which he worked. "But now I got me a slave. Here."

Erlanger pinched the bridge of his nose and stared down at the drawer that Delano pulled from a metal cabinet. The drawer seemed full of tiny, multicolored insects. He blinked rapidly, and reassured himself that the mass was not, indeed, moving. No, they were little brown and green tubes, with stripes of color, and with dull grey or bright silver wires on either end.

"Need these resistors sorted by value, wattage, and tolerance. Mostly eighth- and quarter-watters, some half-watts, damn'fino what else; people been tossing 'em in here for years as we stripped boards for salvage. Sometimes you get lucky; newer types have values printed on 'em. Here's the color chart. Put each type in a separate compartment of these trays."

"Huh?" Erlanger looked from Delano to the clear plastic tray that was divided up like an oversized egg carton.

"I thought you'd worked with phones. You do know what a resistor is?"

"I guess, but tolerance?"

"Hmmm . . . starting from square one, we are. Look, for now, just match up all those with the same pattern of color bands, and the same physical size. Read 'em from left to right, see, starting with the band closest to the left end." He sighed as Erlanger picked up one of the tiny resistors. "No, you got it backwards; turn it around, so . . . red, green, yellow, gold, that's 250K Ohms at 5%, see, quarter-watt. No, suppose you don't see. Cripes, hope you ain't color blind."

"No, red, green, yellow, gold. Just match them like that, and put same size, same colors in separate compartments?"

"Close enough for now; we can label the trays later. Oh, and straighten the leads, ah, the wire ends, with this needle-nose as you sort 'em. I gotta get back to that microwave burst transmitter. Folks in Communications want it up and trotting yesterday."

Erlanger became engrossed in his simple task. Gradually, as he glanced at the printed color chart, he came to recognize the logic. With no little pride, the first time he encountered a resistor with a printed value, rather than color-coded bands, he was able to place it in the right compartment. From time to time, he looked up as Delano muttered something, but the wiry tech seemed to be just swearing at the equipment in front of him. When he heard a strange, high-pitched voice, however, he stood and peered over the shelf-divider that separated him from clear sight of Delano's side of the bench. He was astounded to see a child, a young girl of about ten, who tugged at Delano's sleeve.

"You have one, Mr. Delano. A BQSN-79871 chip?"

"Probably somewhere, Teri. What'cha building now?"

"Reprogramming my robot for perimeter defense surveillance," the little girl said, in a tone that implied all adults were senile.

"That's super, Teri. Let me see . . . BQSN-79871?" Delano leaned over and rummaged through a blue plastic cabinet, then grinned and handed the child a long black thing with silver legs that reminded Erlanger of a fat centipede, if centipedes were flat with square corners.

"Thanks, Mr. Delano. Put it on my bill." The child giggled and skipped out of the room.

"What's with you, Brent? Never seen a kid before?"

"Who was? . . . well no, I mean not at Base. I've seen older teenagers in the commissary, but it never . . . damnit, even the little children here understand all this stuff better than me. I better go down to F and pull weeds; that's about all I'm good for!"

Delano laughed as he came around to Brent's side and clapped him on the back. "No good, no weeds in hydroponics. And don't worry, you'll catch on . . . although you might not top that kid, at that. The little cutie is Teri McKay, Mac's kid; bloody genuis she is. She's been blowing fuses since she was five. Guess it figures, given her parents."

"I suppose I should have known . . . this really is a small town." Erlanger stood and stretched and was relieved to discover that his headache was gone. "But why haven't I seen any little ones before?"

"Got me. Seems like rug-rats are all over the place sometimes." He grinned at his new assistant. " 'Course, not in your favorite spots like the Long Branch." Erlanger groaned. "Most of the families with young children have suites on the north end of D-level; got their own kitchens too, so that's probably why you haven't run across any. The kids got school too, separate from the adult carrels that Connie Sue's had you busy at."

Delano paused and looked over the sorting job that Erlanger had accomplished in the past three hours. "You're doing fine, Brent, but that reminds me . . . we're past due for lunch, and after we eat, you ought to stop by Connie Sue's shop, and get some more computer education. I may want you to read a frequency calibrator some day, and picking red from green ain't gonna do it."

"Jesus, Erlanger, got your tool stuck in that mattress? Hold still, hold your breath, and squeeze off your shots. That weapon kicks to the left, remember."

Erlanger gritted his teeth and tried to follow Pisgah's instructions, but the proper prone position for firing a M-18 automatic rifle continued to elude him. Or, at least, his sheer powers of concentration remained inadequate to guide the bullets to the distant bull's-eye. Pisgah pushed down his ear-protectors and gave him the hand signal; slowly he emptied another clip. The surprisingly soft "pocks" echoed dully from the walls of the narrow firing range, and his nose wrinkled at the acrid odor as shells ejected to his right. Finished, he laid his rifle on the plastic foam mat in front of him, and twisted to look over his shoulder.

"Better, Erlanger, better." Pisgah squinted through a spotting scope. "Still ain't worth much. My Granny could have put them all inside the black and shucked peas with the other hand, but you may be worth my time after all."

The new recruit suppressed a smile and stood. Three days into his training with Pisgah, he had learned to accept the man's rare compliments without expression. The Military man was all business during the morning sessions. He rose, and as the other's black eyes fixed on him, he realized his error, and hurriedly bent over to retrieve his brass. Although he had been told that ammunition could be duplicated, it was still valuable, and he knew at some point he would be shown how to load his own cartridges.

"Strip and clean that weapon, and check it back in, Erlanger. Then report to the gym. Your puny condition looks like something the dog drug in."

Just as he had hidden his grin, he refrained from moaning as well. He had discovered quickly what the gym meant, at least as far as his training was concerned: fast laps, calisthenics, workouts on elaborate metal and padded plastic machines, and—his least favorite—practice in hand-to-hand combat. Most of the time, Pisgah would run him through mock combat, but others were brought in to have a go at him as well. The day before, to his shame, a woman whom he outweighed by 20 kilos had tossed him around the mats like an empty flour sack. Pisgah had been unusually caustic in his encouraging comments, but he got the point; he had a lot yet to learn.

Now, his arduous physical training finished for the day, he allowed a small groan to escape in the privacy of the shower room that was next to the gym. He hadn't thought it was possible to strain any more muscles, but Pisgah's workout had found a few.

"Move it, Erlanger. Daylight's burning up. Report to 413 for survival school," Pisgah bellowed from the doorway.

"Ah, good." He dried quickly, and slipped into the light-weight cotton camouflage suit—fatigues, as he'd learned to call them. Survival school was mostly a snap. He knew much of the woodscraft lore that had been covered thus far, but there were surprises in the information about edible wild plants. And the map-reading, the maps themselves, were completely new, and he found their study fascinating.

His mouth watered as he savored the inviting aromas in the serving line. Erlanger had put in a long day, first the demanding routines of his military training, then the increasingly-interesting work with Delano. Thanks to Connie Sue Nguyen's educational programs, he was becoming more and more confident of his ability to make a real contribution in the electronics shop. He had much yet to learn, that he knew, and had put in a couple of extra hours at the terminal. Of course, Connie Sue's bright smile and encouragement didn't hurt his enthusiasm for extended study-time. He shook his head and grinned as he thought about the petite, dark-eyed psychologist. Either I'm completely out of practice, he thought, or that woman is very interested and . . . so what have I been waiting for?

"You going to stand there all night?"

"Oh, sorry." Erlanger smiled sheepishly at the man in the grey of Maintenance to his left in the serving line, and hurriedly picked from the main courses, then moved on. "Chicken Pot Pie" was what he thought the small green card in front of his choice had said. He shrugged, still lost in daydreams, and picked some kind of brown cake for desert. Now, well past eight in the evening, he was hungry enough to try almost anything.

As he left the coffee urn, and turned to survey the room of mostly-empty tables, he spotted a familiar face, a face he hadn't seen in over two weeks. Lori, sitting alone against the commissary wall.

"OK if I sit here?"

"Surely there are other tables? I'm trying to . . ." She looked up, and the book she had been reading flopped closed as her hand lifted from the pages. Her scowl of concentration changed rapidly, as tiny dimples appeared in her flushed cheeks. "Brent! Oh, of course you may . . . sit, sit. How rude that must have sounded! Sorry, I just was completely wrapped up in Prohofsky's *Recombinant Techniques*, and I . . ." She paused for breath and glanced down at the table.

"Oh damn, now I've lost my place!" She laughed, almost a childish giggle, and pushed the fat book aside. "I must sound like a complete idiot. So, how have you been, Brent? No, eat, don't let your food get cold; you must be famished if you're eating this late. I've wondered how you were getting along, of course, but we've just been so busy . . ."

It was chicken, he discovered, as he tried to follow her rapid leaps in conversation. The flaky crust had kept the large, tender chunks of meat very hot; his mouth worked rapidly, and twisted into a grimace as he sought to avoid burning his tongue.

She fell silent as his face contorted, then said haltingly, "Brent, I'm sorry, I didn't . . ."

He took a gulp of cooler, cream-laced coffee, and shook his head vigorously. "No, no. Nothing to do with you, Lori. The cooks are trying to fry my tongue." He took a deep breath and studied her delicate, feminine face. The skin under her eyes was a little grey and puffy; probably she's still working too hard, he thought, but this was no longer the pinched face of strain and grief that he'd known on their flight from the Ceejays. Something seemed to be stuck in his throat, and it wasn't hot food. "It's me who should apologize, Lori," he finally managed. "I've been busy, too, sure, but that's no excuse for . . . and that night in the Long Branch . . . I've wanted to . . ."

"Oh, that!" The dimples flashed again. "I figured it was your first time there, and you just weren't used to real hooch . . . I was more angry at Cleve and Tom for letting you get so smashed." She laughed again and he forgot about his chicken pot pie. "More flattered, really . . . although Virginia did give me a bad time about dragging in barbarians, but I explained that you had your good points." With her throaty chuckle as punctuation, he forgot his hunger entirely.

"So tell me, Milford man, how have you been getting along? Making lots of friends?"

"Ah, they've been keeping me hopping. Billy Lee Pisgah has been tying me in knots in the morning, then Delano and Stearns have been cramming electronics into me all afternoon. Pisgah's kinda distant, but I understand why that . . . but Tom and Cleve are great guys. Then, I try to spend as much time as possible with Connie Sue . . . I mean, studying and all."

"That's great, Brent. I'd hoped that Billy Lee would train you; he's the best we've got. And Connie Sue's a terrific teacher. I'm sure you're making great progress."

"Ah, Lori, I'd really like to talk . . . and this place, . . . well, would you like . . . ?" He silently kicked himself. As bad as the last time, he thought.

The dimples returned in full flower. "I'd like that, Brent. Your place or mine?"

"You would? Ah, great, my room's just a corridor over."

"Fine. Got anything to drink?"

He still wasn't sure he had heard her correctly, or that he'd heard what hadn't been said. "I've got one of those little plastic jugs from the saloon, but that stuff's pretty raw without watering down."

She smiled. "No problem, they have mixer at the serving counter."

As they walked slowly down the cross-corridor, he tried to get her to talk about her work. She only mentioned generalities, and once behind his closed door she fell silent. Lori watched him fumble with jug, glasses, and the clear, bubbly mixer that she had called "clubsodah." He passed her a drink.

They both started to speak at the same time.

"No, you go ahead. I really am interested, Lori. Do you know whether those Beaks died of a disease we could control yet?"

She shook her head. As she finished her whiskey, she began to talk, all in a rush. He only heard half, and understood less, as she continued in a flat voice: "A prion ... at least we think it's a prion. That's a very tiny, nonfilterable viruslike thing, not really even alive, in the sense of being a complete cell. No protein coat, you understand, but those things replicate. Old records show they're responsible for a number of human diseases, usually rapidly debilitating and fatal, although the prion may be in the system for years before it locks into the cellular DNA. That's another problem, I mean, *Cweom-jik* DNA. Oh, we expected it to be something like ours, like terrestrial species, only so many ways that the base sequences could go together and be compatible with life here, after all. But Ceejay DNA is left-handed, their double helix spirals to the left along the macromolecules."

Lori stared at the corner of the bare room as she paused for breath. "Not that left spirals are uncommon here; we've got some, at least in transitional states. Z-DNA, it's called. With the *Cweom-jik*, though, it seems that all theirs is left-handed, which makes it so much tougher to establish baselines. And we don't even know whether that prion is something they brought with them, something they evolved with, or something new, that they picked up here ..."

She looked up. Her gaze, no longer blank, met his squarely. She placed a firm hand on his chest. Her fingers slid between the buttons on his shirt. "Poor man, I might just as well have been speaking in Swahili. Take me to bed, Brent. Please. Now."

Surprised and happy, he reached up a hand behind her neck, and drew her lips to his. Her eyes closed, she slipped her arm around his back and pulled him closer.

He started to speak, but her fingers moved to his lips.

After, they lay together silently for countless minutes.

Suddenly, a playful slap reddened his belly. "Wha—?" he gasped as breath returned.

"Can't dally here all night, pleasant as the thought may be. I'm for the showers ... want to scrub my back?"

They exchanged wet kisses, and she traded him favor for favor with the soap. Despite his rekindling interest, and her affectionate playfulness, however, a friendly shower was all she had in mind. They dried each other slowly, and with an ample number of exchanged caresses, but try as he might, he couldn't convince her. To his chagrin, he found that she didn't even plan to linger for another drink, even a quiet talk.

"You're a dear, Brent, but not tonight. I've got to make an early start of it tomorrow. Dr. Speigel's coming by the lab for an update, and we've got a fractional distillation series running down in Chem that may give us some partial answers." She dressed quickly and kissed him good-bye. The door latch clicked at her back.

"Any time, ma'am, you're welcome," he muttered to his barren walls. "Women, go figure 'em," he muttered.

"Why wouldn't she spend the night? ... or invite me back to her room? Damnit all to hell, I don't even know where her room is—ah, nuts, who can figure them?"

Disgusted with himself and his confused emotions, he locked his door, switched off the lights, and crawled between sheets redolant of recent passion. He tossed and thrashed for several sleepless hours. Finally, sometime after 2 a.m., he got up and finished the rest of the jug. Colonel Pisgah led him to regret that the next morning.

Chapter

TWELVE

His eyes opened, then closed abruptly as he felt the bright sunlight. He didn't bother to read the bedside clock as he made his way into the shower stall. Not too hot, not too cold. He kept his eyes closed as the welcome fluid trickled down his throat. If she was using him, was that different from the way he had taken his pleasures with women in the past?

"What the hell, don't knock a good lay," he muttered as he turned his back into the spray. Still Lori seemed, somehow, much more of a person than any of the other women he'd been intimate with.

How did she feel about him? That was an even more puzzling problem. Was it just a physical thing with her? No, she had to care something for him— she had, after all, saved his life. Now that they were safe, now that she was home, was she trying to let him down gently?

No. He shook his head again, then vigorously squeezed water from his hair, from his smarting eyes. No, last night had meant more. She must care for him, no matter how she treated him during her cool moods. Inside, he knew that. But something blocked her from full surrender, full expression of her feelings. He thought he knew why. She had lost two lovers, after all . . . twice burned . . . that must be it. Erlanger didn't care to consider an alternative explanation.

Despite his new confidence, the sight of Lori in the commissary again caught him off guard. He waved jauntily as he pushed his tray along the counter. His spirits were hardly daunted as she returned only a cursory nod from the long table where she was seated with several people he had yet to meet.

As he slid, uninvited, into the chair next to Lori, Erlanger nodded hello to the three women and one man around the table.

"Morning, Brent," Lori said softly, with but a trace of a smile.

"Great morning!" He aimed his fork at pink chunks of ham, and grinned. "How're you feeling?"

"Well, thanks. And you?" Her green eyes seemed dark and hooded, her jaw muscles clenched.

"Mmmph," he replied, around a hot mouthful of ham and runny cheese. "Good enough." He silently kicked himself. Much as he wished to recapture the intimacy of the previous night, her signals were plain enough to stop a charging bull. He swallowed too quickly and fumbled with a piece of toast.

"Fine. Brent, I'd like you to meet some of my research associates."

He gave them his best smile, but none of the four names really registered.

"So, the new recruit we've been hearing about," said one of the women, a thin reserved oldster who recalled aspects of Mayor Barlow's ugly sister. "I understand that you are in training. For what do you train, Mr. Erlanger?"

He cleared his throat. "Well, right now I'm just trying to catch up. General study, I'd guess you'd say, on the history here, and our overall situation. They've got me pointed at electronics technician, since that's closest to what I was in my home town. But Colonel Pisgah has me in military training too, and I may join the search teams, since I've been on one mission already . . . eh, sort of." He tried to meet Lori's gaze, to see whether references to their shared adventure would be out of place. He felt more and more uncomfortable before the Bio-med people.

Lori acted as if she had not heard him.

"I see. Two not entirely disparate choices, I suppose," the older woman continued. "So which path will you choose?"

"It's kind of hard to decide," he finally said as he stared at the four strangers. The old woman did seem genuinely interested, and he tried to relax. The others were listening as well. Perhaps his reputation had preceded him? Or was he just a new specimen to them, a bug for their trained examination? He paused, the coffee suddenly as bitter as his first taste of it. "Of course, I've talked it over with several people, including Lori . . ." He looked her way again, but her face was expressionless. "I guess either choice is fine by me. Maybe I'll flip a coin." He tried to grin, as his last suggestion was greeted with polite chuckles.

"Yes, I think that the fifth generation virus is the right direction, Hilda," Lori said suddenly. "Those RNA linkages do mimic the *Cweom-jik* pattern, almost." She sighed and a little life returned to her pale face. "If only we could get it to replicate without enzyme inducement in the second stage."

Hilda, the younger brunette to Lori's left, nodded. "Even Nicholls is stumped on that one!"

Erlanger started to speak, then hesitated. The conversation was so obviously directed away from him that he didn't know how to respond. A quick flash of anger reddened his cheeks, but he realized that he could gain nothing by a protest of Lori's rudeness—especially in front of her colleagues. He fumed silently as the bio-med discussion continued around him, as if he had simply vanished, sudden victim of a Ceejay blast.

His knuckles were white as he clenched his fork, and he set it down with excessive care while trying to decide what was happening. Lori was playing some game. Perhaps he could use her ploy in reverse; let her know that he was aware of what she was doing and that he disapproved.

When the technical discussion reached a lull, he leaned back and spoke, perhaps more forcefully than he should have. "Another search mission to where Lori and I found that crashed aircar might get us more useful tissue samples, I suppose, and I have to admit that I'm the right guy for such a mission."

Silent, polite expressions greeted his announcement. Was that a hint of hostility in the old woman's eyes? A trace of scorn from the quiet, thin man at the end of the table? "Besides," he continued, "I, well, I think I'm about due for some time outside."

Lori turned to face him full on, and stared for a long five-count. "I suppose you could do that, Brent, although I rather doubt that the direction of a search mission would be up to you. And I suspect that the Ceejays will have found that wreck by now. On the other hand, you could serve the Underground well in the shops; you seem to get along fine with the other technicians. It is, of course, your choice. Perhaps, as you say, you do need to get outside. This environment may be stifling, given your background."

He felt blood rush to his ears; his heartbeat seemed to have tripled. What was she doing? Was Lori saying that she didn't care whether he stayed or not? Was this, despite last night, a very cold, very public kiss off?

Even as he said it, as he felt the words form on his lips, he knew that he should have given more consideration. "Yeah, well the choice is obvious. A mission outside is just the kind of action I need."

No congratulations followed his sudden decision. The five seated with him merely nodded, as if a child had announced that his shoes were tied. Lori picked at her waffle, then said: "I'm sure you know best, Brent. The search teams provide a necessary service, and we always need more information, more replacements. Alan and I never did have the chance to look for electron microscope parts, although there's probably not much chance—"

True anger seized him. He stood, his tray forgotten, and glared at Lori, at her startled friends. "Anything's better than this life of a mole here with you."

He stalked out, back straight and fists clenched. He was afraid to look back.

By the time he reached the blue elevator, he was feeling very pleased with himself, sure now that he had made the correct decision. He had, within his own mind at least, become committed to a mission outside—at least one expedition, maybe more. That would show Lori, and all her egghead friends! He started to reach for the button panel, then drew back. No, not the blue elevator, but the red. He turned down the corridor. He would see the Administrator now; would declare his intention immediately.

Nothing had changed about the impressive office or its occupant, as Erlanger found himself once again in the presence of Administrator Boone. Those blue eyes bored into his, and the younger man faltered as he regarded the wise man.

"Do sit down, Brent. You have reached a decision?"

"Yes, sir. I want to go on a mission outside." Erlanger spoke quickly.

"Yes, yes." Boone held up a thin, liver-spotted hand. "Just as we see it. I am sure that you have begun to feel cooped up here? A man your age still craves action, I am sure."

Erlanger tried to relax. He nodded vigorously. "Yeah, you bet. Not that it's getting to me. Don't get me wrong—this is a hell of a place. But I'd like to, well, get out and stretch my legs a bit."

Boone smiled slightly. "To be sure. Perhaps there are too many pressures at the moment?"

His hands now squeezed at his knees, as Erlanger wondered just how much the Administrator might know about his relationship with Lori.

"Fine. Your technical training will continue, of course, and may be completed at a later date. Your potential in that area is too high to waste. But, I believe we can use you outside very soon." The gargoyle smile returned as Boone leaned back, and gestured toward papers to his left. "Recent reports indicate the aliens have removed both the wreck you found and the one you caused, unfortunately. On the plus side, however, there have been no overflights within 50 miles for several days, so we believe that it is safe for a mission to set forth.

"We do need to return to Cincinnati. That is virgin territory for us, and it holds great promise. The *Cweom-jik* spend as little time as possible north of these mountains, and thus many of the smaller interior cities received only nominal destruction. No doubt that is why you were able to find what you did in Cincinnati. Almost all southern and coastal cities were completely leveled, you see, mere slag and rubble."

The old man leaned back in the dark cushions of his chair and sighed. He steepled his bony fingers below his chin, and continued: "What we propose, therefore, is a 10-man mission to Cincinnati, and the Department Heads agree that you should be a part of it. You know something of the area, and you have proven yourself under hazardous circumstances. Mind you, your presence is not considered vital to the success of this mission, but if I were going, I would want you along. Why don't you go over and see Peter McKay—the physicist. He'll brief you fully."

Erlanger blushed, thanked him for his confidence, and said good-bye. He hardly heard Boone's final words, as he strove to contain his enthusiasm.

Although the cluttered, dimly-lit room that McKay called his "digs" was on the same E-level where Erlanger worked with Delano, he was away from his usual place. Erlanger spotted a short figure who was hunched over a display screen in the darkest corner of the room. McKay straightened up, and mumbled something inaudible, to himself. Then he grinned up at Erlanger and shook his hand.

"So, you're going on the great snipe hunt, are you? Congratulations!" McKay nodded his balding head rapidly. "Yes, good that you should go. Action, that's what this place needs. New blood will do it every time. Some excitement for you; some new data, new hardware for me. Really perk things up, it will!" The words tumbled out in a verbal landslide, and Erlanger was more confused than ever about why Boone had ordered him here.

"Yes, the old man said you'd be coming by." McKay's rapid speech paused while he moved something that looked half-computer, half-water pump from a scarred hardwood chair. "Sit, sit. If I'm to fill you in, give you the four-bit lecture, take a load off. Time you learned what you're going to be looking for, what we're fighting for, so to speak. The old man wants you in the picture. Glad to do it. Go on, sit.

Nothing there will bite you . . . I think, yes, power's off to that . . . sit.

"OK, so where shall we begin, h'mm?" McKay cleared off another chair by casually dumping its contents on a dusty workbench behind him.

"What do you know? Ah, no, no! Wrong approach. What don't you know? Do you know about duplicators? Of course you do; all the little villages have duplicators. We have them, too. They were so simple and cheap to make—hell, they can even be used to duplicate themselves. Virtually anyone who wanted one could have one, back when they first appeared, toward the end of the Twentieth Century. Mark you, the circumstances under which duplication technology became available, in many places almost at the same time, well, that's always been most suspicious to the scientific community. Even before the Collapse, many thought that technology most alien . . ."

McKay shook his head. "But I digress, key to the whole puzzle though the duplicators may be. Here at this Base, we've been able to maintain many aspects of pre-Collapse human technology. Common laboratory and production equipment could be duplicated, after all. Basic knowledge, though, is another question. Much has been passed on, has been maintained, but there are gaps and losses. Then too, theoreticians have always been in short supply, and while Base was established as a research center, it was also a repository of knowledge. All well and good, until our big Cray-12 died, and took a lot of our basic data, as well as our research capabilities, along with it."

Erlanger started to ask a question, then recalled that the famous big computer was called "Cray" for some reason. He shifted on the hard chair. His stomach growled, as if it had been many hours since breakfast. Somewhere, he was sure, coffee was brewing.

"To complicate matters," McKay continued, "Base was established more for application than theory. That is, the founders here tried to maintain, to expand upon, *existing* technology—the old ways, so to speak. Other centers had the job of chasing new theories and technology, or so we understand. Thus, there were few facilities here for pure research, especially once it became apparent during the Collapse that we were dealing with an alien science. We're more than a little crippled, short on records and hardware, for original investigation into new scientific principles. Not that we haven't been trying, God knows."

The older man sighed, and began toying with some small gizmo from the workbench that tinkled as he moved it from one hand to the other. "We're up against whole new twists in the physical laws of the universe, don't you see. The alien science uses something that might be called a hole through into Higgs-space, some of us think, where the strong, weak, and electromagnetic forces are all the same. Our research into this science is vital, after all, if we're to have a chance against the *Cweom-jik*; we must understand how the duplicators manipulate those screwy laws . . . how, for that matter, to explain why some items simply will not duplicate molecularly. Don't you see?"

Erlanger continued to nod politely, although he had lost the thread of the lecture entirely.

"Good, good." McKay continued, perhaps dimly aware that he should step down from his soapbox to village idiot level. "We're trying to discover the keys to this alien technology, obviously, just as many other research centers were, even during the Collapse. And we've had some success, I must say. Those pulse-grenades, for example. I understand you've seen them in action, yes? Electroweak pulse-grenades, we call them. They use a room-temperature superconductive magnet that's a primary element in the duplicators.

"Now that's new, something well beyond the scope of human technology before the *Cweom-jik* arrived. The same sort of thing is behind the apparent null-gravity drive of the alien aircars. Good Gracious, the sky's the limit with ... huh-uh, obviously the stars are the limit with such devices. But we don't understand the superconductor. We can make the damn thing but do not understand it yet. If we knew what we were doing with those principles, we could get the big computer back up without liquid helium, which we can no longer manufacture. See, that's what I mean about the distinction between pure research and applied technology!"

McKay finally paused, then sniffed the air. "Oh, the brew's ready. Want some coffee? My own blend, best in the place." Without waiting for an answer, he jumped from his chair and got two cups of coffee.

Finally, Erlanger voiced the one question that he thought was the reason for this confusing chat. "I guess I understand the difference, sir. But what has all this to do with the expedition to Cincinnati?"

"Oh, sorry, my boy. I thought the old man, or one of your friends in the shop would have made that clear. We think—no, we're sure, that research centers and universities in cities like Cincinnati were well into investigation of duplicators and other alien technology before such inland cities were attacked. Civilization went to hell on the coasts first, after all. You can check with our librarian, Virginia Haywood, for all the details, I'm sure.

"The Cincinnati mission will seek records of such research, as well as the usual hardware. But the data, we must have the data!"

Erlanger felt a headache coming on. He massaged his forehead. "Sure, Dr. McKay, but how will we know what we're looking for?"

"Oh, no problem. Let me show you." He scurried

to a wall cabinet and rummaged through stacks of papers.

"Ah!" McKay held out two thick folders, and opened them on Erlanger's knees as he leaned over the younger man's shoulder. Photographs, diagrams, sketches, and printed lists spilled out onto the floor. "Never mind that. Now, Brent, Cleve and Tom tell me that you're getting pretty familiar with electronics. All to the good. While most others on the mission will know what to look for, these photos and manuals will give you a general idea."

Erlanger was surprised to see that some of the photos were obviously made by amateurs—members of previous expeditions, perhaps? He knew a little about photography, for a camera had been used in Milford for citizen identification purposes. But photos of objects, strange equipment, were new to him. Fortunately, everything seemed to be labeled.

"Take this stuff with you, Brent. Study it thoroughly. Ask questions; Connie Sue and Virginia have plenty of programs they can run for you too. Just get these folders back to me before you leave." McKay bustled around the cluttered room. "That should do it. And don't be a stranger, hey? You know where to find me now ... if I can find myself in this mess. Best coffee in the place, remember."

"Sure, and thanks, Mac." Erlanger gathered up the scattered papers and photographs. The physicist had turned back to his workbench and seemed to have forgotten that he had company. He was pushing a thin test instrument slowly into a large, rectangular structure. With a start, Erlanger realized that he was looking at a duplicator with its case opened. He'd always heard that duplicators could not be examined, that they would blow up, somehow. He shook his head and grinned. McKay may be jumpy as a June bug, he thought, but he sure knows what he's doing.

*   *   *

As he dumped his burden of photos and drawings on his bed, Erlanger glanced at the digital clock, then rushed out to find Billy Lee. Despite an early start, he was running behind for his late-morning session with Pisgah, and he knew that the Colonel wouldn't be pleased. At least I've got a good excuse, he thought, as he jogged through the corridors toward the gym. He could hardly wait to tell his military trainer that he'd signed up for the Cincinnati mission. He grimaced as he realized that he would probably be in for even more extensive training.

Pisgah chewed him out for being late, and gave him no time for conversation as they ran through the morning workout. As they moved into the armory for more weapons instruction, however, the dark Cherokee clapped him on the back and said: "I'm glad you decided to join our little party, Erlanger."

"No secrets around here, are there? But thanks." His face flushed; he had expected to surprise Pisgah, and perhaps be congratulated for his bravado. But Pisgah already knew.

"I figure twelve days travel time each way," Pisgah said, in his usual flat voice. His tone never varied, although his hands were busy field-stripping an efficient short range weapon called an Uzi. Erlanger found it hard to concentrate on the voice, as he envied a dexterity that he had yet to master. "We'll spend sixteen days on site, which makes for forty days total. That allows plenty of time for search and acquisition of target materials. We don't make it back by day 50, then Base assumes we've had our ticket punched, and closes up tight, full security, for two months. Maybe someday, another team tries for Cincinnati."

The Cherokee grinned and thrust the reassembled machine pistol into Erlanger's hands. "Course, if we don't come back, it don't matter to us that the doors are locked. We're cold meat."

As he removed the pistol's empty magazine, Erlanger wondered whether Pisgah was trying to test his nerve. If so, he was doing a fine job of it. He tried to keep his face as impassive as the other's. "Understood. Are we going back the same way I came in?"

"No. We have to restock way stations, so we'll carry supplies—heavy packs going and coming. Since there's a good possibility of increased Ceejay surveillance, thanks to the tidy job you and Wysocki did on that aircar, we'll take a different route. Head up old U.S. Highway 27, then 127 north of the ruins of Danville. Don't worry, you'll study the maps until you know every rock and rabbit run.

"Outbound," Pisgah continued, "we make contact with Oneida, Bobtown, and Swallowfield. Those are towns with friendlies, more or less in rebel control, last we heard. We always check out such towns. Very cautiously, of course."

"Makes sense," Erlanger said, as he fumbled with pistol parts. "Any special training for me?"

The Cherokee squinted, as if such questions were particularly stupid. "Got to admit, you're in pretty good physical shape. We'll continue your workouts, every other day. More computer time, of course. Tom Delano will help you with other information and skills you need. Check in with him at ..." Pisgah glanced at his watch. "Say, right after dinner."

"Sure.

Pisgah stood, retrieved the weapon from his student, nodded, and returned the Uzi to its place in the rack. "Glad to have you along, Erlanger, but don't get cocky. We're a team, remember. We depend on you, you depend on all of us. You're still pig ignorant in a lot of ways. No matter what you've done, someone else on the team has done more. Keep that firmly in mind."

"Another little drink won't hurt," Delano said, dumping more ice into Erlanger's glass. "Bit of a celebration we're having, after all."

Despite Delano's light banter, Erlanger detected more than a little apprehension in the other's voice. For all his expertise in electronics, he was very much Base born and bred, and in many ways their roles of teacher and student would be reversed outside.

"Yeah, at least I'll feel like I'm doing something again." Erlanger sipped his rum and cola, and tried to ignore the cloying sweetness. "Not that I haven't been learning a hell of a lot from you and Cleve in the shop, Tom. But, well, you know, now that I know there's a group here, one hell of an organization, that's in a position to do something about those damn Beaks, I just want to . . ."

Delano sprawled back on his bed, and nodded. "We will continue in the shop, right up until D-Day, but we'll both have to hit the library as well." Delano yawned and rubbed his eyes. They had spent the better part of three hours talking about the geography, and the social and scientific history that they would have to study. "Fact is, my man, we'd better call it a night. We have much work tomorrow."

After agreeing to meet the following afternoon in the library on B-level, Erlanger said goodnight. When he returned to his room on C, he found himself too keyed up to sleep. It was almost midnight before he finally put aside McKay's fat folders of information and turned out his light.

To his surprise, the library was actually rather small. The main room, Erlanger was sure, could not be more than twenty by thirty feet. Tables bearing terminals and microcomputers lined two walls, and the remainder of the space was filled with racks of what he had come to recognize as containers for memory cubes and floppy and laser disks.

Off to one side of the main room, a crowded cubicle served as the Base Librarian's office. Erlanger hesitated as Delano made formal introduction to Virginia Haywood. The middle-aged, severely dressed blonde did not offer her hand, and Erlanger felt at a loss to overcome that poor first impression he had made that first night in the Long Branch. Her unusually dark eyes seemed to carry more than scorn, and he wondered if she knew about his recent spat with Lori.

Delano tried to break the obvious tension. "Brought you a new customer, Virginia. We both need a status update on the situation outside, and Brent needs to chow down on technical history, whatever you have on pre-Collapse data collection, that sort of thing, and he needs to know how the library is set up."

Finally, the woman spoke. Her low voice was more pleasant than Erlanger remembered, but there was little warmth in her words. "I've already put together a study program for the whole mission team. Load SPM-27933/BLP on any available terminal. My time is far too valuable to spend with someone completely ignorant of library procedure, of file structure and cross-reference search. This outsider is on his own, unless you wish to help him, Tom."

"No can do, Virginia. Haven't got the time; hell, Brent hasn't got the time. Your job, after all. You know the old man has given this mission Priority One."

She stared at Delano. The temperature in the room dropped several degrees, but his defender continued. "I know you read everything, Virginia, so I'm sure you've already seen and filed yesterday's directive on the Cincinnati mission. So let's get down to it. Unless, of course, you would care to take it up with the old man, himself?"

"All right, damnit!" The angry blonde turned to look at Erlanger for the first time. "But I don't have to like it."

"Nobody asked for hugs and kisses, lady. Just do your job."

Virginia stalked from her office to a seat in front of a terminal near a large printer. The two men watched her fingers move rapidly on the keyboard. "Don't worry, Brent, she'll do her thing for you. Just make you feel like a day-old turd while she's at it."

Erlanger laughed uneasily. "She's done a fine job of that already. But what the hell, she can't kill me."

"Too right! Sticks and stones, and all that."

Within a few minutes, she returned with a large stack of printout. "Here are your maps, your topographical contours," she said as she thrust the papers into Erlanger's arms. "Also the latest socio-cultural reports on the friendly towns you'll pass. This is the cross-reference listing, here the file category codings, here the general layout of the stacks." She took a small breath, and continued to create an untidy pile at Erlanger's chest. Her final additions were prefaced with a sneer. "And these are the file numbers for the programs we use to introduce our young children to the library. Come back later for the rest of the printouts, and I'll post a schedule for your terminal time, for the audiovisual material."

"Thanks, I—" Erlanger began.

"Just get out of my office, both of you."

Chapter

THIRTEEN

As Erlanger and the others on the mission team prepared for the trip north, the level of alien activity in the region increased suddenly. The reports were a trickle, at first. Reynoldsburg, Maysville, Oneida, Richmond, Hendersonville, Jellico—all the small towns that lay near or between the old population centers noted unusual visits by Ceejays. Then the trickle became a flood. Overflights in all areas were frequent, and at least two of the Base's outside contacts reported as many as five aircars flying in formation. Fortunately, the flight patterns and town visits did not become concentrated near the Base itself.

"The Ceejays have finally got cold feet ... yuk," announced Cleve Stearns, one evening in the Long Branch. "They've found out how big and nasty we are, and they're working out a way to surrender gracefully!"

His tongue-in-cheek remark brought grins to more than a few faces in the saloon, and a small round of applause from those within earshot. Tom Delano,

175

seated between Stearns and Erlanger, added, "Yeah, they want to skip out before the big barbecue!"

Erlanger frowned at the rising bubbles in his luke-warm beer, and finished off the glass, suddenly thoughtful in the jovial crowd. "Hey, guys, just how big are we? I know about our contacts in the towns, but I've been wondering about other rebel groups. Are there others?"

"There are rumors about a secret base, all up and down these mountains," answered Stearns. "And to the west, as far as old Tex, people whisper about an Underground somewhere in the east . . ."

"Just like folks toward the East Coast and up north are positive that a major resistance center is located in the west," Peter McKay supplied, as he slid into the empty chair at their table.

Delano asked, as he licked white foam from his upper lip. "Yeah, Mac, what's shaking with your buddies in California? Talked with them lately, have you?"

McKay folded his arms and glared at Delano. "How in the name of God do you guys hear about things so fast? Who told you that we'd been in communication with the Sierra group?"

"Aw, Mac, you know that you can't keep a secret around here." Delano clapped the older man on the back and chuckled. "At least, not while that bug is still in your shop!"

"I'm seriously tempted to believe that you clowns *have* bugged me, along with everybody else. But I'll let it pass. I know how the rumor mill grinds here, to be sure. And we were going to announce the fact that we've talked with Sierra, tomorrow, anyhow.

"But, to answer what I am inferring is Brent's original question, yes, there are other Underground groups like us, scattered all over the country. Most of them are former United States government installations, defense, weapons research, that sort of thing. Such facilities were relatively closed environments, and ran under military discipline, thus they were the last to fall under the spell of the duplicators. A few, including this Base, survived the slow rotting of society and civil order ... mainly by closing themselves off completely." McKay paused to wet his throat, and grinned with evident pleasure at the agritechs' brew.

"How did they do that?" Erlanger wanted to know.

"Not easily, to be sure. Oh, it was obvious to a few far-sighted individuals, some even in leadership positions, that the world was going to hell, thanks to the duplicators." McKay downed his beer and pointed his glass at the pitcher in front of Delano before continuing. "Fact is, the implications were probably clear to most people, but even in installations like this the majority of the personnel just drifted away. The appeal of here-and-now wealth was difficult to resist, after all; people tend to forget about their great-grandchildren, especially when they're too young to have any. The long view doesn't come easily.

"So, few organized efforts, few technical facilities like ours survived. And of those that did, some fell apart within a short number of years, thanks to internal friction and the clear alien threat."

"C'mon, Mac," said Delano. "Give with the new dope on the West Coast. What's with the Sierra group?"

McKay waved his hands, as if quieting unruly classroom behavior. "Oh well, nothing much new with Sierra, really. We had five minutes of static-ridden conversation, courtesy of one of the old Oscar satellites. Just enough to assure one another that we are still alive, and to report that neither group has discovered anything new. Oh, Sierra did indicate that they've been fairly successful in exterminating the outlaws in their region. For a while, outlaws were quite a problem for them, and actively tried to locate Sierra Base, but Tagaguichi, he's the Old Man out there, ordered an offensive, and that was that."

McKay shook his head, as if he had tasted something foul once again. "Sure hope people are holding on like that in the rest of the world."

He fell suddenly silent, stretched, and glanced at his watch. He gulped the rest of his beer. "Gentlemen, I'm afraid I must leave, much as I'd like to remain and turn to more pleasant topics in this good company. Tomorrow I have a new run to make on *Cweom-jik* technology with a bag of tricks called Kaluza-Klein spacetime, and these old bones need sleep."

Soon after McKay left, Stearns excused himself as well, with a wink that suggested he didn't plan to sleep alone. Erlanger was surprised to discover that he and Delano were left to close the place. They chatted for a while about their work together and the upcoming Cincinnati mission preparations.

"Tom, you must know about this thing between Lori and me. I mean, we were close . . . I thought we were getting . . . and then, once we got here, well, except for a couple times, she's just been so damn cold . . . damnit, I can't figure what's going on, and it's eating away at me."

Delano looked embarrassed, and took a long ten count with his beer. "Oh hell, it's obvious, man. Probably shouldn't tell you this, but more than a few people have been talking about you two. Most folks seem to think that she's doing you wrong, if it makes you feel any better. Sure don't care for it myself. But, nobody can figure Lori out, leastwise, nobody who'll talk."

He sighed, then threw back his head and finished the last of his beer. "I have an idea that Virginia

Haywood knows how Lori's head is screwed on, but you'll play hell getting anything out of her!"

"Yeah, you got that right." Erlanger gagged quietly, a sudden lump in his throat. "Still ... I ... well, I wish sometimes that I'd never met her."

"That you don't, brother. Indeedy no," Delano grinned. "Then you wouldn't be here, midst all this good company. And we'd be shy your jovial presence too."

While Delano's remarks cheered him somewhat, no real solution to his dilemma had been offered. Later, once alone in his room with darkness for company, the painful loneliness returned, as it always did.

In the brief moments while the elevator carried him to B-level, Erlanger glanced at his hands. He grimaced at how pale he had become, even though special lamps were available to compensate for the missing sun.

As he stepped off the elevator and headed for the library, his thoughts took an abrupt turn. Odd, how people change, he said to himself. Or is it just me? More and more of late, people were opening up; fewer cool glances seemed to meet his greetings in the halls and chow lines. Of course, Delano's recent remark that many thought that Lori was "doing him wrong" had changed his perspective on a lot of things. From his rude introduction to the Base, through his gradual acclimation, he'd felt like an outsider, as if he faced united hostility to his relationship with Lori.

As he walked briskly along, his soft shoes silent in the long corridors, he acknowledged sheepishly that he may have had things backwards. He had been misreading others, because of his tangled emotions and, yes, his own hostilities about Lori. Everyone wasn't against him. Everyone, that is, except Virginia Haywood. He paused before the painted steel door labeled "LIBRARY KEEP CLOSED" and shook his head. No doubt about it, the witch within was not on his side. What did the Haywood woman resent so strongly? He entered quietly, promptly on time.

Virginia was at her desk, as usual. Erlanger waited a long moment before letting her know that he was there; an old memory had just come to him. Something from his Grandfather Owens, about apologizing even when you are right. Perhaps, just as he had been transferring his hostility and uncertainty about Lori to others, maybe Virginia Haywood had been projecting her own worry and fear about something to him. OK, he told himself, take that a step further. What did they have in common, this faded blonde and he? Lori, of course. But, Virginia had no claim to her . . .

Wysocki! That was the connection. The flash of intuition delighted Erlanger; rarely did his problems suggest their own solutions. Somehow, Virginia was associating him with the loss of her brother, through Wysocki. An odd connection, but he'd had equally strange emotional tangles in his own life. So. Lori represented something of the dead Donald Haywood to Virginia. Loss of Donald . . . loss of Alan Wysocki . . . now him. Convoluted as hell, but there was an internal logic. Perhaps he had an approach, a way past Virginia's cold stone shell. It was worth a try.

"Good afternoon, Virginia," he said in his friendliest tone.

She whirled to face him, nearly toppling her chair. "Don't ever slip up on me again!" she almost screamed, her face pale and pinched.

"I'm very sorry, I had no intention of . . ." Erlanger mumbled, his eyes downcast. Then, in an instant, he knew what he had to do. He took a deep breath, looked directly into her hostile eyes, and said, "I'm sorry about Lori, too. I mean, that she lost Alan after losing Donald. I'm sorry that you've had those losses, as well." The words tumbled out, and he braced himself for a verbal attack. But this had to be said, and he felt better for it.

She looked at him strangely, and for a moment, he thought that she was going to leap forward and strike him. Then the sharp planes of her face seemed to melt, and he noticed an increased gleam in the corner of one eye—a tear?

"You . . . you're . . . thank you, Brent."

Startled, still unsure, he looked at the disturbed papers on her desk, at the long racks of computer media outside the door.

"Brent, it is I who must apologize. I'm afraid that I've known all along that I have been blaming you for Lori's problems, when you really don't have . . .

"Well, Lori is all I have left of Donny. We were very close, Donald and I. Our parents were both killed on a mission to Memphis when we were very young; Donny was all I had left." She paused to brush away a tear. "I married late, you see, and when Don . . . Donald died, Lori was my only connection to . . . well, and then, when anything else happened to Lori, it was like it happened to me. I hurt for her, if you can understand that."

She motioned for him to sit. "Lori's had more losses, more hurts, than Donald and Alan. Her relationships with men were all rather quick and painful, after Donald was killed. With Alan, finally I thought that she had found peace. Then Alan was gone in the same horrible way.

"It was too much to hope that she would ever find anyone again who she could hold onto, become a part of like that. I figured that you were going to be like all the others, the cruel ones who played on the emptiness in her soul. I thought you were like those

other men she sought out, after Donald, before Alan
... men who only gave her a little pain to mask the
deeper despair ... quick meaningless affairs."

Virginia straightened up. "That may be putting too
much of my own feelings onto Lori, but she must not
suffer more, Brent. I felt I had to ... given your
background and all, oh, I'm sorry, Brent, but I've
been telling Lori to avoid you."

"What?" Erlanger was astounded. Her dislike had
been clear, but he hadn't understood. "You mean
that you've actively turned her against me?"

"Yes, yes. Even though the evidence has been plain,
from her, and more recently, from you, that I was
wrong. You must know how skittish Lori is, how she
doesn't really trust a relationship any more. I suppose I just pushed her that extra bit." She stood and
offered her slim hand. "I can only hope that you will
forgive me, that you'll be more decent than I have
been toward you."

He took her hand and squeezed it. "Sure, I understand ... it's like I only figured out part of it a bit
ago myself. I hope we can be friends, Virginia."

"And that you'll be more than a friend to Lori, if
that's what she decides. She still hasn't recovered,
you know, and you need to convince her to trust her
feelings again, to stay with you. I see now that you're
good for her."

Erlanger nodded, then turned away quickly. He
walked to his usual study area, and sat. Some time
passed, quiet time bordered by the soft hum of the
terminal's fan, before he could concentrate on the
words on the screen.

Chapter

FOURTEEN

"Oops, sorry." Erlanger returned to Delano's lab early and found his friend in Lydia Rutledge's embrace. They made an unusual pair, the wiry Delano and the short, dark med tech, but their relationship had obviously progressed considerably in the months since Erlanger had entered their community.

"Hell, man, come on in. You've seen people kiss before. With any luck, it's a disease you can catch."

Lydia squeezed her lover's waist, then pushed him away with a sly grin.

Still embarrassed, Erlanger fumbled with the bulky papers in his hands. "Tom, I was going to drop this stuff off with Mac, and I wondered if you wanted to come along. But you're . . ."

"No, that's OK, Brent," Lydia said. "My break's about over, anyway, and I know how much work you guys have to do." She brushed Delano's lips with two fingers, then turned away. In the doorway, however, she paused. "You've been such a stranger lately, Brent. Seems like we never see you in the Long Branch any more, or the game room, either. I understand that this mission comes first, but you've got to relax sometime. Why don't you and Lori—"

Frown lines appeared in Delano's normally cheerful face, and he started to speak, but she silenced him with a wave. "Oh, hush, Tom. You men can be such idiots sometimes. Damnit, Lori's my friend, and I know that she's miserable. She's let herself become totally wrapped up in her work, just like Brent here. Both of them are trying so hard to hide the obvious, it's pathetic!"

She moved back into the room, and took Erlanger's arm. "You go to her, you big dummy. Lori needs you, just like you need her. Maybe neither of you fools can say it, so somebody's got to kick you out of this sorry, prideful mess you've made. Lori hurts, you know that. She's got lots of sad memories. I suppose you've got a pain or two of your own. Put all that in the past where it belongs, and find what joy you can . . . while you can. Oh, damnit—"

Her eyes filled with tears abruptly, and she dropped his arm and fled the room. Erlanger stared after her, puzzled, yet somehow very pleased with her outburst.

Delano looked after her. "Geez, Brent. I'm sorry about that, truly am. Lydia's getting a short fuse lately, worrying about me off to Cincinnati, and all this talk about funny things happening with the Ceejays. But she shouldn't have poked into your business like that."

Distracted, Erlanger shook his head slowly, then finally turned back to his friend. "No, Tom, Lydia didn't tell me anything I haven't been rattling around in my head for days now." He paused, then thrust the packet of papers into Delano's hands. "Here. Do me a favor, and drop this stuff off with Mac. Tell him I'll stop by his digs later. Right now, I've got to check on something in the library."

*   *   *

The tour wasn't difficult to arrange. Erlanger explained his needs to Virginia, and she agreed that he could learn more on a trip through the Bio-med research labs than he might pick up from a dozen of her computer programs. Of course, the librarian had understood his ulterior motives, as well—perhaps better than he did himself.

One call to Dr. Speigel, head of the Bio-medical Department, gained Erlanger his invitation to a research section seminar, conveniently scheduled for the next day.

"Seen you around, of course, Erlanger. Nice to meet you, finally." Vincente Nicholls was older than Brent expected, but like McKay, he seemed friendly and full of energy. "C'mon in, son," Nicholls continued. "Dr. Speigel said to give you the full tour, that you'd have lots of questions. Preparation for the forthcoming search mission, as I understand. So, physical chemistry and quantitative analysis is what we do here."

"I wanted to see what kind of research goes on here, get an idea about what is known about the Ceejays. I understand there's to be some kind of seminar this afternoon, where you Bio-med people will be talking in general terms?"

Nicholls' dark eyes narrowed, then he nodded. "Yes, the intersectional seminar may well be a valuable experience for you."

"I've never really seen anything in this Department, and I thought before I headed outside again . . ."

"Sure, son." The older man grinned and took his arm. "Let me show you the sights. No words over six syllables, that's a promise."

By the time Erlanger and Nicholls arrived in the molecular genetics laboratory, the younger man was suffering another case of information overload. Each room, each research team, had presented a new set of strange equipment, a puzzling array of sounds and odors. Names, faces, technical terms, all were a muddle of confusion. Few of the Bio-med people had done more than nod or smile; most seemed quite intent on their work. As they moved from ultracentrifuge to starch block electrophoresis equipment, Nicholls continued his brief description of each project, and Erlanger struggled to maintain a coherent picture of the research goals.

Two factors gradually became apparent as the tour continued: The facilities were larger than the staff that manned them; and many pieces of apparently vital equipment functioned poorly, or not at all. For all the size and population of the huge underground Base, Erlanger came to realize, for the first time, just how massive the Ceejay problem was, in terms of scientific research. Second and third generation people, many of them self-taught, labored at tasks that once must have involved many thousands.

Nicholls sighed and patted a large console from which a stovepipe-like column rose to a sharp peak. "Here's the baby we really need back in service," he said softly. Erlanger tried to make out the outlines of the bulky machine, most of which was hidden by an opaque plastic dust cover. "Oh, sure, we've got a smaller electron microscope that's still running, and the big Phillips SEM in DF-16 is some help as well, but this Zeiss EM 309 has an oh-point-three angstrom lattice, and we really need it." Suddenly the older man's melancholy mood seemed to lift. "Ah, here's somebody you know. Perhaps she'd best take over the explanations."

Lori had just come in. Erlanger was shocked by her appearance. Her brown hair hung limp and stringy, and her face was pale, her cheeks sallow.

"Brent! What are you doing here? Nicholls, what's

going on?" Her free hand moved to smooth her unruly hair.

"Didn't mean to startle you, Lori. I assumed you knew that Dr. Speigel asked us to show Erlanger around today, before the seminar. I was just saying that you could—"

"Oh my God, the seminar." Her eyes widened and she checked the time. "I'm sorry, Vincente, but I've got to get these tissue cultures into . . ." She paused and met Erlanger's troubled gaze. "Good to see you, Brent. Really. But I must finish this before my talk, and I just haven't a moment. Maybe Hilda can answer any questions you have. After the seminar, we can—well, give me a call later, Brent." She hurried away.

Nicholls frowned and scratched his ear. "Did I . . . ?"

As he watched her retreating back, Erlanger shook his head. "No, it's hard to explain, just something Lori and I have to work out."

The older man seemed to understand. "Yes, I hope so, son." He cleared his throat, then moved toward Hilda's work station.

"Welcome to the gene bashing shop, men. Only can spare a few minutes, okay? I want to catch the seminar too."

"We understand, Hilda. The kindergarten lecture is fine."

"Okay. Erlanger, you know what a virus is, I hope?"

"Just generally. A tiny germ that causes disease?"

Hilda laughed, and punched keys rapidly. A multicolored, lacy object appeared on the flat screen in front of her. "Must speak to Connie Sue about those Ed programs . . . germ indeed! Well, here's what we're working on. We think it's a prion, a slow virus. We isolated it from those Ceejay tissue samples that you and Lori brought back."

She leaned away from her keyboard so they could get a better view, and rubbed her shoulder through her faded green lab coat. "Now, a prion is a very strange and nasty critter, Erlanger, at least in humans, and we hope that this one's equally nasty for Beaks. One of the first human prions was identified for a disease called kuru, a disease passed by human cannibals, of all things."

Nicholls chuckled, for he had heard the story. Erlanger found his mouth open, and closed it quickly.

"It turned out," she continued, "that a lot of debilitating neurological conditions and diseases were caused by these little suckers, these slow viruses that often took 20, 30 years to manifest any symptoms. Things like Alzheimer's Disease, and muscular dystrophy. We had those licked, before the Collapse, but reports from the towns tell us that they're back."

She sighed, and fingered the keyboard again. The lacy, crystal-like display began to rotate through three dimensions. "Anyway, that's what we think we've got here. This is what we hope is behind those recent reports of sick Ceejays . . . you'll hear more about all this from Lori's presentation this afternoon. Do you want me to . . . ?"

"No, no, thanks. I didn't realize that Lori would be talking about your project at the seminar. Sorry to take up your time." Erlanger paused, and offered his hand to Nicholls. "I appreciate the tour. It's really given me a much better idea of what happens in Bio-med, even if I didn't understand most of the shiny gizmos you pointed at."

"Didn't mind at all, Erlanger."

With the exception of the commissary, the D-level lecture hall held more people than Erlanger had yet seen together at one time. He estimated that there were well over a hundred present for the seminar. He was surprised to see Connie Sue Nguyen among the five on the platform, but her presence was explained when Dr. Speigel made his brief introductory remarks.

The stoop-shouldered Deputy Administrator slowly returned to his chair, and the petite psychologist moved to the microphone. The room lights gradually dimmed, and life-sized images of a pair of Ceejays appeared on the screen.

"Thank you, Dr. Speigel," Nguyen began. "I'm honored to join you life scientists at your quarterly xenobiology seminar. I've been asked to present an overview of *Cweom-jik* behavior and cultural heritage, xenopsychology if you will. While much will be familiar, I hope to suggest new and fruitful avenues for your research."

She paused for a sip of water from the glass at the podium, then nodded toward the screen. "Here we have a typical pair of the aliens, the taller and more robust female or *een*, in relatively uniform tan, and the slightly smaller, more colorful *kepwoi* with his bands of blue and green. Although the sexual dimorphism in size is opposite that of most terrestrial avian species, the differences in feather colors and the prominence of the male sagittal plumes do suggest some parallels with gallinaceous, ground-living species on Earth. We believe there are behavioral parallels as well.

"But first, let us consider where they came from." The display changed to a split screen. On top, Erlanger recognized a conventional view of the Solar System; below, a similar, yet different diagram. "As you know," Nguyen continued, "the aliens have revealed little direct information over the years. What we know of their background comes from reasoning based upon observation, and—more recently—from bits and pieces supplied by a few mayors and other townspeople who have defected to our cause. Since our vocal anatomy can never hope to master *cweomki* speech, the invaders have had to learn English, and some have been quite talkative, albeit in a condescending manner. While we're not sure where the *Cweom-jik* home system is, we estimate that their G$_2$ star, *Rushokmee*, is within 100 lightyears of our system."

The two displays expanded to show only the innermost planets, which began to move in their orbits. The small dot of Earth's moon appeared above, and was matched by two tiny dots about the second planet in the bottom half of the screen. "Piveea, their home world, as you can see here, is in a slightly less eccentric orbit and has less axial tilt than Earth. Hence, the seasonal variations are milder, and the average surface temperature is probably about three and a half degrees Celsius higher. The two moons, Hss and Seinaw, are both much smaller than Luna but they are in much closer orbits, with periods of about one and three of their local days respectively. These factors lead to some interesting speculations about their biological and cultural evolution."

She continued to outline the physical parameters of the alien planet for a few minutes, and then the screen display changed to show a stylized version of what she described as a primitive "flock-village." A number of Ceejays, including young, were shown among round huts of some sort.

"Civilization and technology came much more slowly to the *Cweom-jik* than to humans, we believe. Here, we see the way they probably lived for hundreds of thousands of their years. After all, their planet was a tropical paradise for such a ground-dwelling, flightless species. Food was plentiful, year round, for these omnivores. Their flock system—and *Cweom-jik* means 'unity of the flock people,' you will recall— was ideal for defense against both ground and aerial predators. And that includes," her oval face turned grim, "the arboreal primate-like *zlekk*, which they're so fond of comparing to us, even though it became extinct on Piveea millennia ago.

"With their male-dominated harem system, social stability within the flock was regulated by a status hierarchy. Pressures from sexual rivalry or territoriality, as we know them in the context of our behavioral biology, were considerably less important in *Cweom-jik* heritage. Their major problem was overpopulation, for their females are indeterminate layers and ovulate about once every ten of their days during most of their short year. Before technology allowed them to move to artifical incubation, they went through frequent 'boom and bust' population cycles, and ate their own eggs and newly-hatched as a means of birth control. These factors, in conjunction with their apparent innate fear of large bodies of water, slowed their cultural development. Even with the communal care of young, too much energy had to be devoted to population factors to permit free time for precursors of science and arts."

Nguyen took another sip of water and continued to illustrate her discussion of the alien's development with sketches on the large screen. Finally, the image changed to an actual pre-Collapse picture of a huge, egg-shaped "mothership" in Earth orbit, with a number of the familiar aircars—tiny by comparison. "But they did finally become sophisticated tool makers," she continued softly, "and began to move into space about 8,000 of our years ago. After about 7,000 years of gradual exploitation of their own system, they discovered a faster-than-light drive, and began to look for other habitable planets. We know we're not the first one they found.

"One of the puzzles about their invasion is why they would want Earth, or at least, why they would want this colder, higher-gravity planet in the way they took it. We certainly assume that they have history of aggression—those four-clawed feet are obviously quite lethal, and we know that their ancient history even includes nuclear warfare. But why did they come as conquerors, and not as friends? There, I think we have to look to their ethnology and their evolutionary history.

"On their home world, potential predators were simply eliminated. We must assume that they wanted no rivals from space, either. Then too, despite long-term population stability, they carry that drive, that biological imperative if you will, for room to expand. It may not make much sense, perhaps it's not even a rational motivation for them, but it's part of their nature. Otherwise, the enslavement of humans to supplement their robot agricultural machines in our midwestern and western grain lands is totally inexplicable. After all, the economics of interstellar grain shipments must be hard to justify, on the basis of food requirements alone."

She answered a few questions, then returned to her chair. Erlanger was lost in thought, and failed to catch the name of the next speaker, a physiologist. He began paying attention again as he realized that the young man was talking about *Cweom-jik* sensory systems. Such information might come in handy someday.

"We assume good visual acuity, except for the red end of the spectrum, of course, in what must be the equivalent of a retina that is mostly cones. We must be cautious about speculation from our own birds, however, and it may be that the aliens have greater UV sensitivity than we do."

Again, Erlanger was conscious of the gaps in his piecemeal education, and he failed to appreciate many of the details that were presented. The speaker moved on to discuss their best guesses about the Ceejay auditory system. The salient point, which Erlanger gained from the displayed charts and diagrams, was that he shouldn't try to sneak up on a Beak. Their hearing was excellent, although the thinner atmosphere of their home world might make them less sensitive to the highest frequencies that men could hear.

Then the physiologist turned to the chemical senses, and presented a number of displays of "possible analogous terrestrial olfactory structures." As near as Erlanger could figure it, the Ceejays didn't smell too well. He felt a tickle in his throat and had to hold his hand over his mouth to stop a laugh at his private joke.

The physiologist concluded his talk and a short, yet heated discussion followed. An older man in the audience argued that the Ceejays had no night vision at all, and several others, including Connie Sue Nguyen, countered with the suggestion that use of strong artificial lighting at night was merely a cultural response. The argument became very technical, and all finally agreed that final resolution of such questions would have to wait upon an actual autopsy of a fresh alien corpse.

Finally, Lori took the podium, and he sat up straighter. She began her presentation very quietly, and a man to his right asked that she speak up. Erlanger was shocked; this was not the dynamic woman he thought he knew.

"Sorry," she said, somewhat louder. "I was saying that our group has only negative results thus far. We have been unable to get the alien virus to replicate. If, in fact, it is the sort of disease vector we hope it is, we have yet to discover a means of genetic manipulation that would lead to a selective bio-weapon."

Lori continued for several minutes, with screen

displays of the sort that Erlanger had already seen in her lab. She explained her group's approach to the suspected prion. Research strategies were shown in detail. Erlanger became aware of soft conversation around him, and realized that he was not alone in recognizing her depressed mood.

Her voice rose slightly. "I know many of us were quite hopeful, during the past few weeks, as reports of increased Ceejay activity reached us, reports that included clear indications that alien individuals were ill. On the basis of our research, we may, I believe, consider those reports of alien sickness correct. The *Cweom-jik* have certainly been on Earth long enough for such a prion factor to arise, either from a mutation within their own microfauna, or from a terrestrial source." She paused for a drink of water, and the microphone amplified a distinct sigh. "We must recognize, however, that the aliens are as advanced in their biological sciences as they appear to be in physics—perhaps more so, given the biological imperatives of their early population problems. We cannot hold much hope for what I know some of you have come to call 'the H.G. Wells Solution.' If, as seems likely from intelligence reports, and our own limited research, the Ceejays have a disease, we must acknowledge that they also have a cure. It may be that the alien body I examined on my return from the first Cincinnati mission ..." She paused and looked down at her notes. Her audience fell completely silent, in apparent understanding. ". . . it may be that those remains were of one of the very few actual victims. Military informs us that no further indication of sickness has been observed in the last week."

She looked down again, and seemed to stack the papers in front of her. "We will, of course, pursue our search for a useful weapon. Any questions?"

There were questions, and she answered them in the same flat tone. Erlanger wanted to ask something, anything, that might give encouragement, but was at a loss, painfully aware of the inadequacies in his background.

Then, the seminar was breaking up, and he tried to catch her eye, but she was quickly surrounded by a small group. Before he could reach her, she left through a side door. He returned alone to his own familiar corridors, to his final mission preparations, with a hollow feeling in his stomach.

"I know that I should have called earlier, Brent. Somehow we just kept missing connections."

Erlanger nodded, and stared into her deep green eyes. Lori looked better than she had on the day of the seminar, although there were still signs of lack of sleep. Her hair shone with newly-washed luster, and her close presence filled his nose with pleasant memories. She tried to smile in response to his intent gaze, and a hint of familiar dimples appeared.

They sat together, knees almost touching, in the most secluded corner of the Long Branch.

He smiled in return. "We're here now. Tomorrow I start out for . . ."

She brushed his lips with her fingertips, and his whole body tingled. "Not that, not now. Let's talk of other things."

He nodded again and took her hand. She didn't seem to mind. Lori leaned close to his ear. "Let's get out of this place, okay? My room's a lot quieter. Shall we pick up a jug on the way out?"

"Good idea, but no jug, I really shouldn't drink much tonight, early start tomorrow . . . Do you love me as much as I love you?"

"You know I do. But I'm so scared. Please come back to me alive."

"Don't worry, baby. As long as we love each other, I'll be back."

Chapter

FIFTEEN

The first part of the journey to Cincinnati was easy, although the team's progress was slower than expected. Pisgah led them parallel to the old state route that ran between the ruins of Oak Ridge and Warburg. They avoided the road itself, and other open areas where Ceejay overflights might be a threat.

The leg north to Oneida was tougher, but the promise of an overnight in that friendly town made the day-long hike seem pleasant after their first night out in the chilly fall weather.

When the expedition roster was first posted, Erlanger was surprised that two women were among the ten selected for the trip north.

As team members, Ana Munoz and Jane Rinehart were certainly competent. The group had barely left the Base when Erlanger lost any doubts about their abilities, their coolness under pressure. Pisgah had the point; Ana walked a few meters behind, while Erlanger followed her. A startled timber rattler rose from a rotten deadfall and struck Pisgah's leg. Fangs wet with venom brushed the heavy leather of the Cherokee's boots.

Erlanger let out a yelp when the brown snake struck and recoiled, then he stood transfixed. The Munoz woman was more prepared; almost as quick as the snake, she pulled her machete. In her hand, the flat blade fairly sang as she slashed at the snake. Her first swing missed, as the rattler moved to strike at the long knife. With her second swing the upper third of the snake's body fell to the ground, writhing, while the rest of the reptile landed somewhere in the deep brush. Ana shrugged, made a face, and wiped her blade on a clump of dead grass.

Pisgah nodded to her. His pistol now pointed unnecessarily at the snake's head. He frowned and holstered the weapon, outwardly calm. "Let that be a lesson," he said to the group, who had drawn up behind Erlanger. "A threat may come from any direction."

Erlanger grimaced and made a mental note not to get the short, brown woman angry at him.

While he now appreciated the company of the women and was pleased that his friend and mentor, Tom Delano, was a part of the team, one other member of the group was not to his liking. Fred LaFayette, his former guard, was not one he counted as a friend.

None of the four others were known to him, although Erlanger was familiar with one, Eric Steuben, because of Steuben's reputation as a deadly fighter. Steuben was said to be the only man in the Underground that Pisgah considered his equal in hand-to-hand combat. The other three were technical types who were also well trained in combat.

Oneida proved disappointing. They reached the town well after sunset on the second day out. Pisgah, who was known to the Oneida townsfolk, walked in first.

The others waited in a small forest about a mile off the main road, old U.S. 27. Pisgah came back with two old men, who examined the group, then returned to town without Pisgah. The bizarre cycle was repeated once more; when Pisgah returned again, he was alone.

"It's gonna be a quick overnight, people," he announced. "They've fixed up a place for us, but they're a little nervous with all the recent Ceejay activity. We're to slip in and hike out before dawn."

The group was shown to a crudely-finished basement. The sour-smelling room was evidently a late addition to the building, for they were forced to crawl through a trapdoor hidden beneath a wood stove. The floor was damp and covered with straw. The musty odor made Erlanger sneeze.

Somehow he managed to sleep. All too soon, he was shaken awake by Delano. "Time to hit it, Brent," Delano whispered. "Hope you got all of your stuff together, 'cause they don't wanna risk no lights down here."

"Yeah," Erlanger mumbled, as he tried to push the cobwebs from his mind. "Got everything right here." He had fallen asleep with a packstrap still looped around one arm. He struggled up, hefted the pack over his shoulders, and then stumbled toward the thin gray light that marked the trapdoor opening.

During one of the infrequent rest stops on the trail, Erlanger asked Pisgah what all the secrecy had been about.

"They're scared, like everyone else," the Cherokee replied. "Been quite a few strangers through here lately, and it's got everyone worried."

"Outlaws?"

"Hard to say. Could be Ceejay stoolies—spies. But that, along with the overflights, is enough to make them suspicious of everyone." Pisgah paused to scan the immediate area. "Not that they're suspicious of us—they just don't want to be connected with us, if anything should go wrong."

"I see what you mean. So, I guess we proceed with even more caution?"

"Right." Pisgah waved to the rest of the group, sprawled around the small clearing where they'd stopped. "Up and at 'em. We gotta make some klicks!"

The pace slackened as they made for Bobtown. Roads and open areas were chosen only when no other passage was available. Pisgah kept them especially alert for evidence of other parties, in addition to their skywatch.

No other humans were spotted, although the remains of a campfire were discovered, as they sought a safe place for the night. Pisgah estimated that the charred wood and scattered ashes had been there for two weeks, but he insisted that they move on. "Too easy for them to come back," he explained to LaFayette when the tall man tried to argue.

For once, Erlanger found himself agreeing with LaFayette. The area, a half-acre clearing surrounded by pine trees, was perfect, easily guarded, and serene.

LaFayette was not mollified. "But, it's getting dark—"

"You afraid of the dark?" Pisgah cut him off. "We move on and keep our eyes open—the easy way ain't always best."

They did find a rather rocky campground within an hour. No one was happy with it. Pisgah at least allowed them to build a fire, in the lee of a small cliff, but the group around the fire was a cheerless one. Game was scarce—aside from a deer that no one really believed Delano saw, fresh meat was days in their past.

*   *   *

Early on the third morning, just a few miles out of Bobtown, Delano spotted a rabbit in an open field, and tried to run it down. At first, Erlanger thought his friend was running for cover, and was about to dash for the copse of trees ahead. Then, he saw a movement in the pile of dead bushes that Delano ran toward. A brown streak zig-zagged across the field.

Everyone else, including Pisgah, had been caught off guard by Delano's sudden charge, and more than one had drawn weapons. As they watched, Delano pulled out his pistol, but before he could fire on the rabbit, it disappeared. He returned, panting, to a chorus of laughter.

"That's the hardest I've seen anyone work for nothing in a long time, Tom," Erlanger chuckled.

"Yeah, but if I got him, you'd all sure as hell have eaten the rabbit stew!"

"Right," Pisgah snapped, "but let's keep that sort of thing to a minimum. We'll hunt when we can—no one moves away from the group without letting us know what's going on. We want to get back to Base before the first mountain snow, and this sidetracking costs time—not to mention that it might expose us!"

Some hours later they paused on a hillside above the main road into Bobtown. A major rebel group controlled the town, but to Erlanger's surprise, they were not met openly here, either. Pisgah and one of the techs from Base traveled alone into town and returned with two of the local contacts.

After introductions all around, the Bobtown rebels shared out some canned fruit and cold fried chicken that they'd brought up with them. Erlanger would have traded his entire pack for the chicken alone.

When the group finished their most appreciated meal, Pisgah stood and gestured for them to move closer. "Evans, here, has told me what's been going on in this area. I want you all to hear."

Evans, a short, stocky fellow, cleared his throat. "All right, you know from Oneida that we've had more than the usual amount of Ceejay activity, and that's been bad enough. The Beaks covered this area with a fine-toothed comb, and have spent some time with our Mayor." He nodded to indicate the tall, older man with him. "They suspect outlaw activities.

"Now, we're sure that outlaws aren't all they're after. It's plain enough that they're looking for whoever wiped out an aircar a while back, and we all know about that." Erlanger felt a flush rise to his face.

Evans paused to bite on a rough plug of brown tobacco. "According to what they've told the Mayor, they're looking for a big outlaw organization."

The older man spoke up for the first time. "They seem to think that it's centered somewhere in this region, which could be anywhere within a couple of hundred miles. So, lots of overflights. They searched the village from the air, hovering over houses and near farms, and it looked like they were using some kind of instruments to check things out."

"I reckon they would be looking for electrical or radio equipment," Evans added.

Discussion followed about the possibility of real outlaws in the area—versus spies, which was Pisgah's theory. The argument didn't last long, and the talk quickly became an information exchange. Most of the information came from the Base personnel, although the Mayor and Evans passed on rumors from other towns.

Under the circumstances, another chilly night out in the open was their only option. Their discomfort was softened when a delegation of some two dozen townsfolk came up late in the afternoon. The locals brought fresh food, as well as a little friendliness. In return, the team moved off some distance from the town before making camp.

The terrain flattened out as they neared Danville, their first major objective. According to the old maps, Centre College was located there and the area had not yet been visited by rebel scavengers.

They reached the ruins of the Centre College campus early in the afternoon. A preliminary search revealed blasted and collapsed buildings—almost impossible to enter. Still, Pisgah decided they should try to get beneath the rubble of at least one building. On their maps, a long, low pile once contained a library.

The operation was just plain hard work. They cleared away some of the lighter metal, concrete, and roofing fragments by hand. That effort revealed the real problem—boulder-sized sections of wall and floor. Delano and Pisgah organized a work party to cut saplings for levers. Erlanger, Jane Rinehart, and La-Fayette were left at the building site to finish clearing away the small rubble. The others piled their packs next to the ruin, and strode toward a group of young trees, perhaps fifty meters to the north.

Erlanger and Jane Rinehart had barely begun, accompanied by foul grousing from LaFayette, when Erlanger heard the staccato sound of shots. A chorus of shouts followed.

He and LaFayette grabbed their weapons and were up and running instantly, but Jane Rinehart was a good three meters ahead of them. As if guided by one mind, they headed for the cover of a rusted bus that stood between them and the rest of the rebels.

"Some bastards are sniping at 'em!" LaFayette rasped.

Erlanger looked toward Pisgah and the beleagured rebels, now prone or squatting low at the edge of the stand of saplings. From deeper in the woods, Erlanger could hear the hollow booming of shots. He traced the paths of bullets by the leaves they disturbed.

Pisgah and his group were firing back. Erlanger recognized the sharp crack of the small calibre automatics that the rebels had as standard issue, and the hollow *zip* of Pisgah's Uzi machine pistol. Pisgah's fire was echoed by Ana Munoz's Uzi. Brief cries of pain came from the woods more than once, as the Uzis spoke.

Jane Rinehart crawled around the back side of the vehicle, and was squeezing off carefully-aimed shots from her rifle. LaFayette cursed and crawled to the other end of the bus. He raked the woods with fire from his Uzi.

What the hell, Erlanger thought, and dived beneath the upturned nose of the bus. He squirmed his way to a spot behind a huge metal wheel, its rubber long gone, and began shooting into the woods. He tried to aim where the leaves were moving, at occasional puffs of smoke from the attackers' weapons, but he had no way of measuring his success. Bastards are moving around, he thought, but I know we got some of them.

At the woods' edge, the Underground team darted and paused. They worked their way back toward the cover of the bus. He could see Pisgah motioning them to spread out and fall back, although the Cherokee was having trouble moving one arm.

Then someone was up and running toward them. Pisgah was yelling, cursing, and Erlanger recognized the runner as Eric Steuben. Had he panicked?

"C'mon, damnit! C'mon, or die!" LaFayette shouted as he continued to pump bursts into the woods. Steuben, heedless of Pisgah's yells, crouched over and ran faster. He was bare meters from the bus when he fell. Erlanger saw his face clearly, the grimace of pain and surprise, as he fell. He knew that Steuben had not tripped. As Steuben fell, he rolled, and the dark blotch in the center of his back confirmed what Erlanger already knew.

Suddenly, LaFayette was out in the open and running. Pisgah's group was now halfway to the bus, and LaFayette ran toward them. He cursed and screamed, all but incoherent, as he vaulted over Steuben, dived for the ground, rolled, and came up running.

He dove and rolled twice more before reaching the group. LaFayette joined in returning the fire from the woods, which had diminished. Erlanger and Rinehart continued to rake the woods with covering fire, and now and then one of the other rebels would rise to gain a better shot, then drop and roll away.

Erlanger was surprised at how easily they seemed to have bested their attackers. He, at least, had yet to see one of the outlaws, if indeed they were outlaws. Only one gunman seemed to be still firing from the woods.

The surprise wore off quickly when a bullet caromed off the cracked pavement beside him. That one had come from the right, off to the east! Now he knew why the woods to the north had grown so quiet—the outlaws were moving to flank them.

"Jane!" he called. "Up here, move to the front. They're shooting from your side."

Jane Rinehart moved fast. She squirmed along the back side of the bus to join Erlanger, who had rolled out from beneath it. "Fire into the hillside," he said. He pointed out rapid movements to the east, down a hill that was covered with small trees and dense brush.

Rinehart nodded and began placing her shots into the moving brush. Erlanger did likewise, as he monitored the rebels' progress toward them.

"They've moved," he called out to LaFayette, who was closest, but still a good fifteen meters away. "The hill to the east." LaFayette obligingly turned and raked the hillside with Uzi fire.

At that instant, Ana Munoz, farthest away of the group, sat up suddenly, jerked to one side, then the other, and slowly sank to the ground. Erlanger realized immediately that she'd been hit, probably three times. He cursed, powerless to help her, and continued covering the hillside. Pisgah was doing a credible job of spraying the woods with death.

Odd, how she'd apparently been hit from the front, then from both sides, Erlanger thought. Must have . . .

He spun to his left and, without aiming, began squeezing off shots. Two heads ducked for cover into a culvert across the overgrown parking lot. Erlanger fired off a couple more shots to keep them down, and then the hammer clicked on an empty chamber. Cursing, he pulled out the expended clip and groped in his pack for a full one. The heads popped up again.

"Jane—" he began, but she had already turned and was firing. One head dropped, and the other one flew back.

Now LaFayette was with them—then the three techs, Delano and finally, Pisgah. Hunched close to the side of the old bus, they fired to the west and east, pouring round after round into the brush, and into those outlaws who showed themselves.

"The woods!" Erlanger remembered, and dropped down to crawl beneath the bus, to cover the north approach. Pisgah grabbed him. "No, Brent. Give 'em enough rope to hang themselves."

Erlanger wondered at the Cherokee's plan, but deferred to him. He slid back alongside Delano, who squeezed off carefully placed bursts of fire in response to movement in the bushes. The bullets continued to whiz in, but at a decidedly lower rate than they had even a minute earlier.

"Ana bought it," he said, admiring his friend's marksmanship. "Steuben, too. Like he went nuts."

"Yeah, I saw," Delano replied. "What'd they hit him with?"

"Why," Erlanger paused to take aim at a figure heading back up the hillside. "Damn! Missed him. I guess a bullet. Why?"

"I passed him coming back. Had a metal rod sticking out of his side, he does."

"Crossbow!" Erlanger came back. "They've got crossbows too."

Two figures darted up and over the top of the hill. Then all was silent, except for a few bursts from LaFayette and Rinehart to the west. Erlanger looked quickly back, to the ruins of the building they were searching. He saw only the mound of rubble and the empty expanse of buckled concrete behind.

Pisgah was next to him. "Now, when I give the word, you and Tom roll under the bus and start firing! Me, LaFayette, and Rinehart will swing around the front of the bus, and the rest will come at 'em from the rear. Got it?"

"Yeah, but—"

Pisgah didn't wait. He placed the three men who would come from behind the bus, and then he crawled back to the front, with Rinehart and LaFayette.

"They're coming from straight on," Delano explained. "They want us to think that we've driven them away from the original attack point, and they're going to come at us that way. That's what Billy Lee has in mind, anyway."

Erlanger shrugged, and looked at Pisgah, who was peering around the front end of the bus. Suddenly he tensed. "Here they come—get ready!" Erlanger could hear faint scrapings and footfalls. Someone was running. He took a chance and peeked under the bus. Across the way, he could see a group of men—six, eight?—running across the field where Ana Munoz lay. Behind them, the trees moved . . .

"Now!"

Pisgah, LaFayette, and Rinehart were gone with the word. Erlanger took a quick look to see the three men at the rear of the bus dart out of view, then rolled under the vehicle with Delano.

He counted six of them, then lost track. As one or two fell, another would pop out of the woods—running insanely into the merciless fire of the Uzis. Some carried odd-looking, long-barreled rifles, some crossbows. They fired as they ran, and Erlanger could hear bullets striking the metal above his head.

He felt the short hairs rise on the back of his neck. Others could still be coming from behind. He tapped Delano's shoulder. "Tom, behind us. They could hide behind the ruins."

"Christ! Yes."

The two rolled around just in time to catch three outlaws in the open. Both fired, and the three attackers dropped almost as one. Their blood stained the concrete blocks.

By the time Erlanger turned to face north again, the battle was over. The field and parking lot were littered with bodies.

Erlanger and Delano crawled out from beneath the bus and joined Pisgah beside the shattered glass of headlight sockets. Alert, weapons ready, the survivors searched the area. No more attackers appeared. After a few minutes, Pisgah gave a loud sigh and fell back against the side of the bus.

"Jesus!" he exploded. "Those bastards weren't giving up for nothing!"

For the first time, Erlanger noticed the pale, drawn look on Pisgah's face. His eyes, normally hard and glittering, were slitted. He looked down at Pisgah's right arm, which the Cherokee held against his chest. Blood soaked his shirt and dripped off the heel of his hand.

"Let me look at that," Delano demanded. All of the group were trained in first-aid, but Delano carried the large med-kit in his pack.

The Cherokee nodded, and sank to the ground. Erlanger worried that he had lost quite a lot of blood. Delano carefully cut away the man's shirt sleeve, dumped peroxide in the wound, then broke out a camouflage battle dressing.

As Delano worked, Pisgah's face remained calm, impassive, though Erlanger knew that the peroxide must sting like hell. When the dressing was complete, Pisgah asked, "How bad is it, Doc?"

Delano shrugged. "Apparently you haven't lost enough blood to go into shock. Just as well, as that'd mean we'd have to break into a bag of synthe-blood, and you'd have to wear the automatic infusion device for a day or so. Besides, we've only got one of those bulky blood bags. The wound's clean, right through the muscle. Gonna hurt like hell for a while, and you shouldn't try lifting weights for a few weeks."

Pisgah nodded. Delano put together a tourniquet. "This'll help control the bleeding. Soon's I find it, I'll shoot some Vitamin K into you, too. That large a bleeding area, you'll need some help coagulating. After that, we'll change the dressing and clean the wound each day, and you'll be fine."

When Delano was done, Pisgah stood. "Burial detail," he announced. "Brent, Fred, Tom—you guys dig two graves, fast as you can." He looked at the afternoon sun. "I figure we got two and a half, maybe three hours of daylight, and we need to get the hell out of here.

"Get their weapons and anything else useful," Pisgah called.

The graves were finished, the bodies laid in and covered over. Pisgah said a few words in English, then in his Indian language—short, clipped sounds—and everyone stood for a few moments, silent.

"All right," Pisgah said. "We've got to move, double time. Split up the loads from their packs." Few even spared a glance for the crumpled bodies of their attackers. Carrion deserved its own reward.

The day wore on into the night, and still they marched. Pisgah, over LaFayette's protests and those of several others, refused to allow them to stop until well after dark. "An outlaw band that organized has friends—you can bet on it," he explained as they walked. "Those weapons were quality—not thrown-together. Wherever these guys came from, they have a forge, and metal-working tools."

Next morning Pisgah had them up and going at sunrise. Game was still scarce, but the Cherokee pointed out something he called "nut grass" as they walked near a pond. Water chestnuts were also found. While not very tasty, the fresh vegetables were a welcome supplement to the monotonous jerky. Pisgah wouldn't let them eat the nut grass yet. "Have to boil and peel the roots," he explained. "Save it for supper. Damn Beaks must blast deer herds just like they do horses."

After eating his cold meal, Erlanger stretched out in the sunlight for a few minutes. Pisgah sat next to him.

"We'll rest a little longer today," Pisgah said. "The last couple of days have taken a lot."

"Yeah," Erlanger replied. "In more ways than one."

"By the way, I want to compliment you on the way you handled yourself yesterday. Didn't figure that you might panic, but first time under fire ... Then again, you did take out that aircar with Wysocki, didn't you?"

"Yes."

"Well, you did good." He thumped his shoulder. "Those who can't handle it get weeded out early."

Pisgah stretched his legs and closed his eyes. "You know, I'd like to roll some of the arsenal out of Mammoth, to show these bastards what it means to mess with real people! Give 'em a dose of their own medicine. Creeps—they had us at least five to one, but we took 'em anyway!"

Erlanger was intrigued by the mention of an arsenal. "Mammoth? What's that?"

"I guess you haven't had that in your course, eh? Well, about two hundred klicks southwest of here, there's a gigantic system of caves—goes on for miles and miles. Truly mammoth, appropriately named. Many of our people are there; got a pretty sophisticated setup. While we're into research and operations at Base, they're into manufacturing. They have a shitload of duplicators and lots of scavenged spare parts. They're building up cannon, armored cars, even small aircraft, against the day we're ready to move against the Ceejays in force."

Erlanger found himself once again impressed by the extent of the Underground. "Aren't they running a risk? Of being detected by the Ceejays, I mean?"

"Not a chance. They're under hundreds of feet of limestone in some places and the whole area around the cave entrances they use is wilderness."

"So," Erlanger said, as he worried a bit of water chestnut from his teeth, "if we can crack the secrets of Ceejay technology, we've got a force ready to move."

The Cherokee nodded. "Right—against the Ceejays *and* certain humans." He stood up and stretched. "Okay, everybody. Time to move!"

*   *   *

Two more days of steady, rain-soaked travel brought the band to Swallowfield, where the rebel-loyalist Mayor reported that his small town had been carefully searched, in the same manner as Bobtown. The eight weary rebels were able to spend the night in the town, however.

Erlanger found himself tempted, when it came time to leave the friendly village the next day, to argue on LaFayette's side. The grouch wanted to remain an extra day, to rest and recover their spirits. The townsfolk were eager for their visitors to stay on and the feast in their honor was the most pleasurable event in recent memory for Erlanger. But he remained silent as the Cherokee once again faced down LaFayette's challenge. The man stomped off when Pisgah noted his real interest—a comely Swallowfield lass with a misplaced sense of hero worship.

Erlanger lost count of the days as they slogged on toward Cincinnati. The rain let up some, only to be replaced by occasional snow flurries. They knew the elements set a deadline; the mission must be completed before the heavier mountain snows.

Finally, they reached a steep hill overlooking the Hiyo River. Beyond, they could see the ruined city as it stretched out over the flat alluvial plain. Brown, tree-covered hills rose behind and beside the ruins.

Somehow, it looked different. "Blasting," Erlanger told Pisgah as they worked their way down the old interstate toward the river bank. "The Ceejays have been blasting here since we left. They've really worked the place over. Look there—" he pointed toward a slag heap far inland from the river. "I remember four buildings there—at least ten stories tall. Now nothing."

Pisgah nodded. "Makes our job tougher. I don't

suppose they missed the place where you found those books?"

Erlanger squinted and searched the landscape. A sinking feeling hit him as he realized that he could pick out no familiar landmarks. "Yeah, they did. It must have been off to the right there, between the second and third rows of melted-down buildings."

"Well, we can try, hey?"

They reached the river before nightfall, and made camp away from the bank. Despite the massive flow of water nearby, the night air was warm and dry. The next morning they inflated the two boats and quickly paddled across the river, a mile or so downstream from where Erlanger had made his original crossing. He noted that the bridge he had used for part of his passage was no longer there.

After they put the boats under cover, Pisgah held a planning session. "According to the maps, Xavier University is about ten klicks up that way—" he waved toward the northeast, "and the old electronics plant is better than twenty klicks due north. I think that we should still check out Brent's cache of books, just in case it survived the blasting." He glanced at the map, "The University of Cincinnati campus lies between here and the electronics plant."

Pisgah thought for a moment, then issued orders. "We'll do it in three groups. Brent and Delano, you two work over the area where you found those books, while LaFayette and Maynard and Thompson head up to the electronics plant. I'll go with the rest to Xavier, and we'll scout around along the way. Fred, your group can meet Brent and Delano at the University of Cincinnati site, day after tomorrow."

By midafternoon all three groups started for their respective goals.

*　　*　　*

The apartment where Erlanger had found the books, pistol, and gold hidden beneath the trapdoor no longer existed. For three or four kilometers around the city center, almost nothing could be found except curious slag heaps of fused rock and metal. Erlanger was awed at this evidence of Ceejay destructive power. Nothing but anonymous, mountainous globs of black material stood where once huge buildings had challenged the sky. The desolation was more than he could comprehend. He began to doubt the wisdom of threatening the masters of such great forces.

The University of Cincinnati was another disappointment. While the destruction there was not as complete as in the city proper, the burnt and blackened buildings—multistory and ground-hugging—promised little for those without the manpower or equipment to move tons of stone and metal.

Discouraged, Erlanger and Delano cast about the blocks of ruins for a day before finding LaFayette and his party wandering a kilometer or so away from their prearranged meeting area.

The Xavier site was a matter of a few hours' walk, and the two subgroups reached it at sunset on their third day in Cincinnati. Locating Pisgah's group was a simple matter; they'd had a plan of exploration, and had stuck to it. Thus, Erlanger and the others found Pisgah working around the relatively untouched physics building.

The eight rebels fell at once to work. They cleared a path into the partially collapsed three-story building. The upper floors of the brick and steel structure had collapsed down to ground level, and Delano and the other techs from Base hoped to find something worthwhile in the basement.

They hit pay dirt almost immediately. Careful movement of heavy beams and rubble cleared a path through the building's main entrance hall to a stair-well.

Miraculously, the stairwell was clear—a large pre-fab wall panel had covered it and prevented rubble from filling it up. Erlanger was thankful; his back and shoulder muscles ached continually now.

LaFayette and Pisgah remained on watch, while Delano, Rinehart, the three techs, and Erlanger de-scended into a gloom that had been unbroken for nearly a century. Their flashlights dispelled the phys-ical darkness, but he could not shake a different sort of gloom. He watched without comment as Delano made an odd sign across his chest. They entered the long hallway at the base of the stairs.

"Sure is dismal, eh?" Jane Rinehart commented.

"That it is," Delano agreed. "Let's hope that it's too gloomy for ghosts, as well as the living."

About to make a derisive remark, Erlanger jumped as part of the ancient stair railing collapsed behind them. He realized, with no little embarrassment, that he was the only one who had cried out at the noise.

"Hey!" A disembodied voice floated down the hall. "Everything all right?"

"Yeah, Billy Lee," Delano called back. "Just some old junk falling apart."

The hall ran the length of the building, maybe thirty meters. A rubble-filled staircase blocked the opposite end. Delano took charge.

"Two, four, six, eight, ten, twelve," he counted the doors leading off the hall. "H'mm, works out just right. Me and Brent and Jane'll take this side, you guys take the other, and hit every other door."

The six moved quickly down the hall, opening doors and examining rooms. The first one Erlanger opened fell off its hinges. It led into a closet-sized room that contained a large sink, a bucket, and other unidenti-fiable objects. "Cleanup room," he told himself.

He leapfrogged past Delano, who was in a room filled with tables, and tried the next door. Locked. He twisted the handle, kicked it, then slammed his shoulder against it. Heavy metal, it wouldn't budge. With a shrug, he headed down the hall to see whether the others had better luck.

Half an hour later, Delano shared the news with the two outside. "Nothing much but a lot of Old Time junk—day to day stuff, like clothes and furniture. And," he glanced at Erlanger, "one door that wouldn't open."

Pisgah smiled. "Nothing worthwhile's ever easy, right? Want to break out the plastic?"

Delano's eyes lit up. "Sure! Let's have a go at it. Ain't much that can stand up to that stuff!"

The two men opened Pisgah's pack and brought out a small box. Inside rested a coil of wire, a battery, and a glob of puttylike substance. Erlanger was mystified.

"High-temperature, slow burn," Delano said, noting Erlanger's blank face. "Like thermite, but better. Just touchy, sometimes. McKay didn't want us to bring it, but this is just the sort of thing we need it for. Can't blast in these ruins, unless we want to bring 'em down on our heads. This stuff is ideal!"

In the basement of the ruined physics building, Erlanger and the others watched as Pisgah and Delano carefully kneaded the white blob and placed it all around the edges, as well as around the handle of the stubborn door. They strung two-conductor wire the length of the hall. Delano inserted the bare ends of the wire into the putty, while Pisgah held the other ends of the wires in his hands.

"All set!" Delano announced. He hurried up the hall to the stairwell where Pisgah and the others were gathered.

"Right," the Cherokee replied. He touched the terminals on the wire ends to the posts of the battery. The hallway was lit by a blinding flash, followed by a shower of sparks as the entire mass of putty erupted into a white heat.

The stuff sputtered, and a curious grinding sound emanated from the door. Then, the putty burned itself out. "Let's go up for a breath of air," Delano suggested. "It'll be ten, fifteen minutes before this stuff has cooled off enough to touch."

When the seven of them returned to the hallway, an acrid smell filled the air, and a few wisps of smoke still drifted on the breeze from above.

"Ah," Delano said when he reached the door. "Cooked just right."

Erlanger examined the effects of the putty. The amazing stuff had burned through the steel as if it were paper. Delano knocked the door in with a light kick.

Beyond, a cavernous room lay before them. Indeed, tomb it was, for they recognized skeletons of nine humans who had apparently been at their work.

Jane Rinehart spotted the evidence of their research immediately. In the center of the room, on a massive work table, was mounted what appeared to Erlanger to be a cross between a giant melted-down teevee and ... he didn't know what. About three meters across and one meter high, the curving, pebbled surface was studded with glittering asymmetrical shapes, and little glass-like, sawtooth screens. Colored rods protruded at odd locations around the screens.

Rinehart ran across the room and shouted, "Payoff ... look at this! It's a whole damn Ceejay control panel! Just gotta be!" She ran her fingers over the surface of the thing, and was joined by Delano and the three other techs. Erlanger caught snatches of their conversation. "LCD, high-contrast here, and this is definitely pizeo- . . . they would *have* to have this . . . their eyesight . . ."

Despite their excitement, Erlanger wasn't really paying attention to them. He was scanning the massive room, looking at all of the electronic instruments, the bunks, the cabinets which doubtless held supplies . . . and the skeletons. These men and women had been working here, studying this Ceejay whatever-it-was, right up until the building was blasted—maybe longer. He felt pride and sadness.

Pisgah's voice shook him out of the mood. "Let's get it together, folks. We've got the rest of today to strip this place for what we can carry."

Near noon the next day, the rebels departed, their packs much heavier than when they arrived. Each carried several precious bits of Ceejay technology or human knowledge. Erlanger was entrusted with many of the strange "laser disks" that Delano had called "WORMS". The techs were skeptical that any readable data remained on the gigabyte write-only-read-mostly disks, but their potential was too great to ignore. They took careful notes of the unusual disk drive format, for it differed from any in use back at Base.

Delano treasured a piece of a melted-looking circuit board from the Ceejay aircar control panel. It didn't *look* like the controls for anything, but Erlanger accepted the word of Jane Rinehart and the others that they had, indeed, found alien equipment.

The long-sealed underground lab was a real treasure-trove, and several arguments broke out over just what to take. Delano almost cried when he realized that they couldn't take all of the compact mainframe that stood in one corner. He had fought bitterly with Rinehart over allocating pack-space for laser disks, as well as the wealth of papers, manuals, and research diaries. She'd wanted to take nothing but alien technology, for that was her specialty. Delano won out for the most part. Pisgah ordered them to take a little bit of everything.

Whatever the final assessment of their loot, Erlanger was sure the mission was an unqualified success. The deaths of their companions were at least partially vindicated. He set out with the others with a light step, and an even lighter heart.

Chapter

SIXTEEN

LaFayette was arguing with Pisgah again. Erlanger paid little heed, for it seemed that the stocky blonde man was always bitching about something. Then a couple of the other men began to support LaFayette, bunching up around the head of the column—against the colonel's standing orders for single-file march.

Finally, Pisgah, who was on point, had enough. "Cut the goddamn crap, Fred!" He spoke softly, yet his voice carried to all seven of them as they walked along the road's edge in the gloom of dark grey clouds. "The rest of you know better, too. We stick to the same route back. A mission's no debating society. You saw how Cincinnati has been worked over by the Beaks. It's obvious they're very active even in this lousy weather, so we stay on these old state highways. If we headed east through London or Mount Victory like you want, LaFayette, there'd be dozens of places where we'd stand out like a trail of ants on a kitchen table."

The Cherokee paused to squeeze water from the black ponytail that hung over his collar, but his pace didn't slacken, and his eyes remained fixed to the front. "I'm just as wet as the rest of you, and my boots have trod the same number of klicks. Besides, I-75 wouldn't be any damn drier, for all it might be easier on the feet."

Erlanger nodded in silent agreement as he brushed aside damp brown stalks of ironweed and milkweed at the edge of the cracked asphalt. While he sympathized with the complaints, he recognized the sound reasoning on Pisgah's side. He and Lori had been very lucky when they followed that old interstate highway, for large sections of it still cut a broad, open swath through the land. Here, on what their maps called Route 27, the trees and undergrowth made almost a tunnel at times, and good cover was always close. But it wasn't an easy hike, especially in the chill rain of the past two days.

Despite LaFayette's grumbling, the team had made good time thus far. Their generally southerly march was a half-day ahead of the pace of the trip up to Cincinnati, even with the awkward packs and short rations. Erlanger knew that he was not alone in his frustration with the condition of their route, however. The old road was far from straight, as it wandered through the terrain, and followed natural valleys. The mountainous stretches were particularly hazardous, for washouts were frequent; too, they had to skirt major rock slides. The low ground had also seen much spring flooding over the years. At a place once called Dayton, the old highway disappeared completely. Many bridges were heavily damaged, or missing entirely, and their two small inflatable boats were much used.

They passed Bobtown again and were well into the hills that marked the beginning of the major climb through the Cumberland Mountains. Some requested a second visit to that friendly town, but Pisgah vetoed the idea. There was no important reason to stop, and the chance that Ceejays might be in that town again was too great a risk. Thus, they had no opportunity to stock their packs with fresh food.

Erlanger shook accumulated rain water from his hat brim, and eased the pressure on his pack's kidney pads with the palms of his hands. Even though he was well experienced with the load on his back by this point, damp clothing and jouncing packstraps were never a pleasant combination. The load had lightened considerably on the trip up, of course, but then they made the amazing discovery in the ruins of Xavier University. All carried some part of the papers, laser disks, and computer circuit cards from that sub-basement laboratory. Such treasure wasn't so much heavy as it was bulky and unbalanced, for Delano insisted on soft padding around the delicate items.

Lost in thought—wet, aching feet and sore shoulders his major concerns—Erlanger almost bumped into Delano in the fading twilight.

"Huh?"

"Quiet, twinkletoes!" Delano hissed. "Pisgah's signaled us down and spread out. Must have smelled something; he and LaFayette are scouting ahead."

The two friends looked at each other worriedly, and eased out of their packs. Both checked their weapons. Soon, however, Pisgah returned to view, beckoning. As the rest of the team followed the barely visible trail through the darkening forest, Erlanger realized that the Cherokee probably had, indeed, smelled something. The wind shifted, and they all caught the sour odor of wet, charred wood. When they entered the unnatural clearing around their intended resting place for the night, several muttered curses or groaned. The mostly-underground way station was no longer hidden, no longer a welcome refuge. Only a blackened hole remained.

"My God!" Jane Rinehart said softly, "If the Beaks have found our network of . . ."

"Rest easy on that score," Pisgah said, as he gestured for three of the party to spread out and search the area. "Plenty of ordinary boot prints, though some of those boots were in sorry condition. Looks like we have a bunch of outlaws to thank for our missing supper."

"Son of a bitch!" Delano muttered softly, at Erlanger's side. "More pine nuts and nettle tea for supper, if we can even find that much around here. Just what I had my mouth set for." He gazed around at the brown, dripping leaves of the deciduous trees, and shook his head, then raised his right foot. "Anyone for boiled boot?" he added in a louder voice.

Delano's clowning earned a hard stare from Pisgah. "We're some ways from that yet, and your tongue goes in the pot long before old leather, if you don't hold it down. In this rain, we can't be sure how cold these ashes are, or how far off those bastards may be." Their leader squatted down to examine the ground near the position of the former way station's entrance. "Pretty washed out tracks, so they could be long gone from this whole area. One thing's sure, they walked out heavy. Didn't burn our stuff, they carried it off. Even the iron stove's gone."

"Could have been worse," Rinehart offered softly, from across the burned-out pit. "If it'd been Ceejays did this, we'd really be in a pickle. They probably have instruments that could be used to search out all the way stations, once they knew what to look for." No one argued with her, for that suggestion held too many serious implications.

Once satisfied that the immediate area was secure,

Pisgah organized makeshift shelter and a meager meal. Dispirited and damp, the team huddled together for the night.

The next day dawned clear and cold, and the temperature continued to fall as their march led them gradually into the higher ranges of the Cumberland Mountains. They trudged in silence most of the time, ever mindful of their increasing hunger and fatigue. Even Delano's usual banter was absent, and by the second afternoon south of the missing way station, the electronics tech and his friend were actually snapping at each other.

"Wonderful! Just what the hell we need . . . snow!" Delano kicked at the fist-sized rock he had stumbled over, then booted it into space.

Erlanger glanced around, then squinted as he looked up the brush-covered slope to his right. "Be damned, so it is. Kinda rushing the season. Think it'll amount to much?"

"Probably not early for these elevations. And let's hope there's only half a cloud of this white crap."

Delano's wish was not to be. The snow increased. The team pushed on as long as they could, but the decreased visibility and the cold led Pisgah to order an early halt. They made rude camp at a wide, relatively flat place against the rocky mountainside. "Probably a scenic outlook," Jane Rinehart said, one of the few remarks she made that entire day. At the moment, neither the view nor the outlook pleased anyone.

Once again, even were they able to find dry wood, no fire was allowed, for they were too exposed. Enough saplings were available to strip for lean-to poles, and a combination of their ponchos, ground covers, and the deflated boats made a reasonably snug shelter. One of the men started singing something Erlanger didn't recognize, as they passed around cold venison jerky and colder snow-melt water. The singer's efforts to lighten the communal mood were eventually shouted down, and sounds of wind-brushed snow carried them off to troubled sleep.

The snow was even heavier the next morning, and LaFayette wanted to make snowshoes. "We'd freeze our asses off trying," Pisgah insisted. "We keep moving until we find a cave or some other shelter where we can build a fire. If it still looks like we're in for a lot more snow, then we'll see what we can put together. Ought to have enough rope, wire, and leather among us for the job. But let's get over the hump and see what the other side looks like. The crest of this peak is only about 730 meters, and we ought to make that in a couple of hours, even in this snow."

Erlanger wasn't sure how long they had slogged through the knee-deep drifts. He was just brushing frozen crystals from his eyebrows for what seemed like the hundredth time when he heard a faint scream. Visibility was down to a few meters, and it was all he could do to keep sight of the man in front of him. He pushed aside the left side of his hood, so he could listen, but heard nothing except wind ... then shouts. He moved forward, and could now see that Delano, who preceded him today, had stopped. "What's going on?" he asked, between frosty breaths, as he drew even with his friend.

"Damned if I know. Heard somebody scream. Let's keep low, just in case."

Hunched over, half crawling, they continued upslope. Finally they recognized three others of their party, who were standing in a line and pointing out into the whiteness. The three huddled figures didn't seem to signal any threat, so they joined them. Before the two could ask anything, however, Pisgah shouted an order. The colonel had been bringing up the rear, and Erlanger was amazed that he had come up so fast, and so silently.

"It's LaFayette, Billy Lee," one of the three said. The man's hood was laced tight, and Erlanger couldn't tell who had spoken. "He was behind me, shouted something about needing to take a leak. Damn fool must have just walked over the edge. No telling how far down it is there. Suppose we could drop ropes over, but—"

"But my ass!" Pisgah swore, and looked around. Satisfied with his quick head count, he motioned the rest back against the safer side of the road. "We'd just have more cold meat at the bottom of the ravine. It's got to be at least a 30-meter drop over there." He rubbed his gloved hands together as if he'd like to strangle someone. "LaFayette's gone, and we're not getting any warmer standing here. This time we rope together. If you bastards can't follow orders to stay in sight of each other, at least we may be able to save your pack with the rope."

Erlanger looked into the faces of the group. All were impassive, and certainly none were willing to confront Pisgah's leadership. The Cherokee's eyes were cold, his expression harsh, as he began to break out ropes. Practical to the end, Erlanger thought.

They linked up with the mountaineering gear that Erlanger had used before only in the warm comfort of his training sessions. As he passed the yellow and black nylon line through his belt harness, he wondered whether any of them would see that E-level gym again.

The remainder of their climb that day was uneventful. As near as they could figure it out later, LaFayette must have fallen within half a mile of the summit. They reached that point easily, and their ankles scarcely began to adjust to the downward slope when the snow thinned, then stopped. Within minutes, a most welcome sun appeared. Tired, very hungry, and a little frostbitten, the team made it to the Isham way station by nightfall. Erlanger was not the only one to stifle a glad cry of thanksgiving when that safe harbor, just over the old Kentucky-Tennessee line, proved to be both intact and undisturbed.

An impromptu celebration sprang up in the Commissary on the afternoon of their return. Word spread immediately throughout the entire Base, for the team was two days overdue. Erlanger grabbed a quick shower and shave in his room, and went out eagerly to seek a hot meal. Hair still wet, he was back-slapped and hugged a dozen times before he could make his way to the coffee urn.

As he finished his second piece of strawberry short-cake, and accepted Cleve's offer for a coffee refill, he saw his trail companion in the doorway, and beckoned Delano over. The wiry man filled a tray and was just sitting down at their table when Pisgah entered. Erlanger started to stand and wave, but Delano grabbed his elbow, nodded toward the far corner of the room, and shook his head.

"First the report to the old man, then the condolences," Delano said softly. "Standard practice for a good commander anywhere, and they don't come much gooder than Pisgah. Over there, that's Steuben's wife."

He grimaced and nodded. He was surrounded by such a happy bunch, though the only faces he knew well were those of Cleve Stearns and Connie Sue Nguyen. Erlanger vaguely recognized the widow, her head lowered. He didn't envy Pisgah's job, but was quickly shaken from his dark mood.

"So, as I was saying," Cleve began, over the babble of other voices, "we've got great news in Communications. Solid contacts through those rogue comsats, and . . ."

Cleve's voice seemed to fade from his awareness, as Erlanger searched the growing crowd, searched for the face he most wanted to see. His sense of schedule was off; maybe she was working, maybe sleeping. He kept hoping.

Lydia Rutledge appeared from somewhere, and glued herself to Delano's lap, her arms about his neck.

"Oof!" Delano mumbled, around prolonged kisses. "Just what I need to warm chilled bones."

Erlanger looked away from the entangled couple, acutely aware of his solitary status. Suddenly, he felt a hand at his elbow. He turned. It was Lori.

"Couldn't get away any sooner, Brent . . . and I can only stay for a minute . . . right now, we're in the middle of . . . oh, Brent!"

He didn't hear what she said, didn't care. The feel of her, the smell, the taste, communicated past all words.

The best and the brightest from two departments were stumped. After almost four weeks with the material from the Xavier University lab, no useful data had emerged from the laser disks. Their frustration was particularly great, for study of the printouts and research diaries from that long-dead Cincinnati group suggested that the Xavier scientists had been very close to a breakthrough with Ceejay technology. All signs pointed to a wealth of vital data on the laser disks. Delano considered his continuing failure to read the Cincinnati disks a personal affront.

"Tom? I asked for the salt, please, Tom."

"H'mm?"

"The salt."

"Oh, sure, Brent, sorry." Delano passed the metal

container, and stared moodily at his half-finished lunch.

"This is pepper! And to think you used to accuse me of wool-gathering."

"Ah shit, Brent, not you too! Lydia is hardly speaking to me these days, says I don't know she's alive. This damn disk problem is driving me up the wall."

Erlanger glanced around the sparsely-populated Commissary, sure that others wondered at Delano's raised voice, but no one seemed to notice. "Wish I could help more, Tom. I'm doing the best I can, but I'm still playing catch-up with electronics."

Delano scratched his nose and nodded, then lowered his voice. "I know that, man. Everybody in Science and Communications is going all out, but it looks like my original fears are coming true. The heat, or some other characteristic of Ceejay weapons, just destroyed those disks when they killed off that Cincinnati lab."

"Then why do they seem to work? I never figured we'd get that VAX 1390 up and running again, or the disk drives, for that matter. But everything seems to be working fine; just nothing but random crap comes off the disks."

"Don't remind me, that's what's so damn crazy. Refurbishing the old hardware was a piece of cake, really. When we first found those WORM disks, I was pretty sure we could patch together a drive for them, even though they were incompatible with the laser readers we already have here. But to do all that work, and still come up with nothing. And Mac's been counting on that stuff so much. He thinks his Higgs-space hypothesis might . . ." Delano drummed his spoon on the table. He seemed unaware that he'd fallen silent.

"Did I hear my name taken in vain?"

"Mac!" Erlanger was surprised to see the portly

physicist, for McKay usually ate all meals with his family. "Just the guy I need to give Tom a swift kick. He feels like he's let you Science folks down."

The older man's sharp blue eyes regarded Delano for a long moment, as he set his heavily-creamed coffee at their table, and pulled out a chair. "Still no joy with the disks, h'mm? To be sure, I'd almost give my first-born to know their contents, but if they're not readable, so be it. We'll just have to slog along as we have been, one piece of the puzzle at a time. Not that the papers you men brought back haven't been a great aid, no indeed. We've got some marvelous new clues. My colleagues are almost unanimous in agreement there. The whole *Cweom-jik* model begins to tie together—duplicators, aircar propulsion, even FTL drive. If we could only see how they go from N-space to H-space with so little apparent energy, we'd not only have a Grand Unified Field Theory, but a working engineering template as well."

McKay finally paused for breath and a sip of coffee, and Erlanger tried to broaden his education. "Between Connie Sue and Virginia, I almost know what you're talking about sometimes, Mac, but how could there be another form of space, another universe?"

The physicist finished his coffee, grimaced, and patted his lips with a paper napkin. "My old coffee maker element finally burned out and I haven't had time to tinker up a new one. Stuff they make here is terrible." He leaned back and folded his hands over his ample stomach. "Now, in answer to that very good question, son, about which not a few pre-Collapse theorists crunched a lot of digits, think of circles, spheres actually, within larger spheres." He ignored Erlanger's drawn brows and continued. "Our universe is just one N-space bubble, one bit of normal space as we know it, within the greater Higgs-space bubble. And in H-space, the strong and weak nuclear forces, as well as the electromagnetic forces, maybe even gravity, are all the same.

"Now, we hypothesize that neighboring N-space bubbles may have different rules, different physical laws, if you will. Say in the one next door, inertial mass is altered with respect to gravitational mass. That, if we follow the Cramer Model, would give you Ceejay aircar anti-gravity, not to mention interstellar flight, both of which the birds seem to have. The trick is to get from N to H to another N, and human theorists have never been able to envision that without notions of near-infinite amounts of energy. I have a pet idea, which at least one of the papers you brought back from Cincinnati seems to support. I think the Ceejays use something like a Darlington transistor effect—you know, a little push here comes out as a big shove there. Only the aliens must be tapping into an N-space where solid-state physics doesn't work, because the black box in duplicators seems to have very tiny vacuum tubes."

"Really?" Erlanger had followed the explanation reasonably well, for he had recently studied about the Darlington effect at Connie Sue's terminal, but vacuum tubes in duplicators were a surprise.

Whether from the physicist's cheery presence or the nature of his talk, Delano had apparently shaken off his despair. "Oh yeah," he said, with more of his usual spirit, "a little trick Mac pulled off a couple years back, that was. He cracked the 'mystery module' in a duplicator without it going bang. That's the only part we're sure is alien, see. Everything else inside a duplicator looks pretty conventional."

"Well, my friends, I've got a brainstorming session to get back to, although I doubt if the group will come up with anything new this afternoon."

"Thanks for the quick lecture, Mac," Erlanger said,

as he rose as well, and glanced at the wall clock. "Oops, running late for my time in the library. Maybe someday I'll understand all your bubbles, Mac."

He hurried off to the library and spent three hours with advanced technical material. He was so engrossed in his study that he didn't notice Haywood approach.

"Finding what you need, Brent?"

"Oh, hi, Virginia. Yeah, but understanding it is another problem. I thought I might be able to help with the WORM disk problem. It's driving Tom and the others nuts, and I had the crazy idea that I might find a fresh approach. Sorta through the eyes of 'the new kid,' you know. Should have known better; most of this is beyond me." He gestured at the screen full of hex code drive access routines, and shrugged. "Might as well call it a day."

She moved up closer to him and looked over his shoulder. "Ha!" she said, "that's certainly Greek to me too. But what do you mean, WORM disk problem? You're using a write-once laser disk right now."

He nodded, as he pulled the palm-sized disk from its drive and slipped it back into its file box. "No, I mean the ones we brought back from Cincinnati. They're not compatible with this format. But even though Delano has got a working drive and all, they still come up garbage."

She frowned and began to pace.

"Oh yes," she said. "I know about those. I sent a request through to Admin as soon as I heard. Data bases belong here, in the library, where they can be properly stored and handled. But no, I was overruled. Too vital to the research effort. Must stay with Dr. McKay's team. As if I didn't understand the importance of new records, new data! You'd think that I was ..."

She noticed his expression, stopped walking in small circles, and smiled. "Don't mind me, Brent. Curse of the librarian since the days of clay tablets, I suppose. Tell me about these disks, do they seem to be blank? Or is it a directory problem?"

"No . . . well, that is, Delano's sure that the drive is functioning properly and can access the tracks, but all we get on the screen is seemingly random numbers and symbols, and—"

She held up her hand and frowned. Dozens of wrinkles crossed her forehead. Then her face transformed, blossomed and she started to giggle. "Oh those silly fools," she said as she dashed to her own terminal and started punching keys rapidly.

He followed, amazed. "Virginia?"

"A minute," she muttered. "I know that those old codes are filed . . . ah, there they are."

"What are?"

She looked up from her keyboard and smiled, then gestured at her display. "See, the records on all the original Base security codes. I bet nobody has considered that those disks are under high level encryption lock. You found evidence that the Xavier University people were working for what survived of the U. S. Department of Defense, am I correct?"

"Uh, yeah, that's what some of the papers suggested to Pisgah, but . . . ?"

"It should have been obvious then. Base was established by DoD types, too, don't you see. They were paranoid about security; they coded all their data. After the Collapse, after the *Cweom-jik* made their invasion blatant, wiser heads prevailed, and all that nonsense was dropped for us. But just maybe I've had the right code key here all along."

"You mean that?"

"Sure is worth a try. Let me dig through the files for a while, see what still runs, then I'll ask Dr. McKay for the disks that should have been sent to me in the first place."

As realization of what she offered dawned, he was grinning along with her. "Maybe you'd better just pass your code cracker on to Tom Delano first. I mean, Mac's pretty busy, and I wouldn't want to get his hopes up unnecessarily, in case this doesn't work."

She nodded. "Fine, so long as I can gloat if it does work."

"Oh my everlovin' God! Bingo!" Delano jumped from his stool and rushed to the commmphone on the wall. He punched buttons furiously, paused, scowled, punched more buttons. "Mac, that you? Get your precious brains down to my shop, we've got it! What? Tom, Tom Delano . . . yes, I mean right now . . . you see this, you won't care what Mrs. McKay has just set on the table. We've cracked the encryption . . . yes, it's scrolling down my screen right now, living color. Right as rain, our frosty librarian was, oh, it's lovely . . . c'mon, get down here."

The excitement was contagious. Erlanger grabbed Delano's hands and they swung around and hopped together.

"Whew, this is whacko!" Delano broke free and returned to his terminal, where he tried to catch his breath. The images on his screen changed rapidly:

"AUTHORITY: 20 USC 7082 Secretary of the Air Force . . . charged air movement designator for travel by military airlift command . . . Aeronautical Systems Division (AFSC), Wright-Patterson AFB . . . and HQ USAF levels, and upon request, to other Federal, State and local agencies in pursuit of their official duties . . ."

Erlanger squinted at the screen, then pounded on his friend's shoulder. "Tom, slow down the scroll rate, for cryin' out loud. This looks fascinating, and I'm trying to read."

"Be serious, man, I'm into a bunch of 90-year-old

travel vouchers and accounting records here. There's
more than half a gigabyte on each disk, after all, and
a lot of it's bound to be paper clip counts and shop-
ping lists. We'd get very old and blind spending much
time with this sort of thing. Let's try switching directory paths."

As his practiced fingers moved over the keyboard,
Erlanger moaned in mock distress. "Damnit, just when
it was getting interesting."

"Hey, you really want to do something useful? Run
down the hall and see if Cleve's still working, or hunt
him up wherever. Grab anybody you see. We got a
whole basket of golden eggs here, and I want to share
the wealth!"

Stearns was off-shift and it took several phone
calls to run him down. By the time Erlanger returned to EK-0956 with all of the Comm techs who
had been working in that section, as well as a few
near strangers that the growing crowd attracted in
the corridors, Delano had rigged quite a show. A
large screen now hung from the fluorescent fixture,
against the wall. Erlanger stared at the slowly-rotating
picture for quite a while before the excited background conversation penetrated.

"Run that sequence again, Tom, and I'll die a happy
man. This is too good to be true!"

Erlanger's eyes tracked rapidly from screen to the
last speaker. It was Kaz Ohira, head of Engineering.

"Oh, bless their dusty bones," McKay said, "will
you look at that! Somehow, our sneaky American
ancestors actually captured a Ceejay aircar and took
the damn thing apart . . ."

"Hey, Mac, is that for real?"

McKay spun around, clasped Erlanger's hand, and
squeezed almost painfully hard. "Oh, Brent, Brent,
do you see what you've brought us. This changes
everything. Tom says that this disk alone contains
engineering specifications, control layouts, and spec-

ulations about their propulsion systems. Just think what might be on the other disks. This will jump us years ahead. Think what that Xavier group might have accomplished had they survived a little longer. For all we know, they did solve the major riddles, and it's just a matter of digging through all this wonderful data."

Then Mac let out an uncharacteristic shout. "Enough, Tom. Cut it off."

In the shocked silence that followed the physicist's command, Mac sought aid from those near by, and was hoisted to the top of the workbench. "I'm just as excited as the rest of you, but we can't stand here all night. All this new information has got to be catalogued and duplicated. Then, just as soon as we can, we'll spread it out to the proper divisions and teams for analysis and action. Plenty here for all, I'm sure." Scattered claps and whistles made him pause. "But right now, my friends, somebody help me down from here, because I'm hosting one hell of a party in the Long Branch." Amidst mass cheering, eager hands lifted him off the bench. Erlanger wasn't sure whether the happy mob carried McKay all the way to the bar, or let the embarrassed man walk under his own power. He was too busy trying to get Lori on the phone.

By the time he had dragged Lori from her lab, and reached the saloon, it looked like half the Base was already there. Somehow, Mac and Delano made room at their table.

"Something's different tonight, Brent."

He filled her glass from the pitcher of beer on the table, then paused. She was right; the room even smelled different somehow, almost the feeling of an impending thunderstorm. Even the raucous jukebox was silent. He studied other tables, standing knots of people. Everyone was talking, expounding, arguing, not just drinking. He turned back to Delano, but couldn't find a lull in the other's intense discussion with McKay and Ohira.

"Sure, Mac, but before you came in, I was jumping through a section on weapons systems, and I think the ground work's already been done. Look here." Delano began to sketch rapidly on a notepad that he'd taken from his shirt pocket.

The physicist twisted his neck to follow Delano's design, and shook his head. "Don't we wish, Tom, but that violates conservation of momentum ... besides, we've never seen any evidence that the *Cweomjik* utilize the principles of the duplicator over any appreciable distance."

Ohira, who wore a most Buddha-like expression as he folded his hands around his glass, cleared his throat. "That's the trouble with you theoretical types," the engineer said softly, "no vision. Who says we have to be limited to what the aliens have thought of? Young Delano is on to something here. Obviously some spatial displacement is involved in duplication, even if too small to measure. Why not over kilometers? Handy little weapon that would make, yes? Pull out a chunk of aircar, put in a ticking present from mankind. Would be so nice to crawl out of our holes finally, and pluck a few feathers."

Erlanger stared at Lori. She took his hand. "Do you have the foggiest idea what they're talking about?" he asked.

"Nope, I'm just a chromosome cracker, remember? But it sure sounds like fun. You boys are going to be busy."

"Not too busy for—"

Clapping and the sounds of moving chairs, interrupted him. Many in the room were standing. He and Lori turned to the door, where a very flustered Virginia Haywood was being congratulated. As the librarian made her way through the crowd, Lori got up and kissed her cheek.

"I just heard about your brilliant detective work," Lori said as she hugged the older woman.

"I'm surprised that all these whizkids gave me any credit," Virginia muttered, but her eyes were sparkling with suppressed laughter. "But I guess now they've learned who to see when they really need to know something."

Chapter

SEVENTEEN

"They're going for it!" Delano almost shouted, as he returned from the TAC/OPS meeting with Administrator Boone and the other department heads.

Erlanger looked up from his work, and joined in the spontaneous applause that rippled through the electronics lab. He would have given anything to have attended that strategy planning session, but understood that he lacked the necessary status. He would have to be content with a full report from Delano.

The other techs began to gather round. Delano grinned and declared an unofficial break. He even sent one of the others down the corridor to invite those from Cleve's section. "No sense repeating myself six times," he said. While they waited, he clapped Erlanger on the back, and added: "I'm on the mission, can you believe that! Going to eat his heart out, Cleve is."

The man in question limped in with three of his colleagues. Cleve wiggled his white plaster-covered foot in Delano's direction, as he took a seat on a low stool beside a faded red tool cabinet. "Like to boot your butt, Tom. The dummy transmissions were my idea, after all, and I should be the one to go along to set up the radio. If I hadn't been such a bonehead in that storeroom last week and tripped over that damned transformer . . ."

"I suggested they tie you to a cart, but Pisgah wasn't amused. But seriously folks," Delano continued, "here's the plan."

He unrolled a sheaf of yellow printout, then rolled it back up again—toying with his audience. "We've got to go for a limited test of the defensive weapons, and the site has been chosen." He leaned back against the long bench, and chuckled. "Kaz Ohira was all for a full-scale operation, tests of both offensive and defensive prototypes, but the others shouted him down. We're just not ready for an offensive battle yet. Boy, that little guy is a real tiger, now that we see a chance to hit back at the Beaks with their own technology. Anyway, we're going to try to capture one aircar with that force projector gizmo that Mac designed . . ."

"And we built," one of the others added.

Delano frowned at the interruption and waved the papers in his hand. "Yeah, well, we all had a piece of those units . . . We've run all the static tests here that Mac and the others can think of, and it looks like it'll do the job, that it'll cut out the aircar propulsion system, and nullify their force bubbles too. So it's time to set the trap. Lots of input on that, you can bet. Every department seems to want a piece of the action."

As his friend paused again, Erlanger wondered what site had been chosen. From earlier discussions, he knew of Cleve's original suggestion to set a trap for the Ceejays. The plan called for a location that was both a safe distance from the Base, yet not so far as to call for difficult travel—especially now that snow-storms were reported outside the Base. Also, the site had to be credible, at least to the aliens, as a revived high-tech operation. As the plan had evolved, first out of McKay's group, then in the Military Department, and finally at the Administration level, Stearns and Delano had pushed their own ideas. Apparently, their arguments had been accepted: An aircar would be lured down, incapacitated, and captured. The bait would be a phony research laboratory, from which equally bogus, yet overt, radio transmissions would be sent. The plan was simple, but there were many "ifs." Would the *Cweom-jik* investigate such a signal, especially in the dead of winter, or would they merely blast the site from high altitude? And most importantly, would McKay's force projectors truly work?

Erlanger rubbed his chin, suddenly mindful that he'd skipped shaving that morning, and considered the rapid progress that the rebels had made. The Xavier disks had acted as a final catalyst—he almost smiled as he realized how recently he had learned the meaning of that word. Not only did they now have a good idea about the internal layout and operation of the aircars, but the physicists and engineers had discovered the basic principles of Ceejay devices as well. Finally, they were in a position to turn the Beaks' own science against them. Mac even argued that they had come up with a few new surprises of their own, weapons the aliens didn't have, and wouldn't expect. As his thoughts drifted back to that Bio-med seminar, to Connie Sue Nguyen's remarks about the slow pace of *Cweom-jik* cultural evolution, he wondered if man actually was the quicker, the more innovative species. Lost in thought, he missed Delano's dramatic announcement.

"Where did you say?"

"Damnit, Brent, pay attention. I said that Military

ruled out both Knoxville and Chattanooga. The former's too close, and Chattanooga has seen too much flooding since it was smashed. The trap site will be on the campus of Tennessee Tech. That's about 170 kilometers west of Base, in the hills. Used to be a town called Cookeville. A mission went through there about ten years back. Usual ruins, of course, but the report mentioned that several buildings are still in pretty good shape, and should fit our needs just fine. We'll follow I-40 most of the way, so if the weather gives us a break, it should be an easy four, five day hike."

Several others began to ask questions, all at the same time, and Cleve shouted them down. Whether from his injury or his seniority, they deferred to him. "Who's going?" was the straightforward question he finally asked.

"Not set yet, except no clubfoots allowed." Delano's tone and expression tried to make light of it, but Cleve was visibly hurt. "Sorry, Cleve, you know you'd go in my place if you could. Oh, Pisgah will lead the mission, that's decided. And, while both Mac and Kaz wanted to go, the old man nixed that right quick. This is a game for the young and expendable is what he said in so many words. So probably three or four from Science or Engineering, to set up and monitor the weapons; yours truly, for the 'c'mon, sucker, come and get it' radio transmitter; and probably somebody from Bio-med. The timetable will be posted, usual bulletins. Anything else, Admin will let us know in their own sweet time."

That evening, he and Lori shared a dinner together with Lydia and Tom. Delano and Rutledge had recently moved into larger quarters together, and the couple now had their own kitchen facilities. Delano claimed most of the credit for the pineappled ham and new potatoes with peas, but Erlanger was quite sure that Lydia had done the real work. "Hey, how-cum I don't eat this well every night?"

Lori smiled at him, and pinched him playfully above his belt. "Feels like you're doing fine. Never heard you complain about the Commissary before."

The smile left Lori's face quite suddenly as she put her hand on his forearm, and said quietly: "Brent, I'm going too."

"Going . . . ?" As he realized what she was talking about, his mouth dropped open.

Delano looked at her. "Say, that's great, Lori. Glad to have you along. Knew that someone from Bio-med would be included, but how did you swing the appointment?"

Lori continued to face Erlanger, who stared at her with a puzzled expression. He was both hurt and angry—especially since she had given him no hint of her intentions.

"Wasn't easy," she answered. "Dr. Speigel wanted to send someone else, but I made my case on the basis of greater experience. I've been on several previous missions, after all, and have the best background with regard to aircar attacks. It's got to be someone who knows the xenobiology. This is our first, our best shot at live specimens. Why, the Military people even hope for actual capture and interrogation. Even if we don't get Ceejays alive, the potential for physiological and biochemical research is tremendous."

"Damnit, if it's a matter of experience fighting Beaks, then I should be included!" Erlanger took Lori's chin in his hand, none too gently, and turned her face to his. "And if you think you can just run off from me, woman, you've got another thing coming. First thing tomorrow, I'm going to see the old man and get on that team."

Eyes moist, she stared at him. "Please, Brent, now's

not the time to . . . besides, you can't just burst in on the Administrator. A mission has to be carefully planned, and . . ."

"Why the hell not? He's seen me before. I think Boone likes me, and there's every reason why . . ."

Delano looked to Lydia for support, but she was off in the kitchen. "Wait now, you guys, you know that Pisgah will vouch for you, Brent, so I would think . . ."

Lori shook off Erlanger's hand, and rose from the table. "Tom, please, I shouldn't have just come out with it like this. Brent and I need to . . ." She raised her voice, and Lydia returned to view. "I'm sorry, it really was a lovely dinner and I . . . we'd better go. Lydia, I'll talk to you tomorrow, really I will."

"Told you you couldn't get away from me that easily." They shared Lori's bed again, for the first time in three nights.

"You are the most stubborn man I've ever met. When you get set on something, you just bull ahead. Administrator Boone must be going senile, to let you talk him into going. Still, even with my overprotective Cro-Magnon along, it's not going to be easy. What do we do once we knock out their systems? Their weapons may still be operational, and those beams are deadly, as we know well from the first time—"

"Lori! Enough shop talk, okay? We're together now on the mission planning, but that's for the bright of day." He tried to nibble at her earlobe, but she twisted away.

"No, be serious a minute, Brent. This problem is driving us up the walls. If we're going to try for living prisoners, how do we incapacitate Ceejays? Some in Bio-med have suggested drugged darts, but that's pretty chancy, even with open targets. Besides, we don't know enough about their physiology to figure vehicle and dosage. Pisgah isn't keen on that idea, anyway."

He sighed in frustration, and moved up beside her. "All right, if we've got to think about this now, of all times ... let's see, we can't just blast away with automatics and hope to miss vital organs, pleasant though the idea may be."

She grimaced and brushed his cheek with two fingers. "Oh, Brent, don't be so blood-thirsty. I hate them as much as you do, more probably."

He slid down, tucked his head under her chin, and hugged her. "Too bad we won't be fighting in an old coal mine."

"What?" She jerked to stare down at him. "What do you mean?"

"Oh for ... can't a man get laid in peace around here any more! We had one. Old coal mine, that is, near Milford. Helped a lot in the bad winters, especially when a guy didn't have a warm body ..." She pinched his neck, and he rolled his eyes back to glare at her. "Yeah, I get the message. What I was thinking; something my Grandfather once said, about how they used to use canaries in mines to warn against gas. Some folks thought it was because they could smell it better than the miners, but from what I've learned here, most birds and probably the *Cweom-jik* too, don't have any sense of smell at all. So my grandfather must have been right, that birds just don't breath the same way we do, that they need more air or something ... hey!"

She slapped her pillow, and slid away from him in one smooth motion.

"Lori, have you gone nuts? Who are you calling at this hour?"

She gestured for silence. "I've been such an idiot ... it's so obvious, somebody in our section should have thought ... Hilda? Yes, Lori ... yes, I know what time it is ... just listen."

Erlanger quickly became lost, for her discussion was very technical. She said something about "smoke combined with CS," whatever that might be, and seemed to argue about the availability of "a proper fluorocarbon propellant." She nodded and smiled as she spoke rapidly for a few more minutes, then hung up the phone. She turned off the light, and all but fell across his chest.

She squirmed around and began to kiss the corners of his eyes. "And now my very bright darling Cro-Magnon gets his reward!"

"Lori, you're driving me crazy. First you're on, then you're off ... what was that all about?"

"Your idea, of course! Hilda agrees that gas grenades will be easy to make; simple canisters like the old military tear gas, only nonflammable because we don't want to risk burns on either side. We'll have to guess a bit at Ceejay respiratory mechanisms, of course, but they should be close enough to the terrestrial avian model, once we factor in their apparent thinner native atmosphere. Concentrations that will only give us watery eyes and a cough should really knock them silly." She bent her elbows and wiggled her whole body on top of his, pleased at his response. "U'mm, you've really earned this."

"Well I'll be ..."

"Screwed ... now shut up and enjoy it!"

Operation Turkey Shoot, as the entrapment mission to Cookeville came to be called, was delayed an additional week by bad weather. Limited as they were to a few small external meteorological instruments, the Base lacked much in the way of accurate weather prediction. A break finally appeared, and warm rains melted most of the accumulated snow

from the area. Yet, the best estimates that anyone
was willing to make gave the team only three or four
days of clear conditions.

Pisgah kept the team of seven busy during the
delay, as Turkey Shoot was clearly a Military mission, for all the hopes of the Science and Engineering
Departments. Erlanger and Delano suffered through
refresher courses in tactics and survival. Lori, to their
consternation, actually seemed to enjoy them—perhaps
because such exercises were a welcome physical
change from her usual research work. The four young
scientists and engineers, two men and two women,
who were the specialists in the anti-Ceejay devices,
complained about Pisgah's training as well. The stern-
faced Cherokee ignored all such gripes. Erlanger knew
that he wouldn't have approved the other four, if
Pisgah hadn't found them as proficient with conventional weapons as they were with the newly-discovered
secrets of alien technology.

For his part, Erlanger enjoyed the sessions with
Mac and the other physicists. He and Delano spent
long hours in trying to learn as much as possible
from the Xavier disks. Mac bobbed in and out of
their meetings, always cheerful and full of new speculations. Unfortunately, no one could assure the team
that all Ceejay weapons would be disabled by the
force projectors. While the scientists had been unable
to duplicate the Ceejay protective shields thus far,
they did believe the projectors would be effective
against the aircars and the aliens' individual belly-
pack bubbles.

Once the weather finally cleared, the mission got
off to a good start. Their packs were heavy; no way
stations were available along their planned route.

Everyone took his or her turn with one of the two
light metal carts, as well. While the three cone-shaped
force projectors and the radio transmitter did not

mass more than a man, they were bulky in their waterproof plastic wrappings and it would have taken two people to carry each one, without the carts. And the necessary electrical accessories—the storage batteries, the efficient little steam-powered generator—were too much for a packboard. Thus, as they left the hidden south cave entrance, and cut across open country to Route 58, there were times when two or three others had to aid the one at the handlebars of the pushcarts. Once the team reached the old highway beyond the ruins of Oak Ridge, however, they traveled relatively easily.

A few miles east of the ruins of Harriman, they picked up the old interstate highway, and turned west through the brown, rolling hills. As expected, ancient floods had washed out sections of the concrete bridges around Harriman, but the water was low this time of year, and they forded the breaks in the highway without difficulty. Right on schedule, on the afternoon of their fifth day of march, they reached the highway exit for Cookeville.

Pisgah kicked over an old aluminum sign, and nodded. "S. Jefferson Ave." they all read in sun-faded green letters. The Cherokee consulted a paper map, and pointed to the northeast. Once again, Virginia Haywood had found gold in the old Base records. For many years before the Collapse, Tennessee Technological University had shared research facilities with laboratories at Oak Ridge, and Virginia had found detailed information about the former campus in the files. "Can't be more'n five klicks," Pisgah said. "We'll sleep under a roof tonight."

"Maybe," Delano muttered, as he and Erlanger shared the handlebars on one of the carts. The bicycle tire on the right side had a slow leak again, but Erlanger thought they could make their destination without stopping to patch it.

"All of a sudden, you like camping out?" Erlanger asked.

"No, man. But look around you. Pre-Collapse, Cookeville boasted 25-30,000. Look at it now. We'll be lucky to find an intact roof, let alone much of anything on the old campus."

He had a point. As they came down a small hill, the ruins were some of the worst Erlanger had ever seen. Some time in the past, a forest fire had spread through the area—perhaps caused by lightning, perhaps by alien attack. Only debris-filled basements and a few lonely brick chimneys lined the broad, trash-covered street. New growth was plentiful, as always, but brush, scrub oak, and thin locust predominated, amidst the blackened stumps of what had once been stately trees.

Erlanger was about to voice his agreement with Delano, when Pisgah signaled for silence. He should have known better. Given the history of the area, they had to be alert for scavenging outlaws. Gently, he and Delano pulled their M-22s from the top of the cart, and clicked the thumb safeties.

Only the chill wind, and a few nonmigratory birds, replied to their vigilance. They turned past the collapsed multistory buildings around the town square, and continued north along what their maps called Dixie Avenue. After fifteen more minutes, they passed the worst of the fire damage, and Pisgah quietly began to point out landmarks on their left. Large, open areas of cracked asphalt and concrete were dotted with rusted automobile hulks at the sides of a square of red-brick buildings. Pisgah gestured for the group to close up around him. "That should be Quentin Hall behind us, and we're looking at what's left of the Periodicals Library." Erlanger nodded, for they all had memorized the maps.

As Delano handed off the cart to the blonde physicist, Erlanger began to appreciate the size of the former science and engineering campus. He was amazed that so much ground had once been devoted solely to education, even though he knew that this hadn't been one of the country's largest universities. From the campuses in Cincinnati, he expected close clusters of tall buildings, not acres and acres of what must have once been open areas, tree-lined paths, and—to him, that most strange concept—parking lots.

"Christ," the stocky redhead from Engineering said, "somebody really torched those libraries. Doesn't look like Ceejay blasting either."

They moved down the leaf-covered road to where the Whitson Memorial Library, now an empty X-shaped shell of blackened brick, shielded them from the worst of the near-freezing wind. Lori stood between Erlanger and Delano, and shook her head sadly. "Imagine the information those wrecks once held. Goddamned Luddites!"

"Who?" Erlanger asked.

"Near as we can figure," Delano answered for her, "the Beaks didn't destroy most of the libraries in the country, most of the knowledge bases. Good ol' *Homo sap.* did that for them, during and after the Collapse. Fear and ignorance, my friend, do it every time. The big cities cleared out first, mainly for the lack of food, but rural areas like Cookeville probably could have gone on just fine. It was all the fault of the 'mad scientists,' don'cha see. The duplicators were seen as the technology that brought the evils to the land, so libraries, universities, and research institutes were attacked. Didn't matter even when the word went out about the true source of the duplicators. By then it was too late. We'd fallen for the Trojan horse from the stars, and the crazies brought down the fabled towers of Ilium . . ."

Delano fell silent and blushed, when he realized

that everybody was staring at him. "Tom, I never realized you were a poet," Lori said softly.

Pisgah coughed, and broke their rough circle. "Let's move out. You know the drill. If it's still in any kind of shape, we want to set up our base in Bartoo Hall, then see which one of the former engineering labs looks like the best bet for the trap. Keep a sharp eye out for any human sign, any newer than 80 years, anyway." He moved on around the ruins of the libraries, and the rest followed.

After a few moments, they had to stop and reorient, for the once-open main quadrangle was overgrown with trees and vines. Through the stark, brown branches at the north end of the long field, Erlanger could see a large and surprisingly intact three-story building with white pillars and a tilted, greyish-white tower on top. As he paused to check his own map, the wind gusted in from the east, and he heard bells. All turned their heads, as distinct, melodious tones filled the eerie silence.

"Be damned," Pisgah muttered, as he pointed to the west and moved off. "The Derryberry Hall carillon survived."

"Sheesh!" Delano wore his usual grin. "Probably some venerated old geezer whose ghost still haunts this place."

The next four days were full of heavy labor, as the team worked to clear the basement of Clement Hall, and the nearby parking lot on 12th Street. Back at Base, the original plan had called for them to lure the Ceejays down onto one of the intramural fields or into the football stadium, but all fields were heavily tree-covered. Once on location, Pisgah thought the parking lot was a better potential landing site. The three projectors were set up in a triangle, therefore, with the base toward the former stadium. The old buildings around the parking lot gave them a covered field of fire for their conventional weapons as well.

Erlanger grunted as he shifted a rotted beam, and began to load tumbled bricks into his cart. "Don't see why we have to pretty the place up quite so much," he said to the engineer who worked on some old equipment on the other side of the basement. He worried about Lori. She and Delano were on patrol, and even though no signs of recent activity—human or alien—had been discovered, he would feel a lot better when she returned.

"We're supposed to make this look like a working lab," the other said, his voice echoing from the bare concrete walls. "Otherwise, only one Beak would poke his bill in, and then scram. We want him to call the whole crew out of the aircar." The thin man chuckled, and wiped dust from his high forehead. "At least Pisgah hasn't asked us to get any of this old crap up and running. The guts of this scintillation counter aren't good for anything but mouse nests."

"Could have fooled me." Erlanger laughed in return. "Far as I know, that's the milk protein analyzer you guys hauled back from the College of Agriculture yesterday." He grunted as he pushed his load up the improvised ramp over the old entry staircase.

"Great!" the man shouted at his back. "If we can fool you, we just may be able to fool the damn featherheads."

By the time night fell, the technical specialists were satisfied, and Pisgah took a final tour around the area, then announced that he was also pleased with the trap. Delano mounted a short dipole FM antenna on the roof for the radio, and set up the transmitter in the second dummy lab that they created in the basement of Clement Hall. The steam generator had performed perfectly, and all batteries for the force projectors were at full charge. Erlanger still marveled at how little energy those weapons needed, once McKay had found the way to jump universes the way the Ceejays did.

"Dawn will be about 7:10," Pisgah said, as the team huddled around their makeshift woodstove in the east corner of Bartoo Hall. "I want everybody in position by 8 a.m. Delano will turn on the radio, and haul his ass out of there at 8:15. Check your watches." He paused and held up his left wrist to the fading light from the high, broken windows. "By my mark, the time is now 6:49 . . . mark."

Erlanger and Lori moved off together. By unspoken agreement, they had slept separate from the others, although not so many rooms away that they couldn't hear the person on guard duty, if necessary. In the light of the small flashlight, they unrolled their sleeping bags and zipped them together.

Chapter

EIGHTEEN

With almost serious formality, Erlanger shook Delano's hand. Then, he moved off toward his own position, the thick grove of trees at the west end of the roughly-cleared parking lot. He and Lori had shared a quick kiss a few minutes earlier, and she was already on her way to the south end of the football bleachers. In the grey light of morning, he considered asking Pisgah to change their assignments, to put him with Lori, but she talked him out of it. Her job was to provide covering fire for the dark-haired physicist who manned the force projector site below that white wedge of concrete.

Despite the implicit danger that an actual aircar would represent, he hoped they wouldn't have to wait long for the radio transmissions to attract Ceejay attention. The ground under his knees was damp and cold, and the dark clouds that covered the southern sky threatened rain, at least—if not sleet or snow.

In the basement "lab," Delano checked the repeating tape loop one last time, and chuckled at the strange words that the little transmitter would beam to the north. "Birddog Base, this is Cupcake One, over ... read you five by ... we need more supplies for ..." A short period of static followed, as if the equipment malfunctioned, then more of what they hoped was an intriguing message continued.

As he shifted his weight, Erlanger searched his hiding place for something he could sit on. He watched a man walk across the far corner of the lot. Delano held up his right thumb and waved as he hurried from the phony lab in the basement, and took up his own firing position. Delano disappeared from view, as he crouched down behind the fallen wall at the east end of Bruner Hall. At the other end of that red-brick ruin, Pisgah and the woman from Engineering stood ready with another force projector.

Erlanger stared down at his hands, at the gloved fingers that clutched the plastic stock of his automatic rifle. Then, with a start, he realized his failing, and began to search the sky. Was that something, way off to the right? He lowered his head, and rubbed his eyes. As he turned to stare up again, he caught movement out of the corner of his eye, and swore. "What the hell's the matter with those idiots!" The blonde physicist and the thin engineer he had worked with the day before were walking up the street toward the east corner of the parking lot. They held hands, as if their only concerns were for each other.

Pisgah will skin them alive, Erlanger thought. Lucky the Colonel can't see them yet from his position. Those two are supposed to be on the third projector in Foster. He looked from the couple to their assigned position, in the remains of the burned-out building almost directly across from his vantage point. Even if they run, he thought, it'll take them five minutes to work their way up that shaky staircase to the projector, and that's got to be at least ten minutes past what Pisgah ordered. What's with those two, anyway, some romance starting? He shook his head, both angry at the young couple, and a little envious.

He scanned the area between his position, that of Pisgah, and the couple's destination. Although the team had cleared quite a bit of the former parking lot, many trees still poked through the cracked asphalt. They just might make it, he thought. No reason to expect anything to happen for hours yet, and Pisgah could be looking the other way. He wouldn't have bet a lot on the Cherokee's lack of vigilance, but maybe the new lovers would escape his notice.

The couple lost their foolish gamble to a far more serious threat. Just as the blonde appeared in the open again, Erlanger heard a shout. He thought it sounded like "seven o'clock high," but he was never sure. He saw the couple look up, and he turned to his right as well. His mouth fell open. From the southwest, approaching so rapidly that its size seemed to double as he watched, a Ceejay aircar made directly for the parking lot. He stared upward, his head turning to follow the aliens' trajectory, then he remembered what he had been watching moments earlier. The blonde and her lover were just disappearing into the staircase as he glanced across the lot. Had they been seen?

In seconds, he thought he had his answer, an answer he didn't like. The aircar didn't land, although it hovered almost exactly over the spot they had hoped the Ceejays would choose. A blue haze seemed to envelop the alien vehicle, and he knew that the aircar force bubble had been activated. The machine dropped to a foot from the ground, and a pear-shaped hatch opened in its rounded, grey side.

In rapid succession, four heavily-armed *Cweom-jik* males jumped to the asphalt. The aliens, their colorful crests bobbing, moved awkwardly, a slow waddle. All of them wore the red bellypacks that signaled personal force bubbles, although Erlanger could not be sure that the individual protective units were active. As the four Ceejays began to spread out, their long necks twisted rapidly back and forth. Clearly they were looking for targets. The aircar, still obviously occupied, began to rise. As he sighted on the third Beak, a green-crested male who was moving in his direction, Erlanger swore silently. This wasn't the plan; the aircar could provide deadly cover fire from altitude.

Suddenly, the flattened grey sphere began to wobble in the air, to drop. Erlanger couldn't be sure, but the blue haze of the protective field seemed to flicker as well. At least one of their own force projectors must be operating. He thought it must be the projector in Foster, the one the couple was late in reaching. They must have switched it on the second they got there—probably not even aiming in their panic. As if reading his mind, two of the aliens swung toward the west end of Foster Hall, and began firing their beam weapons. Flame and powdered brick erupted from that sagging old building.

"We're in for it now," Erlanger muttered, as he opened up on the Ceejay in his sights. "The damn Beaks must have some way of detecting our projector's field, they turned right toward it. Either they were tipped off by the aircar, or they've got detection instruments on those chest straps." Unaware that he was talking to himself, he changed a spent magazine for a full one, and continued firing. Others were firing as well, but none of the Ceejays appeared to be wounded.

He flinched as the deadly red line of an alien beam cut through the trees above his head. His eyes began to water, his nose filled with the odor of cordite and wood smoke. Through increasingly obscured vision, he saw the aircar tilt and fall.

The sound of the crash echoed off distant brick walls. One, then a second Ceejay seemed to explode in a burst of grey feathers. Their force bubbles were out! The other two Underground projectors must be focused. "McKay, bless your shiny little head, the damn things really work!" Erlanger found himself on his feet, shouting, and firing. He paused to reload, and grabbed for a gas grenade at his belt.

At first, his fumbling fingers encountered the smooth roundness of a force grenade, one of the two on his belt. No, not that, not while a chance remained to capture a functioning aircar. As he crouched low and edged past the old truck frame, he recalled his painful first demonstration of those electro-weak grenades. Wysocki had given his life in that effort. His gloved hand continued to search his belt for the longer cylinders of gas, as he squinted through the spreading fog before him. Obviously, several gas grenades had already been used—probably by Pisgah or Delano. With a curse, he stuck his hand in his mouth and wrenched off the thin leather glove, then filled that hand with the correct grenade. He spat out the glove, and used his teeth again on the grenade pin. As the small cylinder began to hiss, he realized that he couldn't throw worth a damn with his left hand, and quickly swapped with his rifle. He made a powerful overhand lob, and watched the canister trail bluish smoke as it sailed out into the lot.

Erlanger poked his head over the flaky shell of a truck fender. He tried to get his bearings. There—the aircar, at a bit of an angle, about thirty feet away. He could just make out two Ceejay bodies. Where the hell were the other Beaks? For that matter, where were the rest of the rebel team? He winced as two red beams cut through the increasing smoke, but both were aimed away from him. Just as they had feared, the alien beam weapons were still operational, still deadly. As if from a great distance, he heard a familiar *wump-crack*. One of their team had used a force grenade.

Then, a far brighter red slash cut across the lot to his left. From the aircar! Despite the crash, its more powerful weapons were still active. And it was firing toward the football stadium, toward Lori! He jumped to his feet, and began shooting, almost at random, his training forgotten. From his left, he heard a shout: "Erlanger, get your ass down!" Pisgah's voice, Pisgah's familiar commands halted his mad rush, and he dropped prone in the dusty grit and damp leaves on the cracked asphalt.

Sporadic automatic rifle fire continued, but it all seemed to come from behind him. He raised his head just in time to see another massive red beam angle across his back. He twisted his neck, and saw the west end of Bruner Hall explode. What man had built, what time and the elements had only wounded, disappeared in microseconds of alien wrath. He watched in horror, as the grey aircar seemed to shake like a wet dog, then right itself to hover a few inches off the ground. He heard a noise to his right, and rolled. His rifle butt caught in a tear in his jacket, a long ragged rip that had occurred without his notice.

"Easy, Brent, I'm on your side." Pisgah's face appeared around the side of a mound of trash. The Cherokee's black hair was covered with dust, and a trickle of blood crossed his coppery forehead above his left eye. "You in one piece?"

"Yeah. How about the others?"

Pisgah shook his head. "Don't look good. You saw the projector where I was get it just now. Don't think the other two are still operational either, from the looks of that aircar. Damn, they came too quick.

They had to be on patrol very close. Almost as if they were on the lookout for our bunch, at least for something high-tech." He spat and wiped his mouth on his sleeve. "Delano's back there, to the right about 20 meters, behind a couple of singed oaks. He took a hit in the side, burned pretty bad. At least he got the shitbird that downed him. You got a count on the four Beaks that dropped out first?"

Erlanger couldn't think, couldn't answer. Tom badly hurt? And what about Lori? Pisgah hadn't said anything about Lori.

"Erlanger!"

"Huh? Ah, sorry, Billy Lee. Two Beaks over there. They gotta be dead. Funny, I never thought their blood would be red, just like ours. But what about everybody else?" He knuckled sudden sweat from his eyes, yet the burning sensation continued. Must be the smoke, he thought, the gas grenades. He looked around quickly, and was surprised at how the air had cleared. He noticed that the wind had picked up, and his bare left hand felt numb.

"Good," Pisgah said, as if he hadn't heard Erlanger's other concerns. "Pretty sure I nailed one with a grenade, so with the other that Delano got, that's four. We still got a chance here, even if the original plan is shot to hell. How many force grenades you got left?"

Erlanger wasn't listening, his thoughts were on the far end of the lot, on the grey concrete bleachers where he'd last seen Lori, so few minutes, so many centuries ago.

"Damnit, Erlanger, pull your head out of your ass! We've still got a job to do here, and we just may be able to pull it off. I figure we can lob smoke from two sides, then creep up close enough to get a force grenade inside. Worked for Wysocki, ought to work for us. If we can't capture the damn thing, sure as hell we're not letting the Beaks get off in that aircar. They know too much now, know we got weapons with teeth."

At mention of Wysocki, at the horrible blast of heat that had turned the bearded man into a column of running fire, Erlanger felt bile fill his throat. Had that been Lori's fate, too? His teeth clenched, as he hunched up on his knees. Without thought, his hand reached for a gas grenade, and he stumbled to his feet. He drew the canister to his mouth, and jerked out the pin, his knuckles white as his hand clenched the arming lever.

"No, Erlanger! Not yet, wait for me to get in position on the other side . . ."

Pisgah's words passed over him, as he moved toward the dull grey craft. He didn't hear, didn't pause. But another heard, perhaps understood. In the rounded, dark hatch of the aircar, an *een* appeared. The tall brown Ceejay pointed a strange object at him. It didn't look like their usual beam weapons, but he wouldn't have stopped, even if it was. With measured strides, as if in a trance, he advanced on the alien vehicle. He didn't hear Pisgah curse, and scramble to the side, to get a clear shot at the female. "Drop, you fool!"

He didn't fall, but he did stop, as if an invisible wall had suddenly appeared in front of him. He was struck smartly in the chest by some grey object, and his muscles simply stopped working. He could still move his eyes, could take puzzled note of the thin wire that seemed to stretch back to the Ceejay in the hatch, but his limbs, his entire body from chest to feet, were immobilized. His vision seemed to blur. Funny, he thought, Lori came to take prisoners, and the Beaks did too. Pisgah's going to be angry. Pisgah won't want us to be taken alive. Should be the other way around. Lori's supposed to take them alive, study them. Feel so strange . . . Lori . . .

He was confused. His eyes wouldn't track, wouldn't focus. Half-conscious, Erlanger watched two Ceejays drag him into the aircar, where they stood him against a row of oddly-shaped seats. Some time later, perhaps only minutes, the two returned with an equally-paralyzed Pisgah, whose left arm dangled at an unnatural angle. The man's face was pale, locked in a grimace of pain. Then the two aliens returned with Delano. The wiry tech also had a grey lump on his chest, with a thin cable that ran beyond Erlanger's line of sight.

"Uggh . . . Tom?" His own croaky voice startled him. He was surprised that he could speak at all, but he discovered that he could move his head just a little. The rest of his body, like that of his friends, was still out of his control. "Tom, are you . . . can you hear me?" Delano's eyes were closed, and he made no response.

Erlanger slowly studied the wounded man, and an involuntary moan escaped his lips as he saw the shallow, ragged movement of his chest, the charred mass of jacket, shirt, and flesh that was Delano's left side. His eyes moved to Pisgah, who met his gaze, and with an effort, shook his head slightly.

"Anybody else? Lori? Pisgah, if you can understand me, what about Lori? Are they picking her up too?"

Pisgah made a brief negative movement again, then winced in obvious pain, as the *een* brushed past him roughly. She stopped beside Erlanger, and bent her long neck down to fix him with one dark eye. Without warning, the alien's wing slammed into his face. He sensed a warmth, a wetness at the corner of his mouth.

"You no talk, *zlekk*. No talk now. Later, you talk

good." Her speech surprised him almost as much as the blow. So few of them spoke English. He understood her well enough, despite the trill whistles that extended her consonants. Her actions spoke even louder, and she slapped him again. As much as possible, given the constraints of the strange grey lump on his chest, he bent his head in the submissive gesture he had seen Milford Mayors use all his life.

He heard movement, shrill patterns of Ceejay speech. Out of the side of his lowered eyes, he saw the other two return—a *kepwoi* and another *een*. They dragged no more humans with them but closed the hatch. He wanted to cry out, to feel a scrawny, feathered neck between his hands. He struggled without motion, his nerves alight with thwarted impulses. Through pain-clouded eyes, he realized that his right hand still clutched a primed gas grenade. He moaned in frustration, as he realized how confident the aliens were in their immobilizing weapon. The Underground's grandiose trap had been completely reversed. He couldn't twitch a finger on the grenade lever. What if the Ceejays could overcome their conditioning somehow? There was no way he could reach the suicide pill in his pocket. He hadn't even considered . . . if he did break down, not only this mission would be lost, but the Base, the whole Underground movement . . .

While his mind filled with anguished thoughts, the two females moved forward in the aircar. Within seconds his stomach told him—with the sensation he once found so novel in the Base elevators—that they were air-borne. Somehow, he didn't know why, he felt that they were heading north, toward the football stadium, toward Lori.

Without warning, with no explanation, the aircar lurched and dropped. His arm swung up, and he realized that he was suddenly free. The paralyzing force gripped him again, but was gone in two heart beats. He staggered against the alien seat, his legs weak, as shrill whistles and clicks came from the front of the craft. The aircar spun to the left, and he crashed into Pisgah, who groaned loudly and clutched at his dangling left arm. As Erlanger moved his right hand to steady Pisgah, he realized that he still held the grenade, that now he could use it. The canister hissed as he tossed it forward, then he was thrown off his feet, as the aircar met the earth with stunning force.

Dazed, bruised, but still mobile, Erlanger leaped at the *kepwoi* who appeared in front of him. The alien was bent backward in the narrow aisle, as his weight pressed the *kepwoi* against the edge of a low shelf of metal. He heard thin, hollow bones snap, and groped for the Ceejay's neck.

"Erlanger, down!" He twisted to the side, almost completely on top of the stunned Ceejay, and saw another gas grenade fly past. With a savage grin, he beat the limp alien's head against the craft's wall, and looked back. Pisgah was on the floor, in the middle of the aisle. Delano had fallen over the last seat, but he couldn't tell whether the wounded man was still breathing. Blue, eye-searing smoke filled the whole compartment, and he couldn't see into the pilot area where the two females must still be.

Pisgah coughed and tried to rise, but his broken arm—the white of bone now protruding from torn flesh above his elbow—left him almost crippled with pain. "It's up to you, Brent. I'm out of it." Pisgah coughed again, and Erlanger found his own breathing labored, his throat raw. "I think the bastards are unconscious by now; probably couldn't use their force bubbles or beamers in here even if they weren't." He tried to drag himself up with his right arm, then fell back. "Got to get the door open, Brent, or we're not going to be breathing much longer, either."

He stumbled forward in the choking smoke, moving more by touch than vision. Dimly, through tear-filled eyes, he could see the two females, their bodies slumped against the backs of low chairs. Neither Ceejay moved, and he pushed one aside and studied the control panel. Under far better viewing conditions, he had seen that panel many times in the Xavier disk diagrams. But so much of the function of those oddly-pebbled and twisted shapes, those thin colored stalks, remained a mystery. He didn't remember anyone even speculating about door controls.

Saw-toothed bands of light were pulsating at different frequencies, and from somewhere on the ceiling, a low warbling sound signaled the aircar's mechanical distress. He coughed, almost doubling over as the irritating gas reached deep into his lungs, and looked out the window above the controls. He was startled as he recognized the concrete triangular end wall of the football bleachers. They had almost crashed into that massive structure. He shook his head and rubbed at his eyes. There, on the left, that oval pattern that had been dark on the Xavier diagrams. Here, on an active control panel, yellow light outlined the entire thing. If that represented the whole craft, then the pulsing section ... Hesitantly, he touched, then pushed firmly. At his back, he heard a grating sound, and the section of the panel he had pushed changed from yellow to a deep blue.

He turned around, stumbled over the outstretched leg of one of the *eens*, and shouted back into the cabin. "Pisgah, did that do ... ?" He could hardly see the other two men, but he had his answer. The pear-shaped hatch stood open—only about halfway, but that was more than enough. He hurried to Pisgah's side, and found the Cherokee barely conscious. Mindful of the broken arm, he dragged him to the open hatch. The aircar rested at a steep angle, and the drop to the ground was only about a foot.

As cold rain hit him in the face, Pisgah revived, and coughed. Erlanger made him as comfortable as he could, against the smooth side of the aircar, then returned for Delano.

Delano didn't look good. His face was pale and cool, and his breathing was so shallow that Erlanger could hardly feel it.

"How's his pulse?"

"Rapid. Gotta be over 120."

"Yeah, figured he's in shock. Get his head down, feet up. Try a little CPR, just the mouth breathing, don't lean on that chest. Gotta cover him best we can. I'd give him my jacket, but don't figure I can get it off this arm. You got any morphine?"

As he tucked his own jacket around Delano, and leaned over to breathe into the man's lungs, he suddenly remembered the first-aid kit that they all carried in the thigh pocket of their pants. After a few minutes, a little color returned to his friend's face. He stopped helping Delano breathe, and fumbled with the flap on his thigh pocket. He turned back to Pisgah, as he opened the thin aluminum case. "How much should I give him?"

"Not Delano, you idiot. Stick that damn ampoule in *my* arm. Don't you remember anything? Morphine's the last thing you want to give a man in shock!" At Erlanger's stricken look, his voice softened, and Pisgah reached out and squeezed his friend's empty hand. "Sorry, Brent, just the pain talking. You're doing one hell of a job, but this arm is like to kill me. Son of a bitch *kepwoi* kicked me after I was paralyzed. Hope you strangled the shitbird. Would have doped myself while you were busy with Delano, but I landed on that side when the aircar hit, and mashed the hell out of my kit."

As he followed his trainer's instructions, Erlanger felt his hands move almost separate from his body. His mind seemed to float, as if some secret switch had been thrown in his head, as if all emotion was cut off. He wanted to finish treating Pisgah properly, to set and splint the arm, but he was reminded forcefully that time was short.

"Got to tape up those Beaks, first. That gas was only supposed to knock them out." Pisgah fell silent and panted as he regained his feet. Through clenched teeth, he continued: "Arm's going numb, I can make it. I can guard your back, at least. Got tape?"

Erlanger fumbled in his jacket pocket for the fiberglass-reinforced plastic tape that they had all been issued ten days ago. Strapping tape, Delano had called it. The Old Timers used it for sealing packages. The Military planners thought it had other uses, practical survival uses, and it was one of the easiest ways to tie up a man—or an alien—quite securely. Pisgah gestured, and he took the roll of tape from the other's pocket, as well as the pistol for the holster at his hip. Then, smoke grenades in hand, they reentered the tilted aircar.

Once inside, Pisgah put down his smoke grenade, and pulled the pin on a round force grenade instead. Erlanger looked at him in surprise, then nodded. He understood. Their roles couldn't be reversed again; they either remained in control, or men and Ceejays all died together.

Pisgah's caution proved unnecessary. The *kepwoi* was dead, its feathers slack. Erlanger couldn't tell whether the gas, or his hands, had done the job. He didn't really care. The two females were still breathing, however, and he secured them quickly and efficiently. He fumbled a bit with their chest straps, before he found the release mechanism. Even well taped, he wanted to make sure they had no unfamiliar weapons. He dragged their limp, unconscious bodies into the main cabin of the aircar. There, Lori finally has her specimens, he thought. Lori! How could he . . . He whirled toward the hatch, and almost collided with Pisgah.

"Good work, Brent. Now you can set my arm; see to Tom."

As if sensing his troubled thoughts, Pisgah led him outside, and made calm suggestions about finding pieces of wood for a splint. Once again, a cloud seemed to settle over his emotions, and he followed directions numbly. Pisgah didn't even cry out when Erlanger put his foot in his armpit and pulled. The bone ends grated, but seemed to settle into place. His hands worked swiftly, with antiseptic, pressure bandage, tape. Then, he turned to Delano, found no change.

"Somebody taught you well," Pisgah said with a forced grin. "Now we scout around, figure how we're going to get out of here. You want me to check over there, where Lori . . . ?"

Erlanger stood, and looked around the parking lot, looked at the sky. The rain had increased, and the cold drops felt good in his reddened eyes. Smoke drifted slowly from the blasted ruin that had been Foster Hall, and a bright fire licked at the collapsed roof beside the other rebel projector site. He looked back up. The cloud cover was too heavy to see the sun clearly, but the lighting indicated that it was still early morning. Could all this battle, this death, have taken less than an hour? Numbly, he shook his head, and followed Pisgah toward the stadium, toward Lori.

"Feldmeyer. At least the poor bastard never knew what hit him." Pisgah leaned against the concrete wall, and shook his head. He added nothing as Erlanger gagged and threw up the remainder of his breakfast. The torso and legs of the dark-haired physicist lay in a rain-diluted puddle of blood beside a shattered pile of concrete blocks. Everything above the shoulders was missing, cut clean away by the powerful beam from the aircar.

Erlanger straightened up and wiped his mouth with his pocket handkerchief, then let the soiled white cloth drop, as if his hands no longer worked.

"No projector ... should have been about here." Pisgah continued talking, as he walked around the end of a twisted, rusty pipe. "Mother of God, will you ... what a woman! Erlanger, maybe you'd better not ..."

Pushed by a cold wind at his back that seemed to settle in the pit of his stomach, Erlanger moved around the low wall to where Pisgah stood. His feet carried him forward mechanically. He knew what he would see, but he didn't want to turn his eyes that way, didn't want to *know*.

He heard the gentle humming before he saw anything. His gaze traveled slowly up the short flight of cracked steps. The first thing to register in his numbed brain was the thin, aluminum leg of the force projector tripod. That leg was twisted, bent. At first, he ignored the pale hand that hung beside the bent metal. His eyes moved up higher, to the projector cone itself, the active anti-Ceejay device that still operated somehow. Try as he might, he couldn't ignore the slumped figure behind the projector. Wait. Was that movement? He rushed past Pisgah and kneeled. Chips of rough concrete dug through his pants, but he never felt them. "Lori, Lori, honey, it's ..."

"I'm sorry, Brent. But she's gone. Pure guts, that one, to have got that projector back up, condition she was in. Must of been grazed by the beam, then tossed back by the secondary explosion. Pulled herself up enough to point the projector, to bring us down. She saved our asses, saved the whole operation." Pisgah paused, aware that he was talking too much.

As he pulled her cool face next to his cheek, Erlanger finally noticed the stickiness. But he didn't really feel it; it wasn't her. The horrible blackened chest could not be part of the woman he loved. Her face seemed to smile back at him. He looked up at Pisgah. Rain, perhaps salty tears, flowed down the creases around the hard man's mouth. "Billy Lee, why does she have her rifle strapped to her leg? Just like the boards taped to your arm, Billy Lee. Does Lori's leg hurt, Billy Lee?"

"Not any more, son, not any more." Pisgah looked away. He surveyed the still, crumbling campus. He watched flames leap from the fallen roof of one building to the brown leaves of a 50-year-old red oak. "Erlanger ... come on, Brent, we've got to ..." He had spoken softly, but realized that no one was listening. He climbed the steps and took the other's arm. Erlanger jerked away. "Damnit, Brent, move out. We're not finished here. Got to check on the rest of the team, although from the looks of those buildings, we won't even find pieces. Time for mourning comes later. This mission isn't over."

No response. The Colonel sighed and swung his flat hand. The crack of his palm against Erlanger's wet flesh sounded like a gun shot. The younger man jumped up, and swung his own fists wildly. Pisgah dodged easily, stepped back. With only one functioning arm, he was unable to restrain the wild man. Finally, like a rag doll with rent seams, Erlanger hung limp. He stared, with eyes of stone. "C'mon, Brent, we've got to go."

"Yeah, I know, I know ... but we can't just leave her here. I'll carry her back to ..."

"To where? All the way back to Base? We can't even take the time to bury her, Brent. We don't know if those Ceejays got off some kind of signal. This place could be crawling with Beaks before long."

Erlanger continued to ignore him. He turned and picked up Lori's body. Disturbed by the awkward feel of the splinted leg, he put the body down gently, and peeled off the strapping tape, released the rifle. Then, he picked up the remains of the only woman he'd ever truly loved, and began a slow march to the aircar.

Pisgah stared at his burdened back, and swore in the two languages he knew. "Erlanger, what the hell do you think you're doing? Get your head back on straight. I'm sorry as hell about Lori. Hell, I'm sorry about the whole lot, but that doesn't change anything." He ran to catch up with the plodding man, and grabbed Erlanger's arm from behind. "Look, I'll go this far, all right. If the carts are still intact back at Bartoo, we'll carry her out of town, give her a good burial among the trees. Need a cart for Delano, anyway."

On some level, Erlanger was quite rational, deadly serious and calm. "We're flying back," he said, as if flying alien machines was something he did routinely.

"Don't be an ass! That was a long shot, even had the original plan worked. Now, shit, the specialists who could do that are ashes and dead meat. Even if Feldmeyer or one of the others survived, it's still not in the cards. The way we came down, that aircar probably has seen its last cloud. You think the Beaks are going to tell you how to fix it?"

Their stumbling march had reached the side of the machine in question. Erlanger laid the body down gently, and moved to Delano. He couldn't be sure, but he thought his friend's breathing was better, stronger. Now Delano's face felt feverish, and he thought that was a more positive sign. He turned to Pisgah, and spread his blood-stained hands wide. "I can fly it, Billy Lee, if it'll fly at all. Even if I have to choke the keys out of these *eens*, I'll fly it. Tom will never make it otherwise. And Lori goes home."

"Sweet Jesus, I believe you will. All right, you stay with Delano, pump him full of that antibiotic-steroid complex in your kit. I'll check the other projector sites, just for the record, then swing around for our packs and the big first-aid kit, if they haven't gone up in smoke." Pisgah looked around the immediate area. "Where the hell was I when they paralyzed me with that grey thing? My rifle's got to be over there, some-place." He frowned, then turned back to Erlanger, and pulled a force grenade for the other's belt. "Just in case we get more company. You look sharp, check the tape on those females inside. Last thing we do, we've got the destroy that functioning projector. We can't leave things like that here. If the Beaks did get off a radio signal . . ."

The Cherokee turned quickly and looked back over his shoulder, then swore as his broken arm twisted in the makeshift sling. "Getting slow in my old age. Our own radio, that dummy lab looks to be still standing. We're still putting out that phony transmission . . ."

He hurried off, his gait lopsided as he favored his arm. Erlanger felt Delano's pulse, then carried Lori's body inside the aircar. He looked around for some-thing to cover, to wrap her with, and after a few minutes of fumbling experimentation with the latch of a wall cabinet, he found what looked like a thin rug of some silky material. Satisfied, he moved forward to check the noisy, flashing control panel. Neither *een* stirred as he passed their trussed forms.

Within a few minutes, Erlanger thought he knew what some of the strange controls would do, although he had yet to touch them. He did succeed in cutting off the eerie warbling tone, and some of the sawtooth lights had stopped flashing. The temperature seemed to have gone up inside the pilot cabin, and he hoped that was merely the Ceejays' normal heating system. The warmer air would be good for Tom, he thought, and he broke off his experimentation to carry the injured man inside.

He felt as if he was waking from a bad dream, but knew that the nightmare was real. As his mind cleared, he recalled Pisgah's worry about the intact projector, and began to walk back to the stadium steps. No reason to destroy it; he could carry that back. Once out in the open, he saw Pisgah across the end of the parking lot. He waved and shouted: "Going to get that projector." Pisgah nodded and waved back, then headed toward Clement Hall and their all-too-effective radio transmitter.

Pisgah didn't even have time to curse his own stupidity. The searing red beam stabbed in, through his stomach, before he even saw the badly wounded *kepwoi* huddled in the basement doorway. He crumpled, out of sight of the alien, behind a pile of rotten lumber that the team had cleared from the phony lab. By reflex, his good hand moved to his stomach. He really didn't feel much pain, just slimy wetness.

"Holy Mother of God, I counted my chickens before they were dead," he grunted to himself. "Should have checked on that fourth shitbird, first thing. God-damn rookie mistake's done killed me. Hope Erlanger has the sense to stay back." Then, wrenching pain struck, and he cried out.

Across the long diagonal to the stadium, Erlanger heard the distant scream, and looked up from the projector just in time to see a second red beam cut through the timbers above Pisgah's head. Erlanger froze where he stood.

When the first spasm of intense pain passed, Pisgah

felt a lesser discomfort at his hip, and slid his right hand down to the force grenade. He grinned savagely as he struggled to lift the suddenly overweight object to his mouth. The round ring on the pin tasted bitter, and his teeth clicked on the slick metal for several long seconds before he heard the snick-click he sought.

He crawled forward slowly, a worm lubricated by his own juices, until he could just see the top of the stairs. "Father, bless me, for I have sinned," he muttered, as he gathered his last remaining strength and lurched out for his final pitch. He was dead before the round grenade bounced down the steps and reduced the male Ceejay, the transmitter, and most of Clement Hall to the flaming hell that he prayed to escape.

The trip back to Base in the pirated aircar took the longest hour in Erlanger's life. He spent a good third of that time with the controls, fumbling delicately. Slowly he gained confidence as his experiments yielded mostly expected results. The controls, the odd-shaped light displays, were apparently designed for unsophisticated users rather than technicians, for which Erlanger was most grateful.

Once he got the aircar up and moving horizontally, he managed to retrace the route they'd walked to Cookeville with minimal difficulty. The external viewscreens took a bit of getting used to, but he found I-40 easily enough, thanks to the low altitude he maintained. He moved at a relatively low speed because he had trouble relating his actions at the control panel to what was happening outside. The pear-shaped door remained stuck halfway open, which was just as well—given the high internal temperature the Ceejays regarded as normal.

Mercifully, Delano remained unconscious. The two *een* overcame the effects of the gas quickly enough—he made a mental note to pass on that information—but lay impassive throughout the trip, their bright eyes constantly fixed on him.

He tried not to think about Lori, so close but ... gone forever.

"Hang in there, Tom," he said, "almost home." The low rise that marked the Base location came into view after what seemed an eternity of standing before the control panel. From the air the winding Old Times road had not been difficult to find, but he had to concentrate fully on the controls. The slightest touch on the lever stalks might cause a disproportionate movement of the aircar.

Finally, he was directly over the Base itself. Then it hit him—how the hell was he going to get in? Surely sentries would spot the aircar as it dropped near whichever entrance he chose to use. He could count on a fast—and deadly—response to the arrival of an alien attack craft immediately outside the installation. No, he shook his head, better to set this thing down a safe distance away and slog it up the hill. Now, after all he'd been through, was not the time to risk a mistake with his own people.

He backed off a couple of miles to the west, and scanned the terrain for a hiding place. He didn't want anyone—rebel or spy, human or alien—to see the aircar too near Base. He finally settled in a steep ravine with an overhanging cliff. Silently, he congratulated himself for a safe landing. None of his passengers complained about the two bounces.

With the aircar safely grounded, he found time again to worry about Delano. His friend was still unconscious, although he did stir as Erlanger adjusted the other thin Ceejay rug-blanket he had found to cover him. Delano's fever seemed to have worsened, but he'd done all he could. Delano needed professional care as soon as possible. "I'll be back soon,

Tom," he said as he stood to go. "You're gonna be all right, I promise."

He was out the door when he thought about the *een*. After an awkward five minutes of effort, he had manhandled the two aliens out the door. He lugged them like sacks of grain, one at a time, and dropped each unceremoniously on the ground next to a small tree. Then he shoved them against the tree and used the remainder of the strapping tape to secure them to the trunk, and to one another. On humans, the wrappings would have been cruelly tight, but he didn't care. He wished no lingering doubts about where those Beaks would be, once he was out of sight.

Some time later he was in the cave through which he had first passed into the rebel stronghold, with Lori, so many months in the past. He refused to think about her now, as he had avoided that terrible pain since Cookeville. His personal suffering, his mourning for Lori, for Billy Lee, must wait—Delano, and the Underground, indeed, the entire human race, depended on his successful delivery of that aircar and the prisoners.

He was inside the cave's cool darkness before he realized the mistake he'd made. He didn't have the necessary flashlight to operate the door-signal device beyond the tight curve.

He shouted his frustration and anger in one monosyllabic burst. Suddenly, he felt drained. All that he'd gone through, only to be stopped so close, because he hadn't remembered . . . it would take him almost an hour to walk to the south entrance, and even then . . . Delano might not last that long!

Sudden light filled the room. Before he was aware of what was happening he was surrounded by armed men. He had never been so happy to face rifle barrels in his life.

*   *   *

By common agreement, the celebration was delayed until Delano was well enough to enjoy it, albeit from a wheelchair. A time for rejoicing was overdue, yet it was time for memories too.

The Ceejay aircar, camouflaged and well-hidden among the metal-rich ruins of the original Oak Ridge National Laboratory, was the subject of feverish study by McKay and his engineers. Ceejay overflights had, as expected, increased in frequency throughout the south and the midwest. Fortunately, the *Cweom-jik* gave no indication that they were aware of the location of their stolen property. The Underground had many reasons to celebrate.

Everyone not on duty—and a few who should have been—managed to crowd into the Agricultural level. Erlanger had never seen so many people in one place. The agritechs would have a lot of extra work when this mob left, but their level offered the most open space. No one worried about that today. The beer and grain alcohol flowed freely, and the safety of a few plants was the farthest thing from anyone's mind.

After many toasts and tearful reunions with friends who he'd seen only briefly in the days since his return, Erlanger was pressed to make a speech. Embarrassed, he climbed to a hastily-erected podium and stood before the portable sound pickup.

"Hello," he began, startled at the sound of his amplified voice as it echoed through the cavern. "Hello, and thank you all for coming together today. I've never been much for making speeches . . ."

He nervously cleared his throat before continuing. "There's been a lot said about me, but I want you to know anything I may have accomplished would have been impossible without those who didn't return, from Cincinnati, from Cookeville—not to mention Tom Delano." There was a short round of applause. Many cheered.

"Billy Lee Pisgah, who led the expedition to Cookeville, and who enabled Tom and me to get out alive through his sacrifice—well, we all owe him more than I can say. And Lou Feldmeyer, Karen Wolfe, Chandra Jacobs, and Ramon Alveraz . . . Ana Munoz, Eric Steuben, and Alan Wysocki—these, too, we owe."

He paused; slowly he surveyed the silent crowd in front of him. Through suddenly blurring eyes, he spotted Cleve Stearns, who stood next to Delano's wheelchair. And Peter McKay, Connie Sue, Lydia Rutledge . . . he closed his eyes, fighting back hot tears.

When he opened them, he focused on Cleve, who was smiling and giving him a thumbs up sign. Erlanger smiled back, nodded, and continued. "Most of all, I . . . all of us . . . owe one incredibly wonderful woman for . . ." The recollection, the memory was simply too painful. He mumbled a quick "Thank you," and moved off the stage.

Administrator Boone was waiting as Erlanger stepped from the wooden platform. He looked Erlanger in the eye, nodded, and clasped the younger man's hand with both of his own. Then he took his place at the microphone.

Erlanger moved to join his friends as Boone began to speak. Beside Cleve and Tom, Connie Sue waited for him, her arms open.

"Friends, brothers and sisters," Boone began quietly. "The credit for the success of this mission—and the future success of humanity—should be shared by all of us here, but the most credit is due those who made the ultimate sacrifice, those who gave their lives that others might one day live free.

"Accordingly, I announce with great sadness . . . and proud joy, that the first human null-gravity attack craft is now under construction at Mammoth Cave. She will be christened *Lorilei*."

The applause began slowly, became universal. Boone

continued finally, but Erlanger didn't hear the old man's gentle words. He was only aware of the scent, the softness of Connie Sue, who held him tightly as his tears mingled with hers. He felt right, somehow—about Connie Sue, about Lori's memory. Lori had been venerated. The Underground had its first saint.

Here is an excerpt from Fred Saberhagen's newest novel, coming in February 1986 from Baen Books:

FRED SABERHAGEN THE FRANKENSTEIN PAPERS

Chapter 1

May? 1782?

I bite the bear.

I bit the bear.

I have bitten the white bear, and the taste of its blood has given me strength. Not physical strength—that I have never lacked—but the confidence to manage my own destiny, insofar as I am able.

With this confidence, my life begins anew. That I may think anew, and act anew, from this time on I will write in English, here on this English ship. For it seems, now that I try to use that language, that my command of it is more than adequate. Though how that ever came to be, God alone can know.

How *I* have come to be, God perhaps does not know. It may be that that knowledge is, or was, reserved to one other, who has—or had—more right than God to be called my Creator.

My first object in beginning this journal is to cling to the fierce sense of purpose that has been reborn in me. My second is to try to keep myself sane. Or to restore myself to sanity, if, as sometimes seems to me likely, madness is indeed the true explanation of the situation, or condition, in which I find myself—in which I believe myself to be.

But I verge on babbling. If I am to write at all—and I must write—let me do so coherently.

I have bitten the white bear, and the blood of the bear has given me life. True enough. But if anyone who reads is to understand then I must write of other matters first.

Yes, if I am to assume this task—or therapy—of journal-keeping, then let me at least be methodical about it. A good way to make a beginning, I must believe, would be to give an objective, calm description of myself, my condition, and my surroundings. All else, I believe—I must hope—can be built from that.

As for my surroundings, I am writing this aboard a ship, using what were undoubtedly once the captain's notebook and his pencils. The captain was wise not to trust that ink would remain unfrozen.

I am quite alone, and on such a voyage as I am sure was never contemplated by the captain, or the owners, or the builders of this stout vessel, *Mary Goode*. (The bows are crusted a foot thick with ice, an accumulation perhaps of decades; but the name is plain on many of the papers in this cabin.)

A fire burns in the captain's little stove, warms my fingers as I write, but I see by a small sullen glow of sunlight emanating from the south—a direction that here encompasses most of the horizon. Little enough of that sunlight finds its way in through the cabin windows, though one of the windows is now free of glass, sealed only with a thin panel of clear ice.

In every direction lie fields of ice, a world of white unmarked by any work of man except this frozen hulk. What fate may have befallen the particular man on the floor of whose cabin I now sleep—the berth is hopelessly small—or the rest of the crew of the *Mary Goode*, I can only guess. There is no clue, or if a clue exists I am too concerned with my own condition and my own fate to look for it or think about it. I can imagine them all bound in by ice aboard this ship, until they chose, over the certainty of starvation, the desperate alternative of committing themselves to the ice.

Patience. Write calmly.

I have lost count of how many timeless days I have been aboard this otherwise forsaken hulk. There is, of course, almost no night here at present. And there are times when my memory is confused. I have written above that it is May, because the daylight is still waxing steadily—and perhaps because I am afraid it is already June, with the beginning of the months of darkness soon to come.

I have triumphed over the white bear. What, then, do I need to fear?

Only the discovery of the truth, perhaps?

I said that I should begin with a description of myself, but now I see that so far I have avoided that unpleasant task. Forward, then. There is a small mirror in this cabin, frost-glued to the wall, but I have not crouched before it. No matter. I know quite well what I should see. A shape manlike but gigantic, an integument unlike that of any other being, animal or human, that I can remember seeing. Neither Asiatic, African, nor European, mine is a yellow skin that, though thick and tough, seems to lack its proper base, revealing in outline the networked veins and nerves and muscles underneath. White teeth, that in another face would be thought beautiful, in mine surrounded by thin blackish lips, are hideous in the sight of men. Hair, straight, black, and luxuriant; a scanty beard.

My physical proportions are in general those of the race of men. My size, alas, is not. Victor Frankenstein, half proud and half horrified at the work of his own hands, has more than once told me that I am eight feet tall. Not that I have ever measured. Certainly this cabin's overhead is much too low for me to stand erect. Nor, I think, has my weight ever been accurately determined—not since I rose from my creator's work table—but it must approximate that of two ordinary men. No human's clothing that I have ever tried has been big enough, nor has any human's chair or bed. Fortunately I still have my own boots, handmade for me at my creator's—I had almost said my master's—order, and I have such furs and wraps, gathered here and there across Europe, as can be wrapped and tied around my body to protect me from the cold.

Sometimes, naked here in the heated cabin, washing myself and my wrappings as best I can in melted snow, I take a closer inventory. What I see forces me to respect my maker's handiwork; his skill, however hideous its product, left no scars, no visible joinings anywhere.

February 1986 • 65550-7 • 320 pp. • $3.50